"THIS IS ANNIE. SHE'LL BE STAYING WITH US FOR A WEEK."

The staff crowded around to have a look, and Annie found herself in the thick of black uniforms and white aprons, polished shoes and curious faces.

"Miss." Were they bowing to *her,* to a little orphan named Annie? Leapin' lizards!

"And her dog Sandy," said Miss Farrell graciously.

"Who'll be staying with *me,*" said Annie, and everyone laughed.

"You're our guest, Annie," said Miss Farrell. "We'll take care of you. You're to have new clothing, and Cecille will help you dress and comb your hair. There will be bubbles in your bathtub, and clean satin sheets on your bed. When you've decided what you want to eat, you shall have it for your next meal, whatever it is."

The saucers of Annie's eyes grew to the size of dinner plates.

COLUMBIA PICTURES PRESENTS
A RAY STARK PRODUCTION
A JOHN HUSTON FILM

ANNIE

Starring
ALBERT FINNEY
CAROL BURNETT
BERNADETTE PETERS
ANN REINKING
TIM CURRY
GEOFFREY HOLDER
EDWARD HERRMANN as "F.D.R."
"SANDY" as himself
and Introducing AILEEN QUINN as "Annie"
Executive Producer JOE LAYTON
Choreography by ARLENE PHILLIPS
Music Adapted by RALPH BURNS
Production Executive HOWARD PINE
Supervising Editor MARGARET BOOTH, A.C.E.
Director of Photography RICHARD MOORE, A.S.C.
Music by CHARLES STROUSE
Lyrics by MARTIN CHARNIN
Screenplay by CAROL SOBIESKI
Produced by RAY STARK
Directed by JOHN HUSTON
From RASTAR
Original soundtrack album on Columbia records and tapes.

The stage play "Annie" was originally presented on the New
York Stage by Mike Nichols. Produced on the New York Stage
by Irwin Meyer, Stephen R. Friedman, and Lewis Allen. Book
of the stage play by Thomas Meehan—Music of the stage play
by Charles Strouse—Lyrics of the stage play by Martin Charnin.

Annie

Leonore Fleischer

**Based upon a screenplay
by Carol Sobieski**

BALLANTINE BOOKS • NEW YORK

Library of Congress Catalog Card Number: 82-1686

ISBN 0-345-30451-9

Manufactured in the United States of America

First Edition: June 1982

*Dedicated with affection to
my dear niece, Gloria Wilkinson*

CHAPTER ONE

Every night, just before she fell asleep, Annie would snuggle down in her warm bed and listen to the murmur of her parents' voices outside her bedroom door. Her drowsy eyes, not yet accustomed to the darkness, would drift slowly around the room, making a last-minute catalog of all her favorite things. Although she couldn't see the pictures on the walls, she had them memorized—Little Jack Horner, pulling a plum out of a brimming pie; Jack-Be-Nimble, leaping over a candlestick with a wavery flame; Little Miss Muffet, jumping up from her tuffet as the spider leered at her; Bo Peep, crying over her lost sheep, not noticing that they were gamboling toward her over the hills. Those dear familiar pictures had been there ever since Annie was a baby; her mother wanted to change them for something a little more suitable to Annie's ten years, but Annie didn't want to let them go. On the shelves across from the bed, Annie could make out the dim outlines of her dolls and books, her beloved stuffed animals, and the other toys that were crowded together so tightly they threatened to push each other off.

In the far corner stood the favorite toy of all—Annie's rocking horse, as gaily painted as a circus pony, tall and proud and very handsome. Annie would pretend that he was real, and that she could ride him out the front door, through the park, over the hills, and far away.

On the other side of the door, in the cozy living room, Annie's mother and father talked quietly together; Annie could barely hear them, and she couldn't really make out the words, but she kept catching the word "she" and occasionally the word "Annie," and she knew that they were talking about her, making plans for her future—college, maybe. It made her feel so warm and safe that her eyes fluttered shut.

She loved them so much! Her beautiful, patient, loving mother, whose hands were soft. Her hair was brushed back from her face and pulled into a neat roll at the nape of her neck. Not marcelled or brilliantined, or cut short like a flapper's. Sometimes Annie would watch her brushing it; her mother's hair fell to her waist, a chestnut brown, with one or two strands of silvery gray. And her father, not very tall, not very handsome, but with a merry, laughing face and a mop of riotous red, curly hair that no barber could tame. And strong, very strong—he could pick Annie up as though she were little more than a rag doll and swing her around.

If she kept very quiet and pretended to be asleep, sooner or later her door would open and Annie's mother would come in to check on the little girl. She'd straighten the covers and touch Annie's brow, feeling for a sudden fever which was never there. But Annie must lie very still, and not touch back. Above all, she mustn't reach out her hand to touch back.

Now the door was opening, and a thin shaft of light from the hallway pierced the darkness. Annie screwed her eyes tightly shut and held her breath as her mother approached her bed. She could smell her mother's violet perfume and hear the rustle of her skirt. And she swore to herself, *This time I won't touch back. I won't even try.*

But she couldn't help herself. She wanted so badly to touch the warm hand that was reaching out to her. She pulled her hand out from under the blanket and reached for her mother and . . .

. . . And the Dream dissolved. It always dissolved when Annie tried to touch it, leaving her cold and lonely and sitting on the windowsill of the third-floor bathroom of the Hudson Street Home for Girls, Established 1891. On the other side of the bathroom door was not a warm cozy bedroom filled with toys, but a bleak, cheerless, airless (unless you counted drafts) dormitory with iron cots for beds and orange crates for bureaus. And there was no mother, no father, nobody but fifty-nine other orphans and Miss Hannigan, their keeper.

Annie had never known her parents, had never known

any other home but the orphanage. Yet she was set apart from the other girls; Annie had her Dream. And one day the Dream would come true at last; didn't she have half a locket to prove it? When they left her at the Hudson Street Home ten years ago, there had been a note tucked in the basket with the redheaded baby. The note promised to whom it may concern that they, Annie's mother and father, would come back as soon as they could, as soon as times got better, to claim their baby Annie. As a token of their promise, half a locket on a chain was inside the envelope. They would keep the other half, said the note, so that everybody would recognize everybody when the great day came. So, strictly speaking, Annie was not an orphan. She had parents, half a locket, and a Dream.

Not that any of it mattered to Miss Hannigan. She was usually fair and impartial in her treatment of the orphans. She hated them all alike. Locket or no locket, parents or no parents, Dream or no Dream, you still scrubbed floors, washed, ironed, and folded laundry, went to bed hungry, and obeyed orders. If Miss Hannigan appeared to favor Annie with a little bit more of her hatred, it was only because Annie was smarter, tougher, bolder, and more independent than the fifty-nine other girls. In Annie, Miss Hannigan sensed a leader, and she detested leaders. Miserable troublemakers. Rotten kids.

Annie sighed and shifted on the bathroom window ledge. It was an uncomfortable and precarious perch, because the window was set up high in the wall, just under the ceiling. To reach it (and nobody but Annie had ever thought of reaching it) you had to stand on the toilet, climb up on the tank, and swing yourself up the hot-water pipe until you could hoist yourself up on the sill. But once there, you had the only privacy in the entire orphanage. Although the window was coated with decades of grime (it hadn't been washed since 1891 and this was now 1933), Annie had wiped a little place clean, and through it she could see the sky. In the winter, you could see a star or two and now and then a piece of the moon. In the summer, the sky was still blue, because the orphans went to bed before eight. Why not? They had to get up before six, didn't they? And what else was there for them to do? They had no books, no radio, no playthings of any kind, no midnight snacks, no Mutt and Jeff or Popeye or Blondie, or anything else to make them smile.

If I try very hard, and keep my eyes tight shut, she told herself, *the Dream might come back. And this time I swear not to put my hand out.* Wrapping her skinny arms tightly around her skinny legs, Annie squinched her eyes shut and attempted to concentrate. Every one of the hundreds of freckles on her face stood out against the white skin with the effort. And the mop of red curls quivered. Although New York City was in the throes of a heat wave and the orphanage was stifling, the stone sill of the bathroom window was like a block of hard ice, and Annie shivered, glad she was wearing her ragged old red sweater over her faded hopsacking underwear. Once the fabric had been new, and had been either brown or gray, although why anybody wanted brown or gray material Annie could never figure out. Her own favorite color was red. But many years of wearing and washing had faded it out to a color neither brown nor gray, but combining the worst features of both. But Annie was used to the color. Most of the orphans slept in their underwear.

The red sweater, on the other hand, had never been new. It had come in the barrel. The Hudson Street Home for Girls was a favorite charity for a number of wealthy society women. Not that they visited there, oh, my, no. Not that they donated money. But twice a year, these society ladies held meetings. In the spring, their chauffeurs carried to the meeting every scrap of castoff and unwanted clothing which their own daughters had outgrown. This clothing was packed up in a barrel and sent to the orphanage.

In the fall, the ladies met again, each one bringing a little gift or two for an orphan child's Christmas. These were new and often very pretty—dolls, books, games—the kinds of things so many little girls take for granted. These were beautifully wrapped and duly sent off to Miss Hannigan.

Now Miss Hannigan was a great believer in popular maxims: Spare the Rod and Spoil the Child being her favorite. But Waste Not, Want Not ran it a close second. Whenever the barrel filled with the secondhand clothing arrived, Miss Hannigan had it brought directly to her room. There she would open it eagerly and paw through the

4

jumble herself. Often the best things, destined for the older girls, wound up on her own back. Silk blouses, for example. What on earth would an orphan want with silk? You can't wear silk while scrubbing floors, can you? Then the barrel was carefully repacked and stowed away in Miss Hannigan's locked supply room.

At Christmas, long limousines would drive up to the Hudson Street Home for Girls, and chauffeurs in black uniforms and caps with shiny patent bills would bring in stacks of gaily wrapped boxes. The orphans' eyes would grow round with excitement and anticipation, then droop in disappointment as the boxes disappeared behind Miss Hannigan's bolted doors.

Every single box would be unwrapped by Miss Hannigan, ever so carefully, so as not to tear the tissue paper or muss the silver and gold ribbons. Then the presents would be stacked in their store boxes along one wall, waiting for Miss Hannigan to take them back to the stores right after Christmas and get her money back. Oh, Miss Hannigan loved Christmas! *Such* a jolly time!

Then, *one* object from the used-clothing barrel would be wrapped up in the gift paper and tied with the gift ribbons and marked with an orphan's name. Useful things, like an old middy blouse with a faded blue tie, or a pinafore with a daisy appliqué and indelible ink stains down the front. Or somebody's old red sweater, wearing thin at the elbows. What else did an orphan need? They might not have gotten even these things (there being a lively market for good used clothing) except for the fact that the society ladies liked to receive thank-you notes for their lovely Christmas presents from the grateful orphans. Every year, Miss Hannigan saw to it that every child wrote the identical ambiguous note: Dear Mrs. Rockesmeller, Thank you so much for the beautiful present. I shall always treasure it and remember your generosity. Sincerely yours, Clara Churchmouse, Hudson Street Home for Girls, Established 1891.

It was a hard-knock life, no two ways about it. Outside the orphanage, things weren't all that wonderful either. The world had been on a free ride for ten years, ever since the Great War in Europe, in which so many men had died in order to end all wars forever. In a fever of optimism, Americans had plunged heavily into the stock market, buying, buying and never selling. The price of stocks soared, way above their actual value, yet people kept on buying. Women shortened their hair and their skirts. The waltz went out and hot jazz came in. You couldn't buy a bottle of whiskey legally, but you could buy it illegally on every street corner. Men plastered their hair down like Rudy Valentino and called themselves sheiks, and their dancing partners shebas. Everybody was having a wonderful time, doing the Charleston on the brink of a volcano.

And then the volcano erupted, and the stock market came tumbling down with a Crash that was heard around the world. Overnight, fortunes were wiped out, men and women thrown out of work, factories shut down. Everybody stopped singing "Boop Boop Be Doop" and started singing "Brother, Can You Spare a Dime?" The Great Depression set in. Stockbrokers jumped out of their office windows; men without work went on the bum and lived in hobo jungles. Other men sold apples two-for-a-nickel on street corners. Veterans, who had been promised a bonus that never materialized in cash, marched on Washington to protest, and were shot at by General Douglas MacArthur and his troops. Times were hard.

By 1932, everybody was so sick of the depression that they did what Americans always do. They blamed it on the president, Herbert Hoover, went to the polls and voted the other party in by a landslide. In this case, they elected a Democrat, Franklin Delano Roosevelt, former governor of New York, former secretary of the Navy. FDR, as he was called (he was called other things by the Republicans), promised a New Deal, with jobs for everybody. No more soup kitchens, no more breadlines, only work and a worker's pay. Things were starting to look a little better, and America began to cheer up. They sang: "Just around the corner, there's a rainbow in the sky. So let's have another cup of coffee, and let's have another piece of pie." They sang: "Who's afraid of the big, bad wolf?" and they meant the depression, which was starting to lift a little.

Lifting outside the Hudson Street Home for Girls, that is. Inside, things were as gloomy as they always were. Terrible food, and never enough of it. Freezing cold in the winter, hotter than a stove in the summer. And never ever was there a spring or a fall.

In theory, life shouldn't have been as bad as it was. According to the state laws governing the orphanage, the girls were supposed to be well schooled, with classes five hours a day. They were supposed to learn English, spelling, geography, arithmetic, music, history, bookkeeping. They were supposed to have two hours of gym and one of art appreciation every week.

In practice, the only school Miss Hannigan believed in was the School of Hard Knocks. She had struck up a deal with the local laundry; they would deliver huge bundles of dirty sheets, towels and tablecloths, and the orphan girls would scrub them clean in huge tubs on washboards, put them through the mangle, hang them on the line, take them down and fold them, or press them out on huge ironing boards with heavy irons that weren't electric. These duties kept the girls much too busy for school, but it put a nice piece of change into Miss Hannigan's pocket.

In theory, any one of the girls could be adopted into a good home at any time. Orphans were always up for adoption, always dreaming of adoption, longing for a mother and a father and a home, yearning for the things that other children took for granted—enough food to eat, a warm place to sleep, a tender hand, a little love, an end to loneliness.

In practice, forget it! Any orphan over the age of three didn't have a chance, unless she was blessed with dimples and curls like Shirley Temple. Prospective parents were interested in something pink and white and tiny, not in a scrawny, big-eyed, hungry girl with scabs on her knees from scrubbing floors and knuckles rubbed raw on the washboard.

In theory, the board of directors of the Hudson Street Home for Girls was supposed to make regular visits to determine if the girls were being well treated, well educated, and well fed. Welfare was their concern, and they weren't cruel men.

In practice, they were busy men, and the welfare of sixty little girls was not so pressing a concern as their business worries, especially now, with That Man in the White House. Besides, they placed implicit faith in Miss

Hannigan, who sent them glowing reports weekly. If anything, the girls were being spoiled with too much food, too much love, and too many presents. Kind Miss Hannigan, who worked so hard for such a small salary. However did she manage to make ends meet?

By feeding sixty little girls mush, in watered-down portions.

Annie's blue eyes were tightly closed, and she thought she could feel the Dream almost beginning again. If only she could get it back. On this hot night, it was impossible to sleep; better to stay up here and hope for the best.

"Annie! *Annie!* ANNIE!"

Annie's eyes snapped open as she heard Molly screaming. The poor baby must be having another one of her nightmares; the screaming had turned into frightened sobbing. Annie caught hold of the water pipe and slithered down, running into the dormitory.

Little Molly, the youngest in the room at six, was thrashing around on her bed and crying. Tears had plastered her dark hair to her cheeks and her nose was running, but she still held tightly to her precious doll, a faceless, shapeless lump of beloved rag.

By now, Molly's sobs had wakened the other orphans, who were sitting up and rubbing their eyes. Pepper, the oldest at thirteen, and mean as a snake, was standing on her bed, her hands knotted into fists and placed squarely on her hips.

"How am I supposed to get any sleep around here?" she demanded, furious, as Annie ran to Molly's side, and gathered the little girl in her arms. "Shhhhhh. It's all right, Molly. I'm here. Everything's all right."

"Molly shouldn't be in this room!" shouted Pepper angrily. "She's a baby! She cries all the time! She wets the bed!"

"I d—d—d—do not!" hiccoughed Molly through her tears.

"Shhhh, blow!" ordered Annie, finding a crumpled handkerchief in her sweater pocket. Molly obediently blew her nose with a loud honk, and Annie mopped at her eyes.

Duffy, ten, but a head smaller than Annie, turned

8

ferociously on Pepper. She loathed a bully, and Pepper was a bully.

"You're the one who shouldn't be in here!" she yelled.

"Yeah!" July chimed in, protective of Molly. "You're the one always making all the noise!" July was eight years old, and tagged along after Annie and Duffy like a small, chubby shadow. She had been left at the orphanage as an infant, with a note pinned to her blanket, saying: "Hear's our dotter July. Pleas take god kare of her." Probably, they meant "Julie," but July she was named and July she was called, like the month. She told anybody who would listen that she was born on the Fourth of July, and if Miss Hannigan had permitted birthdays in the orphanage, that's when they would have celebrated it.

"We're gonna get in trouble," Kate moaned, rolling her eyes. Noise like this always brought Miss Hannigan on the double. At this hour of the night, gin would have made Miss Hannigan unsteady on her pins, but with their luck she'd be able to walk.

"Yeah!" Duffy agreed with Kate. "So shut up, Pepper!"

"You shut up!" bawled Pepper.

With a low growl like a feisty little pup, Duffy took a running jump at Pepper, landing on her with both fists flying, although the older girl stood a good six inches higher and outweighed her by about twenty-five pounds. July, with the instincts of a born follower, raced after Duffy and began to pound Pepper with her pillow. Noise and feathers rose to the heavens.

Molly had stopped crying and watched the fight with a mixture of childish wonder and glee. Tessie, small, dark, and nervous, took a strand of hair into her mouth and began chewing on it, her unbreakable habit when things went from bad to worse.

"Oh, my goodness, oh, my goodness," she muttered through the wet ends of her hair. She burrowed under her pillow in terror.

Before the battle could escalate, Annie's hard little hands were forcing the combatants apart, pushing them away from one another, confiscating July's pillow.

"Cut it out!" she hissed through her teeth. "I mean it!" Annie's small, freckled face wore a look of intense ferocity. "You want Miss Hannigan to come in here?" She gave

9

Duffy a push. "Go back to bed. Now." Then she turned to Pepper, who backed down. "Or you'll have me to deal with."

The fight was over. Muttering, the girls obeyed, climbing back into their own beds, settling down again to sleep.

Molly gave a little whimper as Annie tucked her in.

"I can't sleep, Annie," she said with a tremble in her voice. She had been orphaned only two of her six years, and she couldn't adjust to the harshness of orphanage life.

"I know," whispered Annie sympathetically, smoothing the child's dark hair back over her forehead. "Sometimes it's hard. Close your eyes. Think about your folks."

Molly's grubby little fingers reached up to touch the precious locket dangling from Annie's neck. "You're the only one who really has folks," she said sadly. "Mine are dead."

Annie gave the little girl a quick hug. "Think about the folks who are gonna adopt you. Because they want a little girl with brown hair and brown eyes."

Molly was still young enough to believe, and now she shut her eyes. "Sing something, Annie," she begged. "Please? Sing 'Minnie the Moocher.' Please, Annie. It will help me sleep."

Annie laughed and nodded. "Minnie the Moocher" was her specialty, learned from stolen visits to Miss Hannigan's radio when Miss Hannigan was out returning orphan presents to the department stores. " 'Folks, here's the story of Minnie the Moocher,' " she sang to Molly, rocking the little girl in her arms. But before she could get to the part about Minnie's heart being as big as a whale, the door was flung open with a bang and the overhead light shed a harsh and sickly glare over the iron cots and the few pitiful belongings in the orange crates by the beds.

"Did I hear *singing* in here?" rasped a horridly familiar voice. Miss Hannigan!

Once upon a time Miss Hannigan had probably been a little girl, not too different from the orphans, but it was hard to picture her with a mother and a father and a first name. She appeared to have been born mean, skinny, blowsy, and drunk. Life might have dealt severe disappointments to Miss Hannigan; perhaps she had wanted a home, a husband, and some children of her own. Perhaps.

Or maybe she liked things exactly as they were, sixty little girls living in mortal fear of her. Certainly, she made the most of it at every opportunity.

Yet, Miss Hannigan had her good side. She drank. While other ladies filled their bathtubs with sweet-smelling bubbles, Miss Hannigan filled hers with gin. Foul-smelling, poisonous gin which she manufactured herself in the tub, a leftover from Prohibition days, when gin was hard to come by. By now, she was used to the hideous concoction, and had even come to like it. Several dozen gallons of wood alcohol, a few juniper berries, stir once or twice, let it age slowly overnight and it would start to eat its way right through the tub. Because she drank, Miss Hannigan was frequently drunk. Sometimes she was kind enough to pass out, and the orphans lived for those times. When Miss Hannigan was passed out and snoring, the Hudson Street Home for Girls, Established 1891, knew its only few moments of peace. They were moments worth celebrating, and celebrate the orphans did. They would listen to Miss Hannigan's radio, and dance to the music (both were strictly forbidden at other times). It was from the forbidden radio that Annie had learned of President Roosevelt and the New Deal. The orphans were not allowed newspapers or any other word from the outside world. Or they would go through Miss Hannigan's pile of discarded magazines and rotogravure sections, which she sold to the junk dealer when she was through with them. It was in one of these magazines, the *Woman's Home Companion*, that Annie had seen a picture of the room in her Dream, complete with the nursery-rhyme pictures on the wall and the rocking horse in the corner.

Yes, the orphans could be very fond of Miss Hannigan, when she was asleep and snoring. But it was the phase before she passed out that they hated and feared the most. Because Miss Hannigan could be a very mean drunk.

She was in the mean-drunk phase now; every girl in the room felt the marrow of her bones congeal in terror. A bottle half filled with homemade gin swung from Miss Hannigan's hand as she went marching unsteadily through the bedroom, shrieking her anger.

"Get out of bed! This room's a mess!" she yelled, tugging the frightened and unwilling girls out of their cots.

11

"Who said you could move the beds?" she screamed as she noticed the girls had pushed their cots closer together for what little companionship they could get. "This room's going to be regulation by breakfast, my little pig droppings, or kill! kill! *kill!*"

"It's the middle of the night," protested Annie. A bony hand, covered in cheap glittery rings, with long blood-red fingernails, grabbed her by the collar of her undershirt and yanked her off the bed. They stood nose to nose for an instant, and Annie was nearly overcome by the mingled odors of cheap perfume and stale gin. "And if the floor doesn't shine like the top of the Chrysler building, your backside will!"

Hissing with fury, Miss Hannigan gave Annie such a push that the child went stumbling backward and fell to the floor. Now she glared around the room to make certain that everybody was up and dressing. "Understand?" she demanded.

"Yes, Miss Hannigan," chorused the orphans reluctantly. All except Annie, who was muttering something under her breath, stopping as she caught Miss Hannigan's glaring eye.

Miserable little troublemaker! Rotten kid! "What do we say, Annie?" prompted Miss Hannigan with a vicious leer.

Annie hesitated for a fraction of a moment, then gave in. "I love you, Miss Hannigan," she sing-songed through clenched teeth. Those five words had been drilled into her, into all the orphans, over the years. "I love you, Miss Hannigan." Did the woman think the words were true just because she commanded them to be spoken?

But the woman seemed satisfied now. With a complacent nod, she took another long pull at the gin bottle and headed for the door, shaking her head. "Why any kid would want to be an orphan is beyond me."

Annie stood looking after her. That tears it, she thought. Enough is enough, and I've had enough. Standing still and closing your eyes wasn't the way to have a Dream come true. It was time to go out looking for the Dream. It was time to run away again.

12

CHAPTER TWO

Annie had always been caught, every time she'd run away. Caught and brought back and punished. But it never stopped her from trying again. Because someday she'd make it, bust loose and get free and find her mother and father. They'd know each other on account of the locket, and they'd be so happy to see her, and they'd have the best excuse in the world why they hadn't shown up, and they'd all live happily together, and they'd agree to adopt Molly.

The reason she'd always been caught is that she'd never had a plan. On impulse, she would slip out the front door when it was opened and head down the street, running hard until she was caught. Why, that wasn't even running away, that was exercise! But now she had a kind of plan, and it involved her getting away clean. As clean as dirty laundry could be, that is.

There wasn't a lot of coming and going at the orphanage; it wasn't exactly a hot social center. Every two weeks, the man from the shirtwaist factory came with large bolts of cloth to be turned into blouses, skirts, and dresses on sewing machines. He subcontracted out a number of his contracts, and one of his suppliers was the Hudson Street Home for Girls, Established 1891. Miss Hannigan had set up a little sweatshop in what should have been the schoolroom. Instead of desks, there were sewing and pressing machines, dressmakers' dummies, ironing boards, and cutting tables. Miss Hannigan claimed that she was teaching the older girls a trade and a skill that could not be obtained for money elsewhere, but every penny made on the sewing found its way into her rusty old leatherette pocketbook. Between the laundry and the dressmaking, the Hudson Street Home brought in a tidy little profit, which Miss

13

Hannigan made tidy use of. She spent it on alcohol for the bathtub and lavalieres of brass and cheap glass beads, kimonos of artificial silk, printed with large, sleazy flowers, red hair dye, sling-back mules trimmed with marabou feathers, and a monkey-fur jacket. Miss Hannigan agreed with the French saying: It Is Necessary to Suffer to Be Beautiful. That is to say, she didn't think it was necessary for *her* to suffer, only the orphans.

Every week, on Wednesday, Mr. Bundles came from the laundry to deliver the dirty sheets, towels, and tablecloths for the orphans to wash, and to take away their dirty sheets (they had no towels and, needless to say, no tablecloths) for *him* to wash. It was an odd arrangement, forced on Miss Hannigan by the board of directors, who paid the laundry bills themselves, and who would wonder if there were nothing to pay.

By the time the orphans had scrubbed down the walls and the staircases, the floors and the kitchen, it was Wednesday morning, time to strip the beds for Mr. Bundles. Laundry was piled into a large cart, which was wheeled to the front door and up a ramp into Mr. Bundles' truck. And that was Annie's plan, so simple it was pure genius. She would hide in the laundry and be carried out right under Miss Hannigan's nose.

"Oh, my goodness, oh, my goodness," gasped Tessie when she saw Annie climb into the laundry cart and, holding her nose, duck down underneath the dirty, smelly sheets.

"They'll put you in the cellar with the ghosts," exclaimed Kate. She was the one with the vivid imagination.

"You'll get whipped again," warned Duffy.

"You're gonna get us in trouble!" wailed July.

Molly burst into tears as she saw Annie disappear under the sheets.

"Shut up, Molly," urged Annie, her voice muffled by linen.

Pepper thrust her lower lip out. "I'm gonna tell."

"And I'll rearrange your teeth," threatened the laundry cart.

Molly's sobbing came to an abrupt stop as Miss Hannigan, loaded for bear, came stalking in to chivvy her charges.

"What are you standing around for?" she snarled at the suddenly silent girls. "You have to do the kitchen and the bathroom before lunch, my little pig droppings, and if you skip the corners, there will *be* no lunch." At the gasp of dismay that arose from the orphans, an evil little smile broke out over her face. "And we're not having hot mush today," she purred.

Spontaneous applause, cheers, and whistles, cries of joy.

"We're having *cold* mush," she cackled, enjoying her cruel joke.

A chorus of groans and gripes rose to her ears, past the long, glitzy earrings. *"What!?"* she roared, suddenly furious.

"We love you, Miss Hannigan," they piped obediently.

Miss Hannigan's hackles subsided. "Wonderful," she said flatly. Then, as the new thought struck her, she looked around. "Where's Annie?" she demanded. That little troublemaker. Rotten kid.

"She had to go bafroom," answered Molly, inspired.

"She had to go bafroom," mocked Miss Hannigan in a disbelieving lisp. "Oh, yeah? Well then, why . . . ?"

But her suspicions were interrupted by the announcement that the laundryman was here with his truck.

"Oooohh!" squeaked Miss Hannigan, transformed into a breathy young girl at the mere idea of a man, any man. "It's Mr. Bundles!" And with a pat at her dyed and ratted hair, she was off down the stairs to the street.

As quickly as they could, Duffy and July bumped the laundry cart down the staircase (it yelled *Ow!* twice) and out into the street behind Miss Hannigan.

Mr. Bundles was unloading an empty laundry cart to leave when Miss Hannigan came dancing up, frolicsome as a gazelle, but ten times clumsier.

Oh, boy, he muttered unhappily under his breath. *She's in one of them moods. Better get outta here fast.*

Miss Hannigan batted her eyelashes so hard a bead of mascara flew through the air and spattered on Mr. Bundles' white uniform. "Time for a tumble with the Bundles," she cooed coyly, striking what she considered to be a provocative pose.

Mr. Bundles closed his eyes in horror at the thought.

"Not today, Miss Hannigan. I'm behind."

The word "behind" sent Miss Hannigan into a fit of lascivious laughter, and she made a grab for the laundryman's rear end, nipping it neatly in her sharp fingernails.

"Ouch! My schedule, I mean."

"Schedules!" snorted Miss Hannigan, planting her flat bosom firmly against his shirt and panting into his ear. "What are schedules against the storms of passion?" She began to tug at his uniform, stroking his chest and sides, happily unaware that behind her the orphans were stifling their giggles and pointing their fingers.

"We are just so much flotsam and jetsam on the currents of love," she crooned, as the poor man tried desperately to fend her off. "We are caught in the tides . . . what are you doing out here, Duffy?" The pupils of Miss Hannigan's eyes, dilated with lust, were now narrowed in suspicion as she saw Duffy trying to push the laundry cart up the ramp to the panel truck.

"I'm trying to help you," Duffy called back, her face a mask of sweating innocence. As Mr. Bundles came over to give the child a hand, Duffy muttered in an undertone, "It's heavy today."

"It sure is," grunted Bundles, putting his shoulder to it. "It feels like . . ." Duffy dug a quick elbow into his ribs to warn him, but it was too late. Miss Hannigan was stalking over, frowning.

"Like what?" she demanded. "Let me see in there."

In a flash, Mr. Bundles caught on to what was . . . *who* was in the cart. In a diversionary move, he turned and swept the startled Miss Hannigan into his arms, planting a big wet kiss firmly on her lips.

Well! This was more *like* it! Miss Hannigan allowed herself to grow limp in his arms, passion's plaything. All thoughts of an unusually heavy laundry cart went flying out of her head. As Duffy gave the cart a final shove into the truck. Mr. Bundles let Miss Hannigan go and bowed with a flourish.

"Until next week, Miss Hannigan," and he kissed his hand to her.

Miss Hannigan melted, and her eyelids fluttered like a butterfly in love. "Adieu, my little whippet lips," she trilled throatily. "Adieu." And she floated back into the orphanage.

From the window above, Tessie, Kate, and Molly watched the laundry truck clatter away down the cobbled street and turn a corner.

"Oh, my goodness, oh, my goodness," squeaked Tessie, chewing on her hair in excitement.

"Juju beans! She made it!" called out Kate.

And poor little Molly burst into tears. Who would sing to her tonight? Who would comfort her when she had nightmares?

Scram sighed as he turned the corner and saw the boys standing in front of the butcher shop. This wasn't his lucky day. He hadn't eaten a bite since the day before yesterday, and he was feeling weak and light-headed. But even in his enfeebled condition he could tell that those boys spelled trouble. And in front of that butcher shop, too. His luck was running *all* bad. Not that the butcher was the most generous of men, but in the past he had parted with a scrap or a bone, and sometimes, around the garbage cans in the alley behind the shop, Scram had found a mouthful or two, not the best quality, perhaps, but then Scram had never eaten a mouthful of the best quality.

But with those mean-looking boys standing there—four of them—it wasn't worth the risk. Or was it? Scram took one step forward, then two steps back, then decided against it. He'd go back the way he'd come, and try again later.

But it was already too late. He'd been spotted. The boys were running across the street toward him, shouting. Scram turned tail and ran for his life.

He couldn't run very fast in his present condition; he ran like a wheezing old dog. Actually, he wasn't old in years, just old in the ways of the streets. Experienced, or he wouldn't have survived even this long. A dog without a license in a city without a heart—that was almost as bad as . . . as . . . being an orphan. And why, as Miss Hannigan would say, why would anyone ever want to be an orphan? Or a stray dog?

A stone bounced off Scram's furry shoulder, and he ran harder. No fair. Stones weren't fair. Sticks weren't fair. Tin cans tied to the tail weren't fair. But they all seemed to be Scram's lot in life. If only he could accept it philosophically!

He was a dog without a home, without anybody to love or be loved by, without even a name. "Scram" was what most people called him, but he also answered to "Beat-It" and to "Get-the-Hell-Outta-Here." If by answering, you meant running away. Scram lived by his wits, sleeping under cars, shivering in alleys in the winter, drinking out of puddles and open hydrants, scrounging his food wherever he could find it. He wasn't a large dog and he wasn't a small dog. He didn't have any real color to his fur, and his lineage was as undistinguished as he was. He was your basic nondescript mutt, and the only striking thing about him was his eyes—which were large and soft and brown and miserable.

He couldn't do tricks, but he was smart. And brave. And loyal. And, had he but known it, loving. But these were qualities that seemed little in demand these days. Scotties were the big favorite—even President Roosevelt had a Scottie, Fala, who lived in the White House and probably ate filet mignon off golden plates. Scotties and cocker spaniels, poodles and chows, bull terriers—these were the popular and fashionable dogs. Even wirehairs were big. There was a little wirehair in Scram, a couple of generations back. But not enough to make somebody pick him up and give him a home.

Scram looked back over his shoulder as he fled down the alley. No doubt about it, the gang of boys was gaining on him.

The laundry truck bumped over the cobblestones, and the carts in the back went pitching this way and that. Buried under the sheets, Annie fought to get her head out, but just as she was almost free, another bump sent her flying back into the washbasket. *I'm not gonna live through this,* she thought, *but just in case I do, and I get away, it will be worth it.* But she was getting sick to her stomach, with all the pitching and rolling. It was like crossing the Atlantic in a January gale on a ship with no stabilizers.

At last, at the very moment when Annie was glad she'd missed lunch, Mr. Bundles pulled over to the curb and stopped. A minute later, he was setting Annie down on the sidewalk, where she wobbled unsteadily until she got her land legs back. Then, with a wide grin and a wave of thanks, she was on her way.

On her way where? She had no idea, but the late-summer day was so beautiful, the streets so lively and bustling, that merely to walk down them gave her a sense of well-being and a feeling of freedom. All she knew was that she was somewhere in Hell's Kitchen, on the West Side of Manhattan, walking uptown away from Hudson Street.

New York in 1933 was very different from what it is today. For one thing, there were far fewer automobiles, and many businesses—small ones, admittedly—were conducted by horse and wagon or even by pushcart. Television hadn't been invented, and people looked out of their windows for entertainment. There were no transistor radios, but organ grinders wandered around with little monkeys on their leashes, playing for pennies. Knife sharpeners carried large grindstones on wheelbarrows, calling out for housewives to bring down their knives to sharpen, a nickel apiece. "I cash clothes! I cash clothes!" sang the old-clothes men in the back alleys. They'd climb up six flights of stairs to pay a dime for a wornout overcoat, or a penny for a pair of shoes.

Kids were everywhere, playing in the streets, dodging the traffic. They played stoopball, and stickball, with manhole covers for bases. They played King, a neighborhood variety of handball. They played Giant Steps and Puss-in-the-Corner and King of the Mountain. They threw mumblety-peg and shot marbles and spun tops. Rope-skipping was very popular, because the only equipment you needed was a piece of clothesline, and Double Dutch was the killer game, only for the best rope-jumpers. Annie had never done any of these things, and she was fascinated. She wanted to stop and watch; she wanted to join in, but her instincts told her she'd better keep going. So she wandered on, in no direction in particular.

There is one other difference between the New York of then and now that's worth mentioning. Today, the police ride around in squad cars, two to a car. In those days, a single cop walked a beat, looking for anything and anybody who excited his suspicion. And, generally, a cop knew every man, woman, and even child on his beat.

Officer McVie watched from across the street as a small

redheaded girl clambered down from a laundry truck. Here was somebody he'd never seen before, somebody who was too pale for a kid this time of year, like she'd been kept indoors a lot. Somebody in a faded old dress too big for her and an old red sweater too small for her. Somebody with an institutional look about her, who was gazing too curiously at commonplace people and ordinary occupations, as though she'd never seen them before. No other business was pressing the policeman at this moment; so he took off after Annie, keeping out of her sight but dogging her half a block behind.

Annie turned a corner and came upon a street market, pushcart after pushcart selling old clothes, pickled herring, watches and rings of "real gold," men's hats, cages of live pigeons, mounds of dead chickens, secondhand books in Yiddish, Greek, Italian, German, even Chinese. Fascinated, she slowed down, and behind her, the policeman slowed down, too. He was on to something; he was certain of that now. This kid had escaped from a jail of some kind. He could tell because now she was looking so happy, happier than any kid had a right to be with times so hard.

They caught up with him, as he'd known they would, trapping him against the wall in an alley. Scram had growled and barked, but the boys paid no attention. They knew he was all mouth; this dog wouldn't bite anybody. With a lot of pushing and jostling and yelling they managed to tie a long string to his tail, with three tin cans fastened to the string. Now when that mangy old dog ran away, the clattering behind him would scare him out of his wits and make him run faster. Boy, was this fun! It even beat grabbing shopping bags from angry old ladies. Spike, the oldest and largest of the group, gave Scram a whack on the behind that sent him running and yelping out of the alley, trying frantically to shake the cans loose from his tail. Howling with laughter, the boys took off in hot pursuit of the terrified dog.

The smell of the pickled herring and the garlic sausages hanging from their strings was beginning to get to Annie. Breakfast had been a tiny bowl of ice-cold mush, but even that would taste good to Annie now. She was starving, and the aroma of salami was making her mouth water. Of course, she didn't have a penny on her; well, actually, when did she ever have a penny on her? Time to move on, to arenas less fragrant and tantalizing.

As she passed the alley between the rows of houses, a frightened dog raced past her, his heart pounding, eyes staring, tongue panting. To his tail was attached a string of empty tin cans. Behind him hotfooted a gang of yelling boys. Annie shook her head in disgust. How some people got their kicks!

But as she moved past the alley on her way to somewhere else, a yelp of pain stopped her in her tracks. She peered into the alley's dimness. The gang of boys had the scruffy dog penned in a dead end, and two of them were holding him down while a third one was tightening the string around his tail. In pain, the dog kept biting at the string, turning and turning in terrified circles, as the noisy cans clattered on the cobbles behind him.

Annie marched into the alley and stood there watching, her hands on her hips. Although she was standing as tall as she knew how, she was still smaller than the smallest of the boys, and many inches smaller than their leader.

Who now stood watching the shabbily dressed little girl with a sneer on his face.

"Keep walking, kid," he told her scornfully.

Annie took another step toward him, then another.

"Bug off!" Spike ordered, getting annoyed.

"What's he ever done to you?" asked Annie, jerking a thumb at the cowering dog.

Spike glared at her menacingly. "You want a fat lip?" he inquired, not expecting an answer.

But Annie *did* come up with an answer. She kicked Spike in the shins, good and hard. Now he was *really* mad. Although he rarely beat up girls, except for his sister, he came at Annie with his fists clenched and head down, ready to wipe the alley floor with this nosy redheaded brat. "You little—" he began, but he never got a chance to tell Annie what creature he was comparing her to, because on the way there his jaw met Annie's hard little fist, and he was sent flying. Before he could even begin to recover from Annie's left, her right plowed into his stomach, and birdies began to go tweet-tweet around his head. He slumped to the cobbles with a peaceful look on his face.

The gang couldn't believe their eyes. Spike? Taken out by a girl? By a *little* girl? Gotta be some mistake, right?

But the little girl was turning to them now, fists cocked, eyes flashing, ready to take them all on. "Anybody else?" she was saying. "Then *get lost*."

Now, of course, if they'd all rushed her at once, Annie wouldn't have stood a chance. But somehow that never occurred to any of them. What occurred to them was that they had business elsewhere, pressing business. It wasn't as though they were running away from a girl, right? Just because a fella's remembered an important engagement that required his presence elsewhere? One by one they turned tail and got lost, and within twenty-two seconds the alley was empty, except for Annie and Scram. Even Spike had recovered enough to slink away quickly, so he could pull his story together. He slipped, that was it. Slipped on the slimy cobbles just as he was about to deck the snotty little kid, and he hit his head and . . .

Annie knelt down and gently unfastened the cans from the dog's tail. He lay with his chin on the ground and his paws over his nose. He was a mess. His fur was matted and dirty, and cuts showed through on his skin, where he'd been hit by rocks thrown by those crummy boys. His ribs were showing. What a loser!

"Okay, it's okay. They're gone now. You can take off. Nobody's gonna hurt ya," Annie told him, but the dog didn't move or take his eyes off her. Big brown eyes, the saddest eyes that Annie had ever seen, even sadder and browner than Molly's.

"Hey, you're all right. Go on now." And Annie gave him a little push. The dog gave a kind of sigh and a little shudder and settled closer to the ground.

Annie stood up and shook her head, amused. "Dumb dog. Well, cheer up. I gotta be going. So long."

She headed for the entrance to the alley. Behind her she heard a low whine, then the dog got up stiffly and came hobbling after her.

At the entrance to the alley, Scram caught up with

Annie. He was grateful to her, of course, for taking on that gang and getting rid of his tormentors and his torment. But it was more than gratitude that was making him follow her. Scram could tell by the way she was dressed that this little redheaded girl couldn't stand him a meal, probably didn't have anything to eat herself. He knew there was no percentage in it for him. But none of that mattered. What mattered was that, when she was kneeling beside him, he'd looked into her face and that was *it*. A feeling of such love, such devotion had washed over him that it had pressed him to the ground, and he'd trembled and whined beneath it. This little girl was his destiny; she was his person for life. His canine fate had been decreed, and it couldn't be otherwise.

Not that he wished it otherwise. He'd never loved anybody in his life, not since he'd been a tiny puppy with a mother, and that was long ago. But this little freckle-faced, blue-eyed, redheaded girl belonged to him now, and nothing anybody would ever say or do would alter matters. He'd follow her to the ends of the earth, let alone the mouth of an alley.

Annie turned and smiled down at him, touching his flea-infested head with gentle fingers. "I can't find my own home. So how could I find yours?"

Scram wagged his tail happily, content only to hear Annie's voice. As she moved away from him, he followed.

"Dumb dog! Latch on to someone who can feed you. Give you a bath. Put something on those cuts. Go on now."

Scram, who never had done a trick in his life before, held up his paw for Annie to take.

The little girl shook her head impatiently. "You already told me thank you. I didn't do nothing any decent person wouldn'ta done."

Scram lifted both paws and sat up. Annie stopped dead, and turned to look at him. "You . . . are . . . embarrassing me," she said slowly and distinctly. "Now, *scram!*"

At the sound of his name on her lips, he did the only thing a gentleman could do in the circumstances. He licked her face, wetly and enthusiastically.

"Yuck!" yelled Annie, and turned and ran through the crowded street, with Scram chasing happily after her, enjoying this new game. Annie raced past the tenements with their high stoops, fat ladies in sleeveless summer dresses sitting on the steps with their stockings rolled down and paper fans in their hands. Scram followed her. Annie dodged the peddlers, ran around the Ring-O-Levio games, over a potsy board chalked on the sidewalk. Scram followed her. Annie bumped into people, sending them scattering. Scram followed her.

And the truck from the dog pound followed them both.

The dogcatcher had seen that dog before, but it had always eluded him. But today was the day. He drove to the corner ahead of Annie and the dog and put the truck into park. Then he climbed out, with a collar and leash ready, and when Annie ran past him, he braced himself for the dog.

"Gotcha! You're comin' with *me!*"

Scram let out a single high yelp of surprise as he felt the collar tighten on his neck. At the sound, Annie screeched to a halt and looked back. One glance told it all—the triumphant dogcatcher, the trapped and dejected dog. Something rose up in Annie, a feeling of protectiveness, and a feeling she'd never experienced before—possessiveness. Apart from the locket and the red sweater, what had she ever had to possess?

"Hey, mister! That's my dog!" she yelled, running back to the pound truck, and arriving nearly out of breath.

Scram wagged his tail happily at the sight of her. But the dogcatcher uttered a scornful laugh and began to drag Scram to the back door of the truck.

"Yeah? Where's his license?" he demanded skeptically. "Where's his leash? He's no more your dog than I am your father."

Annie gave him a startled glance, but he didn't have red hair.

"I left his license at home," she pleaded. "By mistake. Honest. Please don't take him to the pound. Please . . ." Now her eyes filled convincingly with tears. "My father's blind. This dog leads him to work. If he can't get to work we're gonna all of us starve. Sir, I beg you—"

"And what's his name?" *I've heard some pretty tall stories in my day,* he thought, *but this tale is taller than that new-fangled Empire State Building.*

"My father's name?" asked Annie innocently, stalling for time.

"The dog's name," said the dogcatcher pointedly.

"The dog's name?" Annie's voice rose to a squeak. She was thinking fast now, fast and furious. "His name. Uh . . . you want his name, right? Uh . . ." She looked hard at the dog, but he offered no clue. Unless . . . under the mats and the fleas and the dirt, his coat was sort of red, sort of brown . . . "His name's Sandy." *I like that,* she thought. "Right, Sandy."

By no means was the dogcatcher convinced. "Call him."

"Call him?" Annie looked panic-stricken.

The pound man loosened the rope, but didn't remove the collar. "Go over there and call him." He pointed across the street.

Oh, boy, thought Annie. *Oh, boy, oh, boy, oh, boy.* "You mean by his name?" she gulped.

"By his name," the man nodded. He was enjoying the girl's obvious discomfort. *This'll teach her, the little smarty-pants.*

Annie squared her shoulders and crossed the street. She turned and faced the dog. "Sandy!" she called. "Come here, Sandy."

Scram cocked an ear. *Is that me? Is she calling me? What is she doing way over there?* He was confused and exhausted. The streets were crowded with people, throngs of noisy voices. Traffic was passing between him and Annie, and Scram had always been afraid of traffic, and quite rightly, too. His deepest instincts were drawing him toward Annie, but his hard-won street smarts were warning him to stay put and keep a low profile.

"Sandy! Sandy! Sandy!" shouted Annie, without hope.

By now the street had become aware that a little drama was being enacted here, with a cast of three. It looked like fun, and several showoffs decided to get in on the act.

"Here, Rover!" called a hot-dog man, laughing loudly.

"Rin Tin Tin!" cackled a toothless old newspaper vendor. "Come to mama, Rin Tin Tin!"

Scram sat up and looked from one calling face to another, now completely bewildered. Everybody seemed to be calling him, which was a novelty in itself. But everybody was calling him by a different name, which threw him further into confusion.

Above all the tooting of horns, banging and rattling of trolley cars, shouting of voices, Scram could hear one voice, one dear voice, raised in a last despairing shout. "Saaaan-deee." He stood up, fell down, got to his feet again, and trotted across the street, through the crowds and up to Annie's side, becoming in that instant Sandy forever. Jumping up, he put his paws on her shoulders, giving her face another moist lick.

This time, Annie didn't turn her face away. "Good old Sandy," she told him as she became his, just as he was already hers.

The dogcatcher came up and grudgingly took the collar off Sandy. "Well, you got yourself a dog, kid. Now go home and get him a collar and leash."

"Yes, *sir!*" She flashed him a huge, freckled grin and the two of them ran off, Annie in the lead, Sandy hobbling gamely after her.

"Gotcha!" Out of nowhere, Officer McVie caught Annie by the collar and brought her up short. He knew who she was now, a runaway orphan, and a call to headquarters had confirmed it. The Hudson Street Home for Girls had reported her missing, red sweater, red hair, and all, only it didn't say anything about a flea-bitten mutt of a dog. "You're comin' with me."

Annie struggled, but the cop was too strong for her. Sandy launched a feeble attack, and got a boot in the chops for his pains. Leading her painfully by the scruff of the neck, the policeman marched her step by step back downtown to Hudson Street. Her moment of freedom had been brief, bittersweet, and too soon over. Now it was the orphanage for her, and another whipping.

Leapin' lizards!

CHAPTER THREE

With a sinking heart, Annie saw the grim yellow brick façade of the orphanage looming up ahead of her. Even Sandy, trotting along behind, seemed intimidated by the institution's menacing aspect, and he hung back, whining a little. The officer pulled the doorbell with a flourish; it was the old-fashioned kind on a chain. Miss Hannigan, large as life and twice as ugly, opened the door. Her face brightened when she saw the grinning face of the policeman, then darkened as she caught a glimpse of Annie.

Annie gulped in fear, and tried a friendly little smile and a wave, without success.

"Look what I found under a rock, Miss Hannigan," crowed McVie.

"Annie!" Miss Hannigan reeled back in fake happiness. "My poor little peach fuzz," she crooned. "Are you all right? I was worried sick." She cut her eyes at the beefy cop, to see how motherly warmth went down with him.

Like vanilla ice cream. "I knew you would be," and the cop edged closer. "Big-hearted woman like you." He leered frankly down into her cleavage, such as it was.

Quick as juice through a goose, Miss Hannigan shoved Annie into the orphanage, and turned her full attention to this person in pants. He was exactly her type—horny. "How can I ever thank you enough?" Her eyes popped suggestively, revealing tiny little red veins in the whites.

But the policeman wasn't turned off. The smell of gin excited him, promising other, more forbidden, treats. "I bet we can figure out something, if we put our heads together." Like an old fire horse responding to the fire bell, Miss Hannigan lifted up her head and whinnied in anticipation. McVie snaked one arm around her waist, and brought his face closer to hers.

27

"Kissy, kissy, kissy!" came from the windows above. Pepper's voice. McVie snatched his hand away as though it were on fire, and took a leap backward. The orphanage windows were filled with spying little girls, all of them grinning and sticking out their tongues.

Her dream of love evaporated, Miss Hannigan became strident. "Kill! Kill! Kill!" she shrieked, and rushed inside to wreak vengeance as the policeman stormed off.

Nobody noticed Annie's hands at the basement window, pulling it open. Nobody noticed the nondescript dog of no special color who leaped inside.

After her whipping, Annie was sent to bed without any supper. That made two bowls of mush she'd missed today; Annie would not have supposed that she'd ever be using the words "miss" and "mush" in the same sentence. But food was food, and her empty belly growled in protest. She waited for hours until the house was dark and quiet, then crept down to the kitchen on what was probably a hopeless errand. Miss Hannigan was not the kind of person who left food out for orphans to help themselves to. The shelves and cupboards were bare, and the icebox held only a block of ice. But Annie, with cunning and patience, managed to jimmy the lock on the larder, and found a half-loaf of bread.

She didn't dare take all of it. If it were missed, every orphan in the place would be punished for theft—all sixty of them—and Annie didn't want to be the cause of that. She took only enough to settle the worst pangs of her hunger. After all, when you've been hungry for ten years in a row, you kind of get used to it. Then, remembering Sandy, she carved off another piece, laid the loaf carefully back on the shelf, and replaced the lock on the larder door. Making her way to the basement slowly, not daring to turn on a light, she whispered softly into the darkness, "Sandy? Sandy, are you there?"

A happy wet lick on her cheek told her that Sandy was indeed there. She sank to the cold stone floor beside him, and wrapped her arms around his neck. *Tomorrow I give you a bath; that's a promise,* she said into his ear. Then she divided the bread between them, giving Sandy the slightly larger slice, and they shared their first meal together. When Sandy laid his head on his paws and went to

28

sleep, Annie climbed the steps to her third-floor dormitory without a sound.

All orphans over the age of eight had to work in the sweatshop, or, as Miss Hannigan put it, "The Sewing Salon." They took it in turns, and the next morning it was the turn of Annie's dorm. Molly, although only six, was allowed to stay with them, and she kept herself useful by picking up pins. Miss Hannigan kept a careful count of the pins, and heaven help the orphan who lost one.

Once they were set up for the morning's work, and Miss Hannigan had retreated to her quarters to check on the gin-filled bathtub, Annie put her fingers to her lips, and went down to the basement to fetch up Sandy. She enjoyed the gasp that went up from her audience when they saw the dog, the first dog that ever penetrated these ancient walls.

"Oh, my goodness, oh, my goodness," squeaked Tessie predictably.

"He smells," Pepper stated flatly.

"His eyes are pretty," Kate put in softly.

"What's his name, Annie?" Molly asked breathlessly, her eyes enormous with excitement.

"Guess," teased Annie with a grin.

"Fifi?" Molly's face lit up.

Duffy howled with laughter. "Fifi! What a name for a mutt like that!"

"How about Champion?" asked Kate.

"What's *he* champion of?" demanded Pepper in scorn.

"We could call him Tiger," suggested July.

Now it was July that Duffy and Pepper were hooting at. "Tiger! A toothless, scaredy-cat kind of a tiger!"

Through it all, Sandy sat happily, his tail thumping the floor, his eyes sparkling, giving impartial wet licks to any young face that came near his tongue.

"I got it! Rover! Rover's a good name for him," yelled Duffy.

But Annie was shaking her head. "Nope. All of you are wrong. His name's Sandy."

"Sandy. Right, I like that. Sandy, yup, that's a good name." The little girls crowded around the dog, patting him, giving him hugs, ignoring his fleas and his odor.

29

Here was something to love at last, and they were determined to love him, scruffy as he was, no matter how smelly.

A sudden footfall outside the sweatshop door sent the girls scrambling back to their machines. Sandy ran to hide under Annie's machine, and she draped a bedspread over the machine and down to the floor to cover him, just as the door was thrown open and Miss Hannigan stormed in.

"We love you, Miss Hannigan," chorused the girls.

Annie spun the wheel on her sewing machine and began to work the foot pedal diligently. She didn't notice there was no thread on the bobbin, but stitched away furiously. After a moment, she looked up, all innocent surprise, to see Miss Hannigan standing over her, eyes flashing with rage, foot tapping impatiently.

"Uh, I love you Miss Hannigan?" Annie took a shot at it, but with little expectation of success.

"You're going to the cellar, Annie." Miss Hannigan's voice was cold and deadly. Gasps of horror rose around her. The cellar was the most feared punishment of all, equivalent to solitary confinement for prisoners. It was dark down there, and cold and creepy, and things moved in the shadows. Slimy things, with eyes that glowed red in the dark. There were spiders in the cellar, and maybe even snakes. The basement was okay, because it had windows, but the cellar below it was a chamber of horrors.

"And *this*"—Miss Hannigan reached under Annie's machine and grabbed Sandy by the tail, pulling him out— "*this* goes to the sausage factory!" With savage glee, she saw Annie's face grow so white that the freckles stood out in relief, and her blue eyes filled with tears. It was a great day for the Hannigans when Annie could be made to cry.

Dragging Annie by one ear and Sandy by the other, she marched them toward the door, intending to lock them both in the cellar until the pound could come for Sandy. A ring at the doorbell made her hesitate, then she marched on. Whoever it was could wait.

But whoever it was at the door didn't feel much like waiting, because the bell rang again, longer and harder this time.

Muttering a curse, Miss Hannigan opened her office door and pushed the guilty pair inside, thrusting them into the supply closet. "Wait here, and don't you stir a muscle!

Don't you budge an inch!" she hissed at them. "I'll be back for you two in a minute."

All the way over from upper Fifth Avenue to the Hudson Street Home for Girls, Grace Farrell had wondered if she were doing the right thing. After all, he'd said an orphan. He hadn't been specific about a boy, just an orphan. His very words. But Miss Farrell knew he'd meant a boy orphan. She was taking an awful chance, wasn't she? And she had no idea what she would find when she got there.

First, she pictured a stern matron, her hair pulled back from her face and knotted into a tight, forbidding bun from which not one hair would ever be permitted to escape. Her image was of a tall, heavy woman in an institutional uniform, starched and pressed, perhaps with a bit of jet at the high neck of her shirtwaist as her only ornament. A stern woman, but fair. The children would be painfully neat and orderly, their uniforms dull and depressing, unsuited to childish faces and forms. Maybe their hair would be cut very short, like their fingernails.

But Grace Farrell was essentially of an optimistic turn of mind, and she turned at once to another mental picture. That of a sweet-faced Mother Superior type, with apple cheeks and kindly eyes. Her voice would be gentle whether in praise or mild admonishment, and the girls would be demure, their eyes cast down, their hands folded in obedience. Love would be the ruler here, and Miss Farrell much preferred this picture. But she was prepared to encounter the other.

What she wasn't prepared to encounter was the woman who opened the door and stuck out her angry face. Miss Farrell gave a small gasp of surprise. This woman was so . . . so . . . she searched briefly for a word, but her vocabulary for the likes of Miss Hannigan was severely limited. So *theatrical*.

She saw a tall, skinny woman teetering on high heels. Her red curls were dyed a garish color and evidently uncombed, because bits of padding could be seen sticking out, the padding that was known as "rats" and that made sparse hair look thicker. She was wearing much too much makeup. Her cheeks were rouged in round red circles like a clown's; like a clown's, too, was the absurdly heavy eye

31

makeup and the false eyelashes. Her clothing clung to her bony body and was cut to a deep V cleavage in front in an obvious and pathetic attempt to appear provocative. And she was a walking display rack of junk jewelry. Bangles of wood and plastic decked both her long thin arms, strings of cheap glass beads were wound around her stringy throat and cascaded down her flat chest, while a pair of long glittery earrings dangled against her cheekbones. She might not have been such a homely woman in a decent oufit, but what she was wearing made her appear like some grotesque caricature of a woman. A Hallowe'en apparition. *All she needs is a broom,* thought Grace Farrell, but she checked herself, because she was not by nature an unkind person.

"Miss Hannigan?" she asked politely.

"That's me. Who're you?" demanded the apparition.

"Miss Hannigan, I'm Grace Farrell. The New York Board of Orphans . . ."

Before she could finish her sentence, the apparition's eyes snapped open wide, and a look of terror crossed her clownish face. "W—wait . . . I have an explanation," she stammered, pulling the startled Grace Farrell out of the doorway and into the entrance hall. Miss Hannigan tugged at her nervously, while she kept talking, her free hand making anxious circular gestures in the air.

"She bribed Mr. Bundles to take her out in a laundry basket," Miss Hannigan was chattering. "I know I should have called Mr. Donatelli, but the truth of the matter is I just saw red, and called the cops. But she's back, now. So all's well that ends well, right? Right. I knew you'd agree. No harm, no foul, my little scissor legs?"

What on earth is this woman babbling about? "I'm sorry, Miss Hannigan, but what are you talking about?"

At once, the wide-open eyes narrowed into slits of suspicion, as Miss Hannigan darted into her office, with Miss Farrell following, and slammed the door shut.

"Hold it, sister. You're peddling beauty products, right? I don't need no beauty products, so you can just pedal right on out of here."

Calmly, Miss Farrell dusted off a wooden chair and sat down primly, crossing her ankles and folding her gloves neatly over her black leather purse. "Miss Hannigan, I'm the private secretary to Oliver Warbucks," she announced quietly.

The eyes snapped open again, and this time the mouth fell open to match, leaving Miss Hannigan looking like a refugee from an aquarium.

"Oliver Warbucks the millionaire?" squeaked Miss Hannigan.

"No, Oliver Warbucks the billionaire."

"The Oliver Warbucks that has more do-re-mi than all the Rockefellers put together?" The voice rose so high it almost disappeared entirely. Miss Farrell repressed the urge to laugh out loud. Although the Warbucks name always evoked the same reaction, it never failed to amuse her. Enormous fortunes seemed to impress people far more than enormous virtue or enormous wisdom.

"I don't think there's more than one," she responded quietly, a smile tugging at the corners of her mouth.

"Holy Mary, Mother of God," breathed Miss Hannigan reverently, slumping back into her chair. Then she sat up and looked Miss Farrell over sharply, to see what this woman had that could induce a millionaire . . . correction, billionaire . . . to appoint her his private secretary. Darned if she could see it. Grace Farrell was wearing the worst outfit Miss Hannigan had ever seen. It was a business suit, cut of gray flannel menswear, perfectly plain, and worn with a white bow blouse that was probably silk, but without flowers printed on it, Miss Hannigan couldn't tell for sure. Her legs were encased in ordinary silk stockings, no clocks or rhinestones, and her feet were wearing a pair of narrow leather shoes with sensible heels. Aside from a gold lapel watch—with no rubies or sapphires in it, Miss Hannigan noted—the woman wore no jewelry at all, not even a ring or earrings or necklaces or bangle bracelets. Didn't Mr. Warbucks pay her a decent salary? What was she spending her money on?

And she was a young woman, too, somewhere between twenty-seven and thirty, and she might have been pretty if she curled her hair instead of wearing it rolled back so plain, and slapped on some lipstick, rouge, and mascara. Well, it was true she looked efficient, and probably that's what suited Warbucks best, but what man would want to look at efficiency after six-o'clock quitting time?

Aware of Miss Hannigan's scrutiny, Miss Farrell sat quiet for a moment. Her own thoughts were racing. Outside, while Miss Hannigan had been babbling on nervously, Miss Farrell had taken a quick look at her surroundings, and what she'd seen had appalled her. The children looked underfed and overworked; she had glimpsed the laundry room, with little girls straining over huge washboards and steaming tubs. Somewhere she could hear the hum of many sewing machines all working at once. Were these girls supposed to be working like this? Weren't they supposed to be in classes? Why were they so pale? Were there no outside exercise facilities for them? No sports or games? No romps through the park? And why were they so ragged? Weren't new clothes issued to them on a regular basis, or at least when they outgrew the old? How ironic that a place like this should be called an "asylum," when the word meant haven, a place of refuge.

She had expected nothing like this, and she was having second thoughts about her errand here. It was intended as a kindness, of course, but what if it turned out to be a cruelty instead? Was it fair to remove a child from these ghastly surroundings—and never had she seen an institution so drab, so depressing—only to throw the child right back again, and make her more miserable than before? Would it not be kinder to leave the child here, before giving her only a taste of what she was missing in life?

If the choice were hers, Grace Farrell would get up right now and leave. But it wasn't hers; she was here on instructions from Mr. Warbucks, and it was her job to carry those instructions out.

"Mr. Warbucks wants to invite an orphan to spend a week with him in his home," she said clearly. "I'm here to select one."

Annie, in Miss Hannigan's supply closet, had been listening hard to every word. She'd opened the closet door a fraction of an inch, and had been looking at Grace Farrell. My, that was the prettiest lady she'd ever seen, prettier than any of them in the Sunday rotogravures. So elegantly dressed, with such a shining, clean face, and such beautiful, kind gray eyes. And her hair was rolled away from her face and pinned neatly back, just like Annie's own mother in the Dream. Annie bet this lady didn't get drunk and call helpless orphans pig droppings. She pushed the closet door open a little and flashed Miss Farrell her very brightest freckle-faced grin, turning the volume on her charm control way, way up.

"Wonderful," Miss Hannigan was saying without enthusiasm, having barely recovered from the shock of Miss Farrell's announcement. "What sort of orphan did he have in mind?" She saw Miss Farrell's eyes widen slightly as she caught a glimpse of Annie grinning from the closet, and she slammed the door hard, nearly catching Annie's nose in it.

"Well . . ." Miss Farrell hesitated, captured by the image of the little girl's smiling face. "Friendly and intelligent . . ."

The closet door opened again, and Annie's face appeared, looking friendly and intelligent with all its might.

"M-I-Double-S-I-Double-S-I-Double-P-I," she chanted, proving her smarts.

Hannigan turned, snarling, and shoved her back into the closet again, slamming the door extra hard. "You're asking for it, my little prune pit."

"And happy," continued Miss Farrell, her amused eyes on the closet door. The door opened silently and Annie mimed being happy, clutching at her ribs and mouthing laughter.

"The trials of a working woman," sighed Miss Hannigan with an elaborate show of put-upon patience.

"I'm in somewhat of a hurry, Miss Hannigan," Miss Farrell replied with a frosty smile.

"Of course," snapped Miss Hannigan, dragging a manila file folder toward her officiously. "How old?"

"Oh, the age doesn't matter. Seven or eight . . ."

The closet door opened a fraction of an inch and Annie's little hand signaled frantically.

"Or nine . . ."

Another frantic signal.

"Or ten?"

The hand gave a little "on-the-button" wave.

"Yes, ten, I think," said Grace Farrell.

The little hand appeared again, this time tugging at a curly lock of carrot hair. Miss Farrell suppressed a grin; she was enjoying this game, enjoying, too, the audacity and spunk of this youngster. The child had formed an alliance with her against Miss Hannigan, and in the most ingenious way.

"Oh, I almost forgot. Mr. Warbucks prefers redheaded children."

Miss Hannigan whipped around suspiciously, but the closet door presented the most bland and innocent aspect a closed door could offer. "A ten-year-old redhead?" she retorted briskly. "Nope. Sorry. Don't have one."

Ta-da! The closet door was flung open wide, and Annie stepped out, to the imaginary flourish of invisible trumpets.

"What about *this* child?" asked Miss Farrell, standing up.

"Annie?" shrieked Miss Hannigan, aghast. "Oh, no, you wouldn't want Annie. She's——" she searched for an epithet dreadful enough to scare Miss Farrell off, "she's a drunk."

Grace Farrell uttered a short laugh, and took the child by the hand. "Oh, fiddle-faddle. Annie, would you like to spend a week at Mr. Warbucks' house?"

The electric lights of Times Square would have been pale candles to Annie's joyous face. "Oh, boy! I would love to! I would really, really love to!" She fairly danced in excitement.

"Hold it!" barked Miss Hannigan, who was really furious now. "You can have any orphan in the orphanage, except Annie."

"Why?" demanded Grace Farrell hotly.

Miss Hannigan snatched the child away from the younger woman and thrust her behind her office chair. Her words came out through clenched teeth, as though every one was being bitten off and spat out. "Because she's got it coming to her, and I don't mean a week in the lap of luxury. This brat needs to learn her place."

"Her place?" Miss Farrell's eyebrows rose toward her hat brim.

"I rent out my older girls as domestics. Annie's entirely too cheeky."

"Mr. Warbucks likes cheeky orphans." Heaven forgive me for that lie.

"Tough," spat Miss Hannigan, and it was obvious to Grace that the other woman didn't intend to yield an inch. And a curious stubbornness was creeping over Miss Farrell herself, taking her rather by surprise, for she considered herself to be a businesslike and practical young woman. Was it something special about this freckle-faced little girl, or was it just the Irish in Farrell? She wasn't sure. But she discovered that she was just as determined to take this child as Miss Hannigan was to prevent her from going. And she surprised herself even further by her next tactic. She didn't think she had it in her.

"I assume your resistance has something to do with Mr. Donatelli and the board of orphans——" she began icily.

"Don't assume nothing, sweetheart," hissed Miss Hannigan.

"Mr. Warbucks and Mr. Donatelli are like this," she continued, holding up her right hand with the two first fingers crossed.

She's lying, thought Hannigan. *She's bluffing.* She gave an elaborate yawn of boredom, then buffed her fingernails on her blouse and studied them carefully. "Is that a fact," she said. It was not a question.

"Yes, that's a fact," went on Grace Farrell, her face betraying nothing. "And it's a further fact that Mr. Donatelli was at the house just last week saying how many people he had lined up for your job." And she, too, studied her hands, as she pulled her gloves on carefully, finger by finger.

She's bluffing, Miss Hannigan told herself again, but with far less conviction. Yet it was far from impossible, very far. "Is that a fact?" And this time it was a question.

"Awful time to be unemployed," Miss Farrell commented.

"Just terrible," agreed Miss Hannigan.

A long moment passed between them, during which time Grace Farrell sent up a little prayer of thanks that Miss Hannigan had babbled to her of a Mr. Donatelli, whoever he was, and a little prayer without words, for Annie.

At last, without a word, Miss Hannigan shoved Annie roughly at Miss Farrell. She couldn't take the chance, not with unemployment figures so high. Besides, the kid would be back in a week, and would she get it then! Miss Hannigan would devote the entire week to devising new and fiendish punishments. *I deserve a treat,* she told herself.

"Leapin' lizards!" yelled Annie ecstatically, and Grace Farrell allowed herself a broad smile.

"Come along, dear. Mr. Warbucks' limousine is waiting." She was rather pleased with herself at the way she'd handled that, and could wish that Mr. Warbucks had been there to see it. Of course, if Oliver Warbucks *had* been present, nothing would have had to be handled. He was accustomed to commanding immediate obedience, and receiving it.

But Annie was hanging back now, her face clouded, her blue eyes anxious.

"My dog," she said simply.

Miss Farrell's gray eyes widened. "Your what?" she gasped, but Annie was already pulling open the supply closet door, and leading out Sandy. He was the worst-looking, scruffiest, dirtiest, least-prepossessing mongrel Miss Farrell had encountered in all her twenty-eight years, but before she could open her mouth to protest, Sandy bounded over to her.

"He's really nice, really quiet, really, really good," Annie was assuring her. "He never jumps up on people."

As if on cue, Sandy jumped up on Grace, his muddy paws on her custom-tailored suit, his hot breath on her face and . . . oh, no . . . gave her a really wet, really slobbering kiss, pushing her hat nearly off.

She took a few steps backward, shaking her head, and tried to get her breath back. "I'm afraid not, Annie. He's very sweet, but Mr. Warbucks—"

"Then I'm not coming," said Annie, not defiantly, but with sad determination.

Both women turned to her in astonishment, but Annie met their gaze firmly. They could see that this was very hard for her, for her expressive face had grown quite pale, and her lips were trembling.

Miss Hannigan recovered first. "Mr. Warbucks wouldn't rather have a good-looking lady?" she wheedled, patting at her ratty hair. "I got a week coming."

Annie took a step forward and grabbed Grace Farrell by the hand. "She's going to send him to the sausage factory," she pleaded. "She said so herself."

Grace gasped and turned a face of outrage upon Miss Hannigan, who defended herself sullenly. "I'm not zoned for dogs."

"We'll take the dog," decided Miss Farrell. *Heaven help me, what am I doing? Mr. Warbucks will have my hide.*

Annie's face reflected her happiness. "Oh, boy!" she exulted.

As they walked toward the front door, Miss Farrell was feeling dazed and even a little helpless. What had she done? Oliver Warbucks had sent her to fetch an orphan boy of good manners and a retiring disposition, and no dog. And here she was coming back with a feisty, rambunctious redheaded girl and a dog of uncertain parentage whose enthusiasm for life and noisy way of showing it matched the girl's own. And to top it off, the dog smelled to high heaven and had fleas! How unlike her usual efficiency; what *would* Mr. Warbucks say?

And yet, as she led the way to the twenty-five-foot-long limousine (*Holy Mother of God!* wailed Miss Hannigan silently. *A Town Car!*) with the license plate NY-1, a license plate that by tradition belonged to the governor of New York until Mr. Warbucks decided he wanted it, Grace Farrell felt that there was nothing she wanted to change. She felt a pull toward this bright little girl with the carroty mop, as though they'd known each other for years, in a dream perhaps. She felt that this was the child she had come to get, pure and simple. Yes, it was only for a week, and back Annie would have to go, into Miss Hannigan's vicious clutches. But a week, well spent, could be a very long time. Who knows what could happen in a week?

Annie didn't take the time to examine the luxurious limousine and the strange-looking Oriental, dressed all in black, at the wheel, she was so eager to get started. She couldn't believe her luck. This day had been so full already, with more to come. Sandy danced into the Town Car as to the manor born, and Annie was about to follow, when she heard a commotion above.

The orphans were crowded at the windows, waving and yelling, and Molly, predictably, was in tears.

"Don't go, Annie!" she wailed, heart-broken.

Annie grinned and waved. A week wasn't so long. "I'll be back!" she promised. "I'll bring everybody presents!"

Then, minding her manners, she carefully wiped her feet, cleaning each shoe on the back of her other leg before she stepped into the Town Car. She could smell the leather and the lovely clean scent of the beeswax that kept the leather polished. The interior was of Honduras mahogany, with solid silver fittings; there were curtains at the windows and fresh roses in little silver-and-crystal vases on the car's walls. Annie looked about her in astonishment, then sank happily back on the leather cushions as the car pulled silently away from the curb and picked up speed.

This has been the very best day of my life, she told herself as they headed uptown. *And it's not over yet.*

This is the worst day of my life, growled Miss Hannigan to herself as she watched the Town Car speed off. *But I'll get even. That miserable troublemaker, that rotten kid, will be the sorriest orphan in the universe when I get my hands on her again.*

CHAPTER FOUR

You've been to Buckingham Palace, haven't you? I know you have, because the Queen asked for you by name the last time I had tea there. And you've been to Louis the Sun King's glorious palace at Versailles, and to the Metropolitan Museum of Art in New York, and to the Vatican in Rome. But Annie had never been to any of these places, so she was totally unprepared for Oliver Warbucks' mansion on upper Fifth Avenue.

First of all, you entered through a tall pair of iron gates, always kept locked, which led to a long, circular driveway. The Asp, who was driving the Town Car, took a mysterious magnetic device out of his uniform pocket and the gates opened as if by magic. The Town Car slid purring up the driveway and stopped without a bump or quiver outside the broad steps and the huge carved-oak doors.

Annie peeked out of the window. A stone and marble edifice four stories high filled two city blocks. It was a villa in the Italian Renaissance style, designed by Stanford White. The windows were topped by arched pediments; there were elaborately carved acanthus ornaments at the house corners. The house boasted a copper roof, which gleamed in the sunlight. Two massive lions of stone guarded the entrance, paws raised in silent warning. It was by far the largest building Annie had ever seen, and she was thrilled at its majesty.

"Are we going on a train? Is this a train station?" she asked Miss Farrell excitedly.

Grace Farrell smiled down at her and shook her head. "No, dear, this is Mr. Warbucks' house."

"Leapin' lizards!" breathed Annie. She tumbled out of the car after Miss Farrell, and Sandy followed clumsily, his paws sliding on the marble steps.

The thick oak doors opened suddenly, and Annie froze on the spot, her mouth open in astonishment. Standing in the doorway, almost filling it, was the tallest man Annie had ever seen. He was so tall he made the stone lions look like kittens beside him. His skin was very dark, almost black, and he wore a strange uniform, with golden epaulets on the shoulders of a long, white, form-fitting tunic. Golden chains were looped around his neck and over his chest, gold flashed on his dark fingers. On his head, the nine-foot-tall giant wore a huge turban made of a rare silk cloth shot with threads of gold, and wound round and round and round until the many yards of it had been tucked neatly into the knotted headdress. From the center of the turban, topped by an egret feather, flashed a pigeon's-blood ruby, the rarest in all India, and it caught the sunlight and turned into a heart of fiery flame. The man's lips parted in what he believed to be a smile, but to Annie it was a grin of such terror-inducing menace that she squeaked in fear and ran to hide behind Grace Farrell's skirts. Annie wasn't afraid of much, but she'd never encountered anything like this man before. Why, his black polished boots were almost large enough for her to hide in!

Sandy, sensing Annie's fear and scared to death of this man-mountain himself, broke into hysterical barking.

In an instant, everything was noise and confusion— Annie hiding and near tears, Sandy almost hoarse with barking. Grace was unable to hear herself think. She glared at the Asp, who, with Oriental calm and detachment, remained seated behind the wheel of the Town Car.

"You're a big help," she told him in an exasperated tone, trying to be heard over the barking.

The Asp shrugged slightly. "I have to put the car in the garage," he said mildly, but Grace had the sneaking feeling he was enjoying all this in his silent way.

She reached around her and pulled the quaking Annie out of hiding. "Annie, this is Punjab," she said, indicating the giant in the Indian officer's uniform. "Punjab and the Asp are Mr. Warbucks' bodyguards. There's nothing to be afraid of."

Punjab raised his hands in the air and made a couple of mysterious passes. At once, Sandy stopped barking, walked up the stairs in a straight line, and stopped at Punjab's feet. There he lay down on his back, all four feet in the air, and a doggy smile on his face.

Annie's fear evaporated. Wow, what a trick! Could he teach her that? She ran up the steps, her right hand extended for a shake.

"I'm Annie," she grinned. "Boy, I wouldn't want to come across you in a dark alley."

Punjab leaned down solemnly and took the little girl's hand into his large black one, where it disappeared entirely. A current of energy passed between them; both felt it, as though electricity had forged them together. He looked deeply into her eyes.

Now they passed into the entrance hallway, where Annie gasped again. Huge and mirrored, with a massive chandelier of scintillating crystal drops reflecting from the marble floors, the entrance hall alone was fifty feet long and forty wide. Heavy paintings hung on the walls between the elaborately carved mirror frames, and below them, on console tables of gilded wood, stood bronze statues, marble busts and gigantic bouquets of hothouse blooms in rare Ming vases. On an easel stood a framed Rembrandt, looking almost lost in the vastness of the space around it. Tall curio cabinets held priceless T'ang horses of jade and other precious stones, exquisite examples of Greek pottery from the fifth century B.C., and tiny porphyry vases of Egypt's Middle Kingdom. At the end of the vast hallway, a graceful staircase of marble curved upward to the higher floors.

"Wow!" Annie breathed, unable to say more. An army of servants was mopping, dusting, polishing, and scrubbing the already gleaming surfaces. One man in a footman's uniform was standing on tiptoe on the highest rung of a fourteen-foot ladder, dusting the moldings with an ostrich-feather duster on a long pole. Another, with a large can of marble cleaner, was rubbing a coat of it into the staircase. Two other footmen, with lamb's-wool buffers strapped to their feet, were skating down the hallway, adding an extra gloss to the highly polished and very slick floor. Standing at a sideboard, the head butler, Drake, was putting the finishing touches on an elaborate Georgian silver tea service, making certain that no stain of tarnish, no matter how tiny, marred the flawless surface of the silver.

Sandy, bounding with doggy enthusiasm into the entry, slipped and skidded on the polished floor. As his paws went out from under him, he scrabbled desperately in the air, found his footing, lost it again, and went skidding and skittering all the long way down the hallway, to fetch up at the disdainful feet of Drake, the head butler.

Drake inclined his aristocratic head only enough to look down his nose at his formerly glistening black shoes, now covered by a scruffy and unpleasant-smelling canine of no discernible ancestry and certainly of no breeding. Drake uttered a disapproving sneeze.

"I take it you've been to the zoo, Miss Farrell?"

"Not recently, Drake." Miss Farrell took on an air of command as she marched down the endless foyer with Drake at her side. She fired a string of questions at him.

"Has the organ been tuned, the pool heated, the floors waxed . . . well, yes"—with an amused glance at Sandy, who was living proof the floor was waxed as he skidded after Annie and Grace Farrell—"is the tennis court net up, the French doors fixed, the elevator oiled, the typewriter repaired, the second teletype installed, and the photographer here?"

It was only then, as the last question brought them to a baronial chair outside the drawing room, in which a little man with a belted raincoat and a slouch-brim fedora sat clutching a huge Speed Graphic with flashbulb attachments, that Drake was able to slip in an edgewise word.

"Yes, Miss Farrell," and he sneezed again, casting a venomous glare at Sandy.

"Allergic to dogs, Drake?"

"No," said the butler, with his nose as far into the air as he could send it, "filth."

Grace Farrell turned to see Mrs. Pugh, the cook, bustling up, tying on a clean apron.

"Is dinner under way, Mrs. Pugh?"

"Yes, miss," and the plump cook beamed all over her rosy face. "I'm preparing his favorite. Texas grapefruit, Virginia ham, Idaho potatoes, Wisconsin cheese, Washington apples, and baked Alaska."

"Good. Now, everybody listen, please. I have an announcement to make that concerns you all."

The staff stopped waxing, polishing, dusting, scrubbing, scouring, and tidying and turned its full attention to Miss Farrell. She, in turn, looked around for Annie, who was standing behind her, half hidden, with her china-blue eyes as large and as round as saucers with sheer astonishment at all this undreamt-of grandeur.

"This is Annie. She'll be staying with us for a week."

The staff came crowding around to have a look, and Annie found herself in the thick of black uniforms and white aprons, polished shoes and boots and curious faces.

"Miss." Were they bowing to *her*, to a little orphan named Annie? Leapin' lizards!

"And her dog Sandy," said Miss Farrell graciously.

"Who'll be staying with *me*," put in Annie, to a general outbreak of laughter from everybody but Drake.

The prettiest of the three chambermaids, Annette, took a step forward. "May I take your sweater, miss?"

Annie clutched at her precious red sweater, which was half of everything she owned. "Will I get it back?"

"Lord love you, yes, miss."

Reluctantly, Annie took it off and handed it over, but kept an anxious eye on it for a minute or two.

"Now, Annie," said Grace Farrell, "what would you like to do first?"

Annie looked around carefully, thinking hard. Then she made up her mind. "The windows," she said decisively. "Then the floors." She began rolling up the sleeves of her shabby smock. "That way, if I drip—"

The explosion of hilarity interrupted and surprised her. Everybody—with the natural exception of Drake—was laughing fit to bust, the footmen guffawing, the maids giggling, Mrs. Pugh holding her ample sides. Even Grace Farrell was laughing as she bent to give the child a quick hug.

"Oh, Annie, you won't have to do any cleaning while you're here."

Annie was totally bewildered now. "I won't? How'm I going to earn my keep?" she asked, her tiny brow puckered with doubt.

Grace Farrell was smiling into her eyes, Grace Farrell

had taken both of Annie's hands in hers, and Annie saw again how lovely she was.

"You're our *guest*, Annie," said Miss Farrell softly. "We'll take care of you. You're to have new clothing, and Cecille will help you dress and comb your hair. There will be bubbles in your bathtub, and clean satin sheets on your bed. When you've decided what you want to eat, just let Mrs. Pugh know, and you shall have it for your next meal, whatever it is."

The saucers of Annie's eyes grew to the size of dinner plates. Could she believe her ears?

"You'll find the swimming pool downstairs," continued Miss Farrell.

"A swimming pool inside the house?" This was too good to be true. "Oh, boy!"

"You do play tennis, don't you? We have a tennis court outside. Two, actually, one grass and one clay."

Overwhelmed, Annie shook her head. "I . . . I . . . never even saw a tennis racquet," she admitted.

"Have an instructor here at noon," Grace said to Drake. "Oh, and get that Don Budge fellow, if he's available." Drake went off to the telephone at once to see if Budge was available. And he was, for after all, he wasn't going to win the Grand Slam for another five years, or the Wimbledon singles and doubles for another four.

Annie's head was whirling so she was afraid it would lift off her neck and go flying around the room. When Annette, Cecille, and Miss Farrell showed her to the room she would sleep in, she almost passed out cold! She had more space than all the orphans in the Hudson Street Home for Girls, Established 1891, had put together. A huge pink bed, with pink counterpane and matching canopy, tied back with sprigs of roses. A full-length mirror framed in gold, in which Annie could see a shabby red-headed orphan with an ear-to-ear grin on her face. Closets that she was assured would be filled with clothes; shelves that she was told would be crammed with books and toys. A bathroom, all her very own, with a thick soft rug and double-thick terry towels. Annie had never seen a terry towel before; at the orphanage, all they had were basins of tepid water, ice-cold floors, and ragged "towels" made of old flour sacks. It was all so overwhelming that she couldn't take it in at once. It was making her dizzy, and she collapsed on the thick carpeting in a heap, followed by Sandy, who melted into a canine puddle next to her, still wagging his tail furiously.

It was time for Miss Farrell to take charge, to put her famous efficiency to use. Annette she sent to the Fifth Avenue shops, De Pinna and Best and Company, to collect a suitable wardrobe for a ten-year-old child and bring it back at once. And, since Annie had no clothes to wear now anyway, why not go swimming first, then lunch? Somewhere there was a bathing suit to fit her; the under-gardener had a daughter just about Annie's size. Would that do?

Would that do! Swimming! Although she had never swum before (a fact she neglected to mention to Miss Farrell), Annie took to it like a baby duck, first paddling around in imitation of Sandy, who never left her side, just in case, and later developing almost a sidestroke. Miss Farrell, watching from the side of the turquoise pool with the Roman mosaics on the floor, made a mental note to see if Eleanor Holm, the swimming star, might be persuaded to drop by and show Annie the butterfly stroke.

Most of the staff, instead of returning to their duties, hung around the swimming pool to watch Annie. They had never had—or ever expected to have—a little girl in this house. They had seen princes and prime ministers come in and go out through the big oak doors, plutocrats, philosophers, poets, pundits, and playwrights (Mr. Warbucks being quite chummy with Mr. Bernard Shaw), but Annie was a novelty, and they watched her splashing around in delight. Her enjoyment brought smiles to their faces, with the exception of Drake, to be sure, who closed his eyes in horror as Sandy spread dirt and fleas in the chlorinated water. They'd have to drain the pool.

Suddenly, what sounded like an air-raid siren went off with a head-splitting wail. All at once, the servants began rushing to the exit, jostling one another aside in their haste to get out. As they ran, they were straightening their hair anxiously, patting hair nets into place, checking the buttons on their uniform jackets, retying the bows of their aprons more neatly.

"What is it?" asked Annie fearfully, climbing out of the

pool. Sandy clambered out after her and shook himself
mightily, spraying water everywhere.

"It's Mr. Warbucks," replied Miss Farrell, distracted.
"Don't be afraid." But she herself was looking anxious,
checking the seams of her stockings, smoothing down the
skirt of her tailored suit. In an undertone she gave orders
that Annie be taken up to her room, dressed and combed
and brought right back down again. Then she herself
hurried off to be at the front door when Mr. Warbucks
came in. The noisy siren had signaled that his car—today
he'd taken the Dusenberg, with the license plate NY-2,
which used to belong to the lieutenant governor—had
reached the garage. The siren was known to the staff as
the Two-Minute Warning, or Oh-Oh, Here He Comes.

Because Annie had almost nothing to wear, and because
her mop of red curls defied any comb, she was down in
time to see the front doors open and Oliver Warbucks
stride in, flanked on either side by Punjab and the Asp.
A sudden shyness seized her, and she hid behind one of
the great marble pillars in the hall, peeping out with curiosity at this man who held so much power over so many.

She saw a tall man of commanding presence, a man
who walked with his spine as stiff as a broomstick, his
head held high. It was a strange head, bald as a peeled
hard-boiled egg, shaven clean every day. The jaw was
strong and jutting, the mouth stubborn, yet it was a handsome face. From where she was hiding, Annie couldn't see
the color of Oliver Warbucks' eyes, but she could see them
glinting and she guessed—correctly—that they were the
color of steel. It was a stern face, but not a mean one. Impatient, arrogant but not vain. Oliver Warbucks looked to
be a man of large faults, but no little frailties. Annie decided she liked him, but she knew she was also a little
afraid of him. Sandy cowered at her feet, his paws over
his eyes.

Warbucks was dressed in a suit of black, with a vest that
bore a heavy gold chain across his middle, from which
hung various golden nuggets. A diamond stickpin glittered
on his shirt. A stiff collar and a somewhat old-fashioned
black bow tie completed the costume of a billionaire.
Annie was to learn that this was his invariable costume,
and that he had vast closets crammed with identical copies

of this very suit, drawers filled with hundreds and hundreds of white stiff-collared shirts. He had no patience with valets, or choosing neckties, or matching blue shirts to brown tweeds. Oliver Warbucks knew what he liked, and when he found it, he stuck to it.

"Welcome home, sir," she could hear Grace Farrell say, as Warbucks marched to the sideboard where the silver tea service was standing ready. He took no tea, however, but accepted the brandy and the Havana cigar that she was lighting for him.

He didn't return the greeting, but asked abruptly, "Did the painting arrive?"

"They're uncrating it now, sir," said Grace quietly, indicating with a slight movement of her head where two men in coveralls were carefully lifting a painting out of an elaborately constructed wooden packing case that bore steamship labels from the S.S. *Normandie*. They turned the painting around so that it faced Warbucks.

Oliver Warbucks stared at it for a minute, scowling.

"I hate it. Send it back," he said finally. "Any messages?"

Grace Farrell had learned to keep her opinions to herself, but she could barely repress a gasp. Hate it? Hate the *Mona Lisa,* Leonardo's masterpiece, the most famous portrait in the history of art? But all she said was, "President Roosevelt called three times this morning. Said it was urgent."

Behind her pillar, Annie *did* gasp. The president of the United States! Why, Roosevelt was Annie's hero! He was going to make things better for everybody, even orphans! Annie had heard it on Miss Hannigan's radio, the last time Miss Hannigan had obliged them by passing out.

Warbucks' scowl deepened. "Everything's urgent to a Democrat," he rasped. He spoke with a slight accent, one that Annie had never heard before. "What else?"

Miss Farrell consulted her message pad. "Mr. Rockefeller, Mr. DuPont, Mr. Vanderbilt, Mr. Carnegie . . ."

"Wait!" barked Warbucks. The men lowering the painting back into the Louvre's packing crate stopped, suspended at the billionaire's command. "There's something interesting in that woman's smile. I might learn to like her. Take her upstairs and hang her in my bathroom."

They nodded immediately, and lifted *La Gioconda* back out of the case, using the utmost delicacy, for no value could be set on this painting; it was absolutely priceless, and the Louvre had parted with it only after Warbucks had rescued France's failing economy single-handed.

"Mr. Warbucks, I'd like you to meet—" began Miss Farrell, but Warbucks paid no attention. Which was just as well, because Annie was still hiding behind the pillar, trying to get up the nerve to emerge and be introduced.

Briskly, Warbucks picked up his briefcase again and headed for the stairs, issuing crisp commands over his shoulder.

"I've no time for dinner tonight, Mrs. Pugh. Send up an American cheese sandwich at midnight." The plump cook's face fell as she thought of her lovely dinner going uneaten. But she didn't dare to do more than nod her acquiescence.

"Come on, Miss Farrell, let's get started," ordered Warbucks, making an abrupt turn, and nearly falling over Annie, who had decided to come out after all, but who'd chosen the wrong moment and the wrong place. As soon as she and Warbucks collided, the photographer leaped up with his trusty Speed Graphic and snapped their picture with a brilliant and noisy pop of his flashbulb.

Between tripping over the child and having a flashbulb go off unexpectedly in his face, Warbucks was totally at a loss, a situation he found himself in almost never. He opened his mouth and let out a roar.

"Punjab."

Like a streak of black lightning, the Indian giant was across the lobby and on the photographer, pinning him against the wall with one huge hand, while the other crumpled the expensive camera as if it were so much cellophane.

"What the devil is going on here?" bellowed Warbucks.

"Forgive me, sahib. Miss Farrell said—"

Grace was talking at the same time, "This is Annie, sir, the orphan who'll be staying with us for a week."

Warbucks looked down at Annie, his brow furrowed, the corners of his mouth turning down in the scowl that was so characteristic of him. "Orphan? What are you talking about?" He pointed a finger at the shaken photographer. "Who's he?"

In her most soothing tones, Miss Farrell reminded her employer gently, "The public relations people? Your image?" Warbucks' scowl was now looking puzzled. It was obvious he had no idea what his secretary was babbling about.

"They wanted photographs of you sharing your home with an orphan, sir, don't you remember? It's just for a week, sir."

Annie held her breath, begging him silently to remember.

"Oh," said Mr. Warbucks. "Yes," said Mr. Warbucks. "Hmmm," said Mr. Warbucks. He looked a little embarrassed and uncomfortable, then he took a long, hard look at Annie.

"But this doesn't look like a boy," he told Miss Farrell. "Orphans are boys."

I was afraid this would happen, thought Grace. *Poor Annie.* "You didn't say you wanted a boy," she spoke up rather bravely. "You just said orphan. So I got a girl," she finished in a much smaller voice.

Warbucks gave her a steely stare. "I want a boy." He turned his back on them both and headed once more for the stairs, but Annie trotted by his side.

"I've got an interesting smile too, sir." She grinned up at him anxiously. "Don'tcha think maybe you could learn to like me, too, sir? Hang me in the bathroom?" She waited hopefully for a response, but he didn't even crack a smile. Oliver Warbucks' mind was elsewhere. He turned to Miss Farrell sharply.

"Why do I smell wet dog?" he demanded.

Grace winced, and opened her mouth to make some explanation, then shut it again. Seeing her predicament, Annie snapped her fingers. At once, a fearful, soaking Sandy, looking like an oversized wet mop with a hangover, crawled out from behind the pillar and slid on his belly over to Annie's feet. He still didn't trust that waxed floor.

"Because Sandy got wet in the pool, sir," said Annie.

Warbucks stared at the mutt in disbelief. That wretched object, under the same roof with his Rembrandt and his Leonardo Da Vinci? He looked across at Grace Farrell, whose cheeks were stained dull red with embarrassment. "Take them back," he commanded, his voice dripping with ice. "Now."

"Oh, sir," pleaded Grace through the lump rising in her throat. "She only got here." She felt far worse for Annie than she did for herself, although it was her own neck and her own job that were on the line here.

But Annie was stepping up bravely, Annie was forcing a smile. "That's okay, Miss Farrell. We'll be okay," she was saying. The little girl turned to Oliver Warbucks and held her right hand out. "It's been real nice meeting you, sir, anyhow. I sure do like your place . . ."

Still a little dazed from the experience of meeting an orphan of the wrong gender and a dog of the wrong everything, Mr. Warbucks finally noticed the small hand, took it faintly and shook it a little.

"Thank you, Annette, I—"

"Annie," interrupted Annie. "I've really had a swell time already. The Asp drove us here in a car the size of a train, Mr. Warbucks, and Punjab put a spell on Sandy, and we made Drake sneeze, and we saw your tennis court, and Sandy got to swim in your pool, and . . . well . . . I've had enough fun to last me for years. It's a really swell idea to have an orphan for a week, Mr. Warbucks, a really terrific idea, even if it's only for a week, and only for your image, and even if I'm not the orphan. I'm glad you're doing it."

Incredulous, Oliver Warbucks finally found his voice. "I'm glad you approve." He turned to his secretary. "Let's get to work," he said impatiently, burning to begin. Time was his most precious commodity; he already had more money than the country of India or the state of Rhode Island.

Going up the stairs, Grace said hesitantly, "Since we have so much to do, maybe I could take her back in the morning?" She snuck a look at Mr. Warbucks to see how he would take this suggestion.

But he was already opening his mail, and paying only scant attention to her words. "Whatever. Let's go!"

Annie and Grace exchanged one brief, joyous, triumphant glance. At least, Annie had been reprieved until morning. And who knows what might happen between now and morning? Why, anything! Then Grace Farrell dashed up the stairs after Oliver Warbucks, ready to put in many long hours of work.

As for Annie, although she had meant what she said to Oliver Warbucks, she was delighted for her sake that she could stay the night. Just to sleep in that wonderful bed, with the counterpane and canopy of roses, and all that room! Just to spend the rest of the day here, in this palace, to try to get every detail by heart to tell the other orphans when she went back in the morning . . . in the morning. Annie sighed, thinking of the morning, but she brightened again. She was going to make this day last, squeeze every drop of joy from it that she could.

"C'mon, Sandy! If we've got only one day, let's make the most of it."

CHAPTER FIVE

After the Town Car had turned the corner, carrying the rotten kid to her unjust reward, Miss Hannigan did what any self-respecting slattern with red blood in her veins would do. She went into her room, locked the door, and tied one on. She got plastered, bombed, looped, stewed, blotto, and all the while she was dipping her flask in the bathtub and bringing it up dripping with gin, Miss Hannigan was contemplating the injustices of this world, and the many and awful crosses she had to bear on the rock-strewn pathway of her life.

"Little girls," she muttered to herself, flinging herself across a bed strewn with torn stockings, dirty kimonos, and old movie magazines with Jean Harlow on their covers, "little girls, how I hate 'em. Look at me, I'm still young, I'm still beautiful [this was a favorite fantasy of Miss Hannigan's], I'd make some lucky man a wonderful wife, but why am I stuck here with sixty miserable, rotten, whiny, nasty, hateful, horrible little girls?" She moaned, and staggered off the bed to wobble to the mirror and contemplate her bleary image.

"I should be out dancing somewhere, somewhere where a tango orchestra is playing, and the night is young. I should be wearing fox furs and a diamond necklace. Not many women can carry off diamonds, but I can," she told her reflection confidingly. "I should be driving around in a *big* car, a Reo maybe, or an Olds, and going to the movies every night with a box of chocolate-covered cherries. Instead, here I am stuck playing nursemaid to sixty of the schemingest, most defiant, freshest bunch of ungrateful individuals that God ever put on this earth to torture a poor, hardworking creature like me who never harmed the hair on the head of a fly." She was in the self-pity stage now, which was usually followed by blind rage, then the blind staggers, and then she usually passed out.

"What have I ever done to deserve all these children?" moaned Miss Hannigan, taking another hefty swig from the flask. "Not that I wouldn't be a perfect mother, kind, gentle, loving, totally unselfish and giving, self-sacrificing, devoted, saintly, caring for the hideous little brats night and day with never a thought for my own comfort or convenience."

Breaking off to take another long drink from the flask, Miss Hannigan drained it to the last lethal drop. *Thish will never do. Gotta filler up again. Mish Hannigan needs her vitamins, or thoshe li'l monshters will get the better of her.*

She wavered into the bathroom on her shaky skinny legs and fell to the floor with her arm in the tub. Fortunately, it was the arm that held the flask in its hand, so she sat there for a minute or ten, listening in rapture as the flask gurgled in the gin stew. Maybe another juniper berry or two . . . give it a li'l bezazz, a little hotcha. Miss Hannigan was so preoccupied with her beloved home brew that she didn't hear any sound at all from the other room, with the result that when she wandered back into her bedroom and saw a strange man and a strange woman sitting on her bed, she was so startled that she let out one loud scream and sobered up almost completely.

"Hi, sis!" said the strange man with a grin.

Miss Hannigan squinted to see him better. There *was* something vaguely familiar about that ratty little face with its pointed weasel nose, squirrel teeth, beady little eyes, and no chin. The ratty little face had grown a thin moustache since the last time Miss Hannigan had laid eyes on it, and that's what had thrown her off. That and the quantity of gin she'd ladled down her throat this morning.

"Rooster!" she cried without pleasure as she recognized her brother. "Aren't you a sight for sore eyes, Rooster? What is this, did they let you out of jail early?"

"On account of his good behavior," simpered the woman, whom Miss Hannigan had never seen before. She was snuggled so close to Rooster Hannigan, it appeared she wanted to force her way through him to the other side.

"Sis," said he with a complacent male grin, "meet a little friend of mine, Lily St. Regis."

Miss Hannigan turned no friendly face in the young woman's direction. She saw a bleached blonde, round in all the places where Miss Hannigan was flat, wearing a tight rayon satin dress, black net stockings, and four-inch heels. Her face might have been pretty if you could see it, but it was hidden under so many layers of makeup that the features were almost indistinguishable, except for the mouth, which was painted in the form of a perfect cupid's bow.

"St. Regis," the young woman giggled. "Named for the hotel." She tightened her grasp on Rooster, as though afraid he was going to make a break for the exit.

"You couldn't find the Waldorf?" Miss Hannigan asked her brother, her voice dripping with sarcasm. She wasn't happy to see Rooster; on the contrary, he never came around unless he wanted something, and that something was invariably money. He had ways of getting it, too, ways that Miss Hannigan recalled were customarily unpleasant. There was no love lost between these two, but at least Miss Hannigan worked for part of her living. Rooster stole for all of his.

Now his arm was stealing, stealing around his sister's shoulder as he turned her attention away from his girlfriend, who was quietly rummaging through Miss Hannigan's personal possessions, helping herself to the bits and pieces she fancied. She slipped rings on her fingers, bracelets on her arms, and tucked lavalieres and strings of beads into her ample bosom.

"Sis, this very afternoon I put me a ten on the nose of this darling horse, eight to one. Sure enough, the scumbum took off and whipped the pack." Rooster's little eyes glittered with the scam.

"Rooster, that's great. Let's celebrate," grinned Miss Hannigan, always ready for another drink.

Now Rooster's voice dropped an octave, and he gave his sister's shoulder a brotherly squeeze. "The thing is," he told her with oily ease, "I got delayed. The joint was closed before I cashed in. Eighty dollars, sis, first thing in the morning, guaranteed. Five is all I need to tide me over," and his voice sank to nearly a whisper.

Miss Hannigan stiffened and shrugged his arm off her shoulder. "Not even a nickel for the subway."

"They got a sucker at Hennessey's tonight," pleaded Rooster, his little skinny bantam body writhing with the effort of extracting money. "I can't get in the game without a five."

"The flophouse ain't good for a lousy five bucks?" demanded Miss Hannigan, meaning Lily St. Regis. As she dropped the remark, she turned to see Lily easing another necklace down the already bulging front of her shiny dress. In the wink of an eye, Miss Hannigan was across the room and grabbing at her precious jewels. She began to pull them off Lily's wrists and fingers and drag them out of the cleavage of Lily's dress.

"I beg your pardon, I'm sure, but I don't stoop to what you're incinerating. I ain't no hooker," complained Lily, unable to suppress a little whimper as she saw the baubles returning to their owner.

Furious, Miss Hannigan dumped her jewelry in a dresser drawer, and turned, grabbing up her purse.

"God, Rooster, if I give you five, will you take the fleabag out of here?"

But Rooster was already backing toward the door, grabbing Lily by the hand. "Hey. Just joking," he said quickly. "I don't need cash. I just dropped by to say howdy doody. Not even a nickel for the subway. C'mon, Lily. Say good-bye." And Rooster in his tight loud suit and Lily in her tight loud dress were gone.

Miss Hannigan was happy to see the last of them, but something wasn't quite kosher. It wasn't like Rooster Hannigan to turn down an unearned five, not even when he was holding. Unless . . . Miss Hannigan tore open her purse and looked inside. Empty. The rotten so-and-so had taken every cent while her back was turned and she was reclaiming her jewelry. That snake in the grass! That toadstool! That . . . that . . . that . . .

"*Rooster!*" Miss Hannigan exploded, and she threw her door open, scattering orphans like flower petals, and took off after her thieving brother. But the street was empty.

Although she had looked forward to sleeping in the huge bed, she hadn't been able to close her eyes. All her life, Annie had been accustomed to sleeping in a room with six or eight other little girls. In this vast and empty room there was no breathing besides hers and Sandy's, no whimpers or little cries in the night, no gentle snoring from childish noses. It was too quiet, too creepy, and by far too lonely. Annie's arms ached to hug Molly; she would even have been glad to see Pepper. Instead, she held tightly to Sandy, who had joined her under the covers, but even his presence and his warmth didn't comfort her enough to let her sleep. Even the Dream didn't help; in the luxury of these surroundings, Annie couldn't evoke it.

Oliver Warbucks' house, set far back from the street behind high stone walls, was isolated from its neighbors. Surrounded by extensive gardens, it was more of an estate than merely a mansion, and one had the feeling, especially at night, when the wind blew around it and the shadows of the tall trees made odd moving patterns on the bedroom ceilings, that one was far from New York City. Annie had this feeling now, sitting up in her bed, her eyes wide with fear, her little hands entwined in Sandy's fur. He wasn't feeling too comfortable himself. It seemed to Annie that Sandy was sensing something. His ears were alert, pricked at every sound, and every few minutes he whined restlessly.

"This room is bigger'n Grant's Tomb," whispered Annie into his furry ear. "Think we're ever goin' to get to sleep?"

Sandy growled in answer.

"Me either," agreed Annie, throwing back the covers and slipping her feet to the floor. Sandy barked loudly in agreement, and scrambled after her, knocking over a huge areca palm tree, scattering leaves and dirt on the carpet.

"Shhhhhh," cautioned Annie, leading the way out of the bedroom.

The hour was late, and the house was very dark and still, except for a light streaming from beneath a closed door at the end of the long corridor. It was Oliver Warbucks' office, and in it he and Grace Farrell were still working. These were the billionaire's favorite hours, when the rest of the world slept. These were the hours when, without interruption, he could get the massive amount of accumulating paperwork out of the way. He could also stay in touch with Europe and the Far East, which were either hours behind or hours ahead of the United States.

Annie

**A Girl's Best Friend
Annie and Sandy**

Just an old meanie
Carol Burnett as
"Miss Hannigan"

Everybody's favorite orphan
Introducing Aileen Quinn as
"Annie"

A lovable and heroic mutt
"Sandy"

The Bad Guys, "Lily" and "Rooster"
Bernadette Peters and Tim Curry

Everybody's favorite billionaire
Albert Finney as "'Daddy' Warbucks"

A kind new friend
for Annie
Ann Reinking as
"Grace Farrell"

"Why would anybody want to be
an orphan?"

The Magnificent
"Punjab"
Geoffrey Holder

Hail to the Chief!
FDR (and Eleanor, too)

Annie comforts little Molly

"It's a hard-knock life"

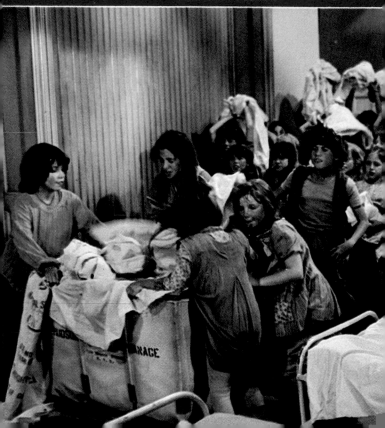

1

Renata Walsh pushed open a door of glittering glass and entered the Camino Real, a shopping mall situated in San Isidro, a stylish suburb of the city of Lima, the capital of Peru.

It was five to nine in the morning and the ground floor of the mall was deserted except for a few hurrying people who, like herself, were making their way to the offices or shops where they worked. Most of the shops were ranged on either side of a wide aisle, the floor of which was covered with yellow tiles. The offices were on the floors above them.

In the centre of the aisle there was a bronze fountain, shaped like a broad-leaved tropical plant. Crystal-clear, light-glittering drops of water fell like rain from the small bronze leaves at the top of the plant to the wider, longer

1

ones at the bottom and then into a circular pool. Above and around the fountain were many real plants, trailing from hanging baskets or bursting from huge pots. Railings protected the fountain area from the walkways on either side and seats were ranged beside the railings. In the middle of the day or in the afternoon the place was usually crowded, not only with shoppers, but also with those people who just liked to sit around and watch other people. The whole area was an indoor Spanish plaza, covered over by yellow, blue and white skylights through which the sunlight was already slanting.

Renata was on her way up to the third-floor gallery that overlooked the ground floor and where her design studio and workshop was situated in the complex of rooms right above the famous Muro fashion boutique. As she walked with her straight-backed, hip-swaying model's walk towards an escalator her attention was drawn to a man who was striding past her. He was

2

taller than most Peruvian men and was dressed in blue jeans and a bombardier-style black leather jacket.

Recognising instantly his distinctive hawklike profile and rough yet short black hair, she stopped in her tracks and, turning, began to hurry after him as fast as her high heels would let her. She didn't catch up with him until he was going to push open one of the exit doors.

'*Señor!*' she called out impulsively. 'Señor Hernandez!'

He stopped and for a moment stood still with his back to her, his shoulders slightly hunched as if he was bracing himself against being accosted by a strange woman. Then slowly, almost reluctantly, he swung round to face her, his eyebrows slanting down in a frown from under which his black eyes regarded her warily. She went closer and smiled up at him.

'You don't remember me, do you?' she accused him lightly. 'I'm Renata Walsh. We met more than a year ago.

You brought me a letter.'

He stopped frowning. His eyes lost their wary expression and a slight smile curved his firm, generously curved lips.

'How could I ever forget you?' he said, with a gallantry that surprised her considering his initial reaction. It also made her feel good about herself.

His glance swept over her dark red hair, which was drawn back severely from her high, rounded forehead and was fluffed out about her ears and shoulders. It lingered admiringly on her golden-complexioned face before drifting down to the suit she was wearing. Made from vivid green cotton, it had a three-quarter-length straight skirt and a long, loose jacket. On her high-instepped feet she was wearing green high-heeled sandals, the same green as the suit. She knew, because she was a model as well as a designer of women's clothing, that her appearance was as striking and exotic as a tropical bird's.

'How are you?' she asked. Accustomed though she was to being looked

at, the way he was looking at her made her pulses begin to throb with unusual excitement. It was some time since she had felt such a purely physical reaction to an admiring expression in a man's eyes.

His expression changed, the sensuous glow of interest in his eyes fading and giving way to the hard glitter of wariness again.

'I am well, thank you. And you?' he replied, stiffly polite.

'Oh, I feel great now. Are you still flying?'

'Yes.' He was stepping away from her, half turning towards the exit again, impatient to be gone.

'The same route?' Renata persisted, going after him, not wanting him to go yet. 'To the jungle?'

'I fly there, among other places,' he replied, and glanced meaningfully at his watch. 'I must go. I have an appointment at nine-thirty,' he murmured, and flashed her another appraising glance. 'Good to see you again, Renata.'

'Wait, please wait a minute!' Noticing

5

how carefully he had been speaking English, as if he hadn't been using the language much recently, she spoke in Spanish and delved a hand into her flat briefcase. She brought out a square of thick white paper with gold writing on it, an elegantly styled invitation that she held out to him. 'Here, take this. It's an invitation to my first solo fashion show — it's next week. Bring your girlfriend, or your wife. Oh, please take it,' she urged when he seemed reluctant to take the ticket from her.

His long fingers reached out and took the ticket quickly from her without touching her fingers.

'Thanks.' He studied the writing on the ticket and then looked directly into her eyes. Was it her imagination or was the glow of warm admiration back? '*Adiós, amiga,*' he murmured, and turned away to push open one of the exit doors behind him.

A flash of light-reflecting glass and he was gone. Wondering if she had really met him and had actually talked to

him, Renata stayed standing where she was, staring at the door through which he had gone, wishing she could have delayed him longer. On seeing him again she had felt that the feeling of kinship with him she had felt at their first meeting had returned. Since Kendal had died she had often felt the need for someone in whom she could confide her problems, someone who would understand and perhaps offer advice or a helping hand . . .

With an exclamation of irritation at her meandering, somewhat mawkish thoughts, she turned and walked back to the escalator. So it had happened. She had met Jason Hernandez again, and the meeting hadn't lived up to her expectations. So what else was new? Wasn't it time she behaved in a more mature way and stopped expecting too much from a chance meeting with a mere acquaintance?

She was twenty-six years of age and had been a widow for over a year. Always independent by nature, since

she had lost Kendal she had learned the hard way to stand on her own feet and fight her own battles. She didn't need any man to protect her or to be a buffer between her and the more unpleasant aspects of life. At least she hoped she didn't.

The studio-office which had been allocated to her since she had become a partner in Carlos Muro's business was quiet and cool, a place where she could spend hours at her drawing-board designing dresses or sports outfits or could meet with clients to discuss the materials that would be used in a particular dress design. Carlos had made sure she had every comfort and every facility she needed, and she was grateful to him for not expecting her to work in an uncomfortable hot garret tucked away somewhere in his garment factory in a more industrial part of Lima.

But then, Carlos wanted a lot from her. Not only did he want to use her talent as a designer to make money for

him and to bring them both fame in the fashion world, he also desired to possess the rest of her. He wanted to own her body as well as her soul. In fact, his possessiveness was fast becoming a serious problem to which she was having difficulty finding a solution.

Sitting down at her desk, she sifted through the papers on the top of it for some notes she had made for the preparations for the fashion show, intending to take them with her to the hotel where she would meet Carlos that morning to finalise the arrangements. But it was hard to concentrate. The meeting with Jason Hernandez seemed to have scattered her wits. Her thoughts would keep winging back to the day when he had arrived at her apartment, with a letter in his hand that her late husband, Kendal Walsh, had asked him to deliver to her.

More than a year ago Jason had come to see her, and yet even now she could feel her stomach nerves tightening as they had when she had opened the door

of the tiny bedsitter where she had been living at the time and had seen him, a dark shape looming against the dim lighting of the passageway. It had been just after sunset, she recalled now, as she slid down in her swivel chair, her eyes half closed as she relived the vivid memory.

★　★　★

Alone at the table finishing her evening meal, Renata felt worried. Nearly four months had passed since Kendal had gone off into the jungle to live with the primitive tribe he was studying. It was to be his last trip, he had told her, and he should have been back a month ago. She had received no word from him since he had gone, and last week, unable to bear the anxiety any longer, she had gone to see Tom Ogden, a friend of her father's who worked at the Canadian Embassy in Lima, to ask if he could find out where Kendal was. Tom had been most sympathetic and helpful

and had said he would do his best to do as she asked.

A sharp knock on the door of the tiny shabby room startled her out of her train of thought. Not expecting anyone to call on her at that time of day, she hesitated for a few moments before going to answer the door. Only when the knock was repeated did she move towards the door and open it, with the chain still on.

'Señora Renata Walsh?' The voice was dark and deep, like the eyes that looked at her out of his shadowy face.

'Yes, I'm Renata Walsh. What do you want?' she replied sharply.

His sudden grin was a flash of white teeth against olive skin.

'I understand your caution,' he said. Much to her surprise he spoke English, with just the suspicion of a Spanish accent, a slight attractive slurring of some consonants. 'I'm Jason Hernandez. I have a letter for you from your husband.'

Still distrustful of him, she said

11

sharply, 'Show me the letter, please.'

'OK.' He shrugged his broad shoulders, put a hand in a pocket of his jacket and pulled out a crumpled envelope. He offered it to her through the narrow gap between the door and the jamb. She took it and looked at it quickly. Sure enough, her name and address were written on the envelope in Kendal's spidery scrawl.

'Thank you,' she said. She took the chain off and opened the door wide. 'Please come in and tell me where you met Kendal.'

'You're sure you want me to come in?' He was as wary as a cat now, regarding her with slitted eyes.

'I couldn't invite you in before because this isn't a very good neighbourhood and I'm always careful when I open the door to a stranger,' she explained. 'There've been several robberies, and a woman in the flat below was raped last month. But I really want to know how Kendal came to give you the letter to bring to me, and I'd rather you came in than have

12

you stand outside and tell me.'

He stepped inside. For a few seconds they stood looking at each other, both of them still very cautious yet both of them staring at each other's appearance with great interest, he as if he liked what he saw, she thinking rather belatedly that perhaps she shouldn't have let him in after all. He looked rough and tough, not the sort of man she usually associated with.

He had thick black hair and it was brushed sideways across the front of his head above his broad, lined forehead. Under black eyebrows his eyes were deep-set yet large and wide and fringed by short black lashes. He was wearing a plain white shirt open at the collar under his black leather bombardier-style jacket, and the cotton was strained tight across his thickly-muscled chest. Renata judged him to be in his mid-thirties and there was about him a sort of devil-may-care quality. His face, with its proud high-bridged nose, firm wide lips, and stubborn cleft chin, had a

battered look, and a new scar slanted rakishly up his right cheek. He looked as if he lived adventurously, as if he liked taking risks.

Quickly she remembered her manners, and breaking the silence between them, because it was suddenly snapping and crackling with all sorts of vibrations, she said, 'Please sit down. Can I get you a drink? Coffee? Or some wine?'

'No, thanks. I can't stay long.'

He moved into the room to sit on one of the rather rickety chairs at the round table and looked round the small, shabby room, at the curtained alcove where the bed was hidden, at the other alcove with its two-burner cooker and small sink. Then he looked back at Renata, his dark eyes studying her appearance now with a cool objectivity.

'A woman like you shouldn't be living alone in this district. It isn't safe,' he said, authoritatively, as if he had the right to dictate to her where she should live.

'I know it isn't.' She also sat at the table across from him. 'But it's all Kendal and I can afford right now. He's a student of anthropology and he's here on a research scholarship from a Canadian university, so we don't have much income.'

'He told me he's in this country for two years to study the life-style of a certain jungle tribe. Then he'll write a thesis about them and will get his doctorate,' he said, but Renata had the impression that he wasn't really interested in what they were talking about, because he was still staring at her as if he had never seen anyone like her before in his life.

'That's right,' she replied, feeling satisfied now that he really knew Kendal. 'I've been working lately as a model for a manufacturer of women's clothing who owns an exclusive boutique in San Isidro, to try and supplement Ken's income, but I haven't earned enough yet to afford an apartment in a better district. Where did you meet him?'

'I've flown him several times to Puerto Maldonado, which is the nearest town to the part of the jungle he's been living in,' Jason continued. 'We've got to be pretty friendly.'

'You're the pilot of a plane?'

'I own an small aviation company based in Cuzco. We fly passengers and sometimes supplies to places in the mountains or the jungle that are inaccessible by other forms of transport. I still pilot one of the helicopters myself, not because I can't employ other pilots to do it but mostly because I'm addicted to flying the things. Can't get the need to fly out of my system.' His quick grin was self-mocking and he rubbed the scar on his cheek. 'I apologise for the state of the letter, but I've been carrying it in my pocket ever since Ken gave it to me some weeks ago when I left him at Puerto Maldonado.'

'But why have you been so long bringing it to me? Why didn't you mail it to me from Cuzco?' she exclaimed, disappointed because he obviously

16

hadn't seen Kendal recently.

'A good question,' he drawled with another grin. 'I couldn't get to a post office, that's why. On the way back to Cuzco after leaving Kendal I flew into a snowstorm and couldn't see where I was going. Rather than be killed when the chopper hit a mountainside, I baled out, dangerously as it turned out, because I fell when I landed and hit the back of my head on some rocks and lost consciousness. When at last I came round it took me a while to find my way to an Indian village, and by the time I got there I'd developed a fever. Took a while for me to recover and return to Cuzco.'

Renata stared at him with a certain amount of awe. She had heard about the pilots who flew small planes and helicopters about the country, had heard that they sometimes took hair-raising risks and sometimes lost their lives while trying to take supplies to remote villages that were often shaken by earthquakes, but she had never met one before.

'I didn't mail it to you,' he continued with his explanation, 'because, as you can see, the address got washed out a bit while I was wandering about the mountains. So since I had to come to Lima today I came here on the chance that you were still living here.'

'Thank you — thank you very much,' she whispered, looking down at the battered envelope and trying not to give way to the disappointment she was feeling because he hadn't any recent news of Kendal. 'I'm very glad to get it. You see, I haven't heard from Kendal since he left four months ago, and I'm very worried about him. He should have been back in Lima by now.'

'I guess he'll turn up soon,' he said comfortingly. His face hardened and his eyes narrowed slightly. 'At the time he gave me the letter he said it was urgent. I got an idea from the way he spoke that you and he had had a spat before he left.'

'He told you he and I quarrelled?'

Renata exclaimed, opening her green eyes very wide, surprised that Kendal, usually so reserved about his emotions, would confide in this hard-bitten macho type of man.

'I told you we'd got to be friendly. He was nervous about flying in a chopper and so tended to talk a lot while we were in the air. He'd often told me he didn't like leaving you behind in Lima and wished you could have accompanied him to the jungle. That last time I saw him I guessed he was upset because you had refused to give up the job you had here to go with him.' Again he gave her a hard glance, not admiring her now but looking as if he disapproved of her. 'Didn't you ever want to go with him?'

'No, I didn't. What could I have done living with a primitive tribe? I'm not trained for anything like that. I've always thought it best for me to stay in Lima to try and earn some money, to be here when he came for a rest,' Renata explained defensively. She picked up the

19

crumpled letter again. As he had said, the address on it had been blurred by rain. 'But that wasn't why we quarrelled,' she added. 'Kendal didn't like the work I've been doing for Carlos Muro as a model. That's why I'm so glad to get this letter. I was upset, too, when he left, still angry with me, still unforgiving.' She was surprising herself now by her own willingness to confide her anxiety to Jason, yet somehow he didn't seem at all like a stranger since he had expressed his friendship for Kendal. She looked across at the dark, watchful eyes in the lean, scarred face and she also smiled a little in mocking knowledge of herself. 'You see, I'm very quick-tempered — it goes with the red hair, I guess. I blow up and say many things I regret later. But just as quickly I calm down and I'm ready to apologise. Not so Kendal. His temper rises slowly and it takes him ages to get over a quarrel, to forgive and forget. Since he went, I've been so worried, thinking that maybe he wouldn't forgive me, that he might

never come back. We haven't been married very long and . . . '

She broke off, not sure how to describe her feelings of anxiety after Kendal had gone without either of them having said they were sorry, without making up after the quarrel.

'Then you'd better read the letter. It will make you feel better,' Jason Hernandez suggested quietly. 'You can be sure that when I last saw him Kendal was still very much in love with you, and I'd guess he still is, wherever he is.'

There was a strange twist to the corner of his lips now, and he rose quickly to his feet and strode to the door as if he was eager to get away from her. Renata followed him.

With his hand on the doorknob he turned to look down at her. Again, as when he had entered the room, there was a moment of strange tension as they stared at each other.

'I hope Kendal is back with you soon,' he said.

21

'I hope he is too,' muttered Renata, looking down at the letter in her hands. 'You might see him before I do.'

'That's possible,' he agreed. 'Anything you'd like me to tell him if I do?'

'Only that I love him and that I'm looking forward to his return. Thank you again, for bringing his letter,' she smiled.

'*De nada.*' He reverted suddenly to Spanish.

'You're a Peruvian?' she asked quickly, also speaking in Spanish, recognising that his accent was the same as her own.

'Partly.'

'I guessed we had something in common,' she said, smiling up at him, pleased to have pinned down that strange attraction he had for her, that feeling of having found in him someone who was a friend, no, more than that, someone with whom she felt an odd sense of kinship. 'I was born in Lima and lived here until I was twelve, when my father, who is Canadian, took us back to Canada. My mother was a Peruvian.'

'My father was a Peruvian and I was also born here, but I also lived for a while in the States,' he replied coolly, as if he didn't like talking about himself.

'So when did you come back here?'

'About five years ago.' He opened the door.

'When Kendal comes back you must come and have dinner us,' Renata said hospitably.

Jason Hernandez half-turned to glance down at her over his shoulder.

'I think that's one risk I'd better not take,' he said, so softly he could have been talking to himself. Then, before she could make any comment, he added more brusquely, 'I don't come to Lima often and I don't have much time for socialising, but thank you just the same. *Buenas noches, señora*. Lock your door and put the chain on after I've closed it.'

He went out and closed the door before she had any chance to say goodnight, leaving her staring in puzzlement at the panels of wood, wondering

what he had meant when he had said that dining with her and Kendal was a risk he had better not take.

★ ★ ★

The telephone on her desk rang and Renata came back to the present with a start. She reached out to the receiver, lifted it. She had hardly spoken into it when a man's voice cut across hers.

'Renata, what are you doing? It is ten-thirty and you were supposed to be here at the hotel at ten!' At the other end of the line Carlos Muro's high, light voice was staccato with irritation.

'Oh. Is it that time already?' Renata glanced at her watch with surprise. Had she been daydreaming about Jason Hernandez for over an hour? 'I came into the studio to pick up some notes and I ran into someone I know and I just had to have a few words with him.'

'Who?' Carlos demanded sharply.

'The pilot of the helicopter who used to fly Kendal to the jungle. Remember I

told you about how he brought me a letter from Kendal once?'

'Oh, that guy.' Carlos's voice drawled in a bored way. 'Why would you let him keep you talking? You can't possibly have much in common with him. Now hurry up and get over here.'

'Yes, yes, I will. Just as soon as I can grab a taxi.'

But as the taxi sped along busy streets and skirted plazas on its way to the centre of Lima her thoughts would run all the time about Jason Hernandez. How much better he had looked than he had at their first meeting, she thought, his face healthily tanned and the scar on his face no longer livid but faded to an interesting pale line.

There was so much she had wanted to talk to him about. She wanted to tell him about Kendal and to ask him more about himself. And what had he meant when he had said, How could I forget you? Had he meant it had been impossible for him to forget her? Or had he meant he *had* forgotten her, but

on meeting her again wondered how he could have done so?

She could only hope he would come to the fashion show and that she would have a chance to talk to him there.

2

The taxi in which Renata was riding approached the Plaza San Martin along Lima's main thoroughfare, called *La Colmena* or The Beehive, by Limenos, although that was not its proper name. As usual the plaza was crowded with candy sellers, shoeshine boys and vendors of tickets for the popular lottery run by the Peruvian government as a way of raising money. Cinemas, office buildings crowned with neon signs, the elegant Hotel Bolivar and the influential Club Nacional and the Circulo Militar were on the east side of the square, but Renata was going to the west side, to a broad avenue lined with airline offices, Italian and French restaurants, foreign banks and the towering Hotel Crillon.

When she arrived at last in the ballroom of the downtown luxury hotel

where the fashion show was going to be held the next day, workmen were hammering together the catwalk along which the models displaying her first collection of *haute couture* fashions would teeter and slink. On the stage to which the catwalk would be attached, slim and sleek in an elegant grey suit, Carlos Muro, who was now her partner in a new enterprise called Renata Fashions, was standing talking to a small dark-haired woman.

Seeing Renata approaching him, Carlos broke off what he was saying and turned to her. About forty-five, he was the same height as she was, tall for a woman but not for a man. She knew he kept himself in good shape by practising aerobics and swimming every day. His brown hair was smoothly brushed straight back from his temples and forehead, any sign of greyness hidden by the application of a colour formula. He owed the healthy tan of his face to sunray lamps. With his neat, aquiline

features he passed as handsome and was outwardly smoothly self-confident and charming. He had always managed to avoid marriage, but assumed arrogantly that he could have any woman who attracted his fancy, especially if she was already employed by him. For some time now he had fancied Renata.

'*Buenos dias*. I am glad you have come at last, *querida*,' he said, reaching out, taking her right hand and raising it to his lips as he always did when he greeted her. 'I would like to present to you Señora Mendoza, the florist. Señora Mendoza, this is Renata, a name I hope you'll hear and see very often after tomorrow's show, for she is going to put Lima on the map as the leading fashion city in South America.

After the two women had acknowledged each other Carlos went on to lay down the law concerning the arrangement of flowers and plants for the show, walking about the stage and then the big room and indicating just what it was

he wanted and where he wanted it, while Señora Mendoza made notes and nodded. Only a couple of times did he ask Renata for her opinion, and she wondered, as she often did, why he had wanted her presence there at all, since it was quite obvious he had made up his mind about the decorations for the show and nothing she could have said would have changed it.

She had known him now for more than two years, ever since she had been taken on as a model for his Camino Real boutique. After finding out that she had been trained in dress design in a Department of Fine Arts at a Canadian university he had soon put her to work to design off-the-peg dresses and suits that were manufactured at the garment factory he owned. When the lines she had designed had been highly successful and had sold well, he had hired her as a full-time designer and had encouraged her to develop some *haute couture* fashions for the wealthier women of Lima. Six

months ago when she had returned to Lima from Canada, where she had gone with Kendal when he had been sent home, Carlos had suggested to her that she should become a full-time designer of *haute couture* women's clothing, with his financial backing, and they had become partners.

And tomorrow the dream she had dreamed for years, ever since she had designed a wedding dress for her stepsister way back in Vancouver, was going to come true. In this ballroom she would realise her ambition to compete with the famous international fashion designers.

If only Kendal could have been here to witness her success! But then Kendal hadn't really liked her choice of career. He had thought fashion design frivolous and hadn't really approved of her modelling for Carlos, in the same way that she hadn't always been able to understand his dedication to studying the life-styles of primitive tribes. Yet in spite of that wide difference between

their chosen careers they had fallen in love with each other, and if only he hadn't caught that fever in the jungle and died, if only . . .

But she could go on like that forever, she thought, and it wasn't her way to waste time in regrets. Kendal and she had had a brief but loving relationship in the heyday of their youth and, apart from that one quarrel before he had left for the jungle, their marriage had been fairly happy. Best to dwell on that, on the times together when they had been close and in tune, and not to worry about the differences that had existed between them.

She became aware that Señora Mendoza was leaving and that Carlos was calling her attention to the fact. When the other woman had gone, Carlos's glance flashed over Renata, missing no detail of her appearance. With a pointed index finger he flicked the silk shirt she was wearing under her open jacket and which was stretched taut across her breasts.

'I like this. Your own design, of course,' he said ambiguously. He often said ambiguous things. Now he could have been referring not only to her shirt but also to her physical shape.

Without answering directly, she stepped away from him.

'Why did you want me to come down here? Is there anything I have to do?' she asked lightly.

She disliked the way he touched her, in a proprietorial way, using any excuse to harass her sexually. If she hadn't been so dependent on him for work as a model and designer she would have long ago slapped his face and told him to get lost. As it was, it suited her, for the time being, to be diplomatic and to ignore his sexually suggestive remarks and gestures.

'We're meeting the manager of the hotel for lunch,' he replied. 'It's good policy, I always think, to entertain such people so that on the day of the show we can expect to get the full co-operation of his staff. He's bringing

his wife who would very much like to attend the show. Do you have any complimentary tickets with you?' he asked, as they strolled out of the ballroom, which was on the second floor of the hotel.

'No, I don't. I just gave my last two to Jason Hernandez, the helicopter pilot,' she told him.

They walked across the wide landing to a wrought-iron railing. Leaning on the top rail, Renata looked down into the spacious foyer with its shining tiled floor across which people were coming and going.

'What a waste!' jeered Carlos, leaning close beside her so that his shoulder brushed against hers. 'You don't really think a rough bush pilot would be any more interested in *haute couture* than your late husband, do you?'

'He might be. Anyway, I thought he might like to give them to his wife or his girlfriend. It was just my way of saying thank you to Señor Hernandez for bringing that letter from Kendal, the

last I ever had from him,' she answered, inching away from him.

She was wishing now that she had never mentioned Jason. Carlos was always so jealous of any men who claimed her attention, and there were times, when he made remarks about Kendal, that she sensed he was glad Kendal had died and that she was now a widow and without any legal attachment to another man.

'I do hope you haven't made any arrangements to see him after or during the show,' he went on smoothly. 'I don't want you distracted at all by any outsiders on Wednesday. Everything must go as perfectly as possible, and that means complete concentration on what all of us are trying to attain. Only with complete dedication can we pull this off, Renata. You understand what I'm getting at?'

'Yes, of course I understand. No one wants the show to be a success more than I do. My future as a designer depends on it,' she said with a touch of

irritation. 'But do you have to sound so much like a slavedriver? I want it to be a success, but I would like to enjoy it too. If I can't think of a fashion show as something to look forward to and enjoy I shall get all uptight and make a mess of everything.'

With one of his mercurial changes of mood Carlos turned to her and smiled.

'Then of course you must enjoy it, *querida*,' he said softly, putting an arm about her shoulders and whispering into her ear. She stiffened immediately but did not shake off his arm, even though every nerve in her body was protesting against his embrace. 'Never let it be said that I would spoil your enjoyment. Not for anything would I like you to get uptight and ruin everything. Come, let us go now and find the manager and take him to lunch.'

'I'll be glad to. I'm really hungry,' she said, turning away from him and setting off in the direction of the escalators, feeling as if she were a wild bird that

had just escaped from the hands of a would-be captor when his arm slipped off her shoulders, wishing she could fly away from him. Only the self-discipline she had taught herself over the years in order to achieve her ambition to be a successful fashion designer prevented her from walking away from him.

The next day, in spite of her resolve to relax and enjoy herself, she was on edge when she opened the show by modelling the first outfit. As she swayed with swinging hips along the catwalk Carlos announced her name and described the style and materials used in the elegant daytime suit. Only when she heard some applause and gasps of admiration did the knot of pre-performance nerves that had tightened within her ease and fade. Slowing down, taking her time, she smiled at the audience before turning at the end of the catwalk, and took the opportunity to search amongst the crowd of wealthy Peruvian socialities for Jason Hernandez. She didn't see him.

Several other models followed her, wearing other day dresses and suits, and it wasn't until she walked out for the second time, wearing a sports outfit, that she thought she saw Jason. He was right at the back of the room and he was standing, leaning against the pale green wall, dark and somehow mysterious, as out of place among the chattering women and their masculine escorts as a condor, that almost extinct bird of prey of the Andes, might look among a group of chirping hens and crowing roosters.

The third time Renata went out, nearly an hour later, she was modelling the last, most romantic and most beautiful of her creations. As she swept slowly along the catwalk wearing a ballgown, an off-the-shoulder concoction of shimmering white taffeta which set off the golden glow of her skin and the rich dark red of her hair, she looked for Jason again. He was still there leaning against the wall. But when she turned to sweep a curtsy to the

enthusiastic, hand-clapping audience he had gone.

She had no chance to feel disappointed because he hadn't stayed to congratulate her on the show. Soon she was surrounded by a crowd of excited people, other designers and garment makers as well as clients, as they all offered their congratulations. Then there were photographers from fashion magazines and the local press to pose for. Success was heady, she discovered, a high from which she had no wish, for a while, to come down, back to the reality of hard work and self-discipline that lay behind any creative art.

Among the women who stayed behind to speak to her about buying one of her model gowns or having one custom-designed and made was a slim blonde with cornflower-blue eyes. Judging her by her casual jeans and sweatshirt, Renata guessed she didn't belong to the usual upper-class clientèle of Muro's boutique. She waited patiently until all the wealthy better-dressed women had

left before approaching Renata.

'I can't really afford to buy one of your models, although I think they're gorgeous,' she said, speaking English with an attractive, drawling American accent. 'But I just had to come and speak to you to thank you for giving Jason the tickets so that we could come to see your show. He asked me to tell you he's sorry he couldn't stay. He had to go off to some meeting with the directors of one of the airlines.'

'Is there any other Jason in your life?' quipped the American, with an attractive impish grin. 'I guess there could be — with your colouring and figure you must have hundreds of admirers and would-be lovers. Yes, I mean Jason Hernandez.'

'Are you his . . . ?' Renata's voice dried up. She didn't really like to ask a personal question of someone she had only just met, and yet for some reason it was important to her to know if Jason was committed to this young woman in any way.

'I'm Cindy Lehrer,' said the blonde woman quickly. 'And I'm in Lima with my father, who's here on business. I just couldn't pass up a free trip to the land of the Incas. Dad represents an aircraft company — they make small planes and helicopters mostly. Dad has come to sell new choppers to the Peruvian Army. Jason used to work for Dad's company as a test pilot before he came back to this country, so of course Dad just had to get in touch with him to try and sell some choppers to the Hernandez Aviation company too, while he's here. Jason flew down to Lima the day before yesterday to visit with us. Coming to this show has so far been one of the highlights for me. I'm studying dress design at a college in the States, and I'd just love to do what you're doing one day.'

Not wanting to let this young woman go without learning more about Jason from her, Renata said impulsively, 'It's nice to meet you, Cindy, but right now I haven't any time to talk with you

41

longer. Could we meet at another time? Not today nor this evening, I'm tied up all day, but tomorrow I'm having a day off. How about you coming to my place for coffee in the morning around ten o'clock?'

'I'd love to, if you'll tell me where you live,' said Cindy with a sort of self-satisfied smile as if she had been hoping to arrange some further meeting.

Renata told her the address of her apartment and gave her directions on how to find it. Cindy wrote everything down in a small notebook.

'Thanks,' she said with her bright smile when she had finished writing. 'Would you mind if I bring Jason with me? He said something about wishing he'd had time to stay and talk to you today.'

'Of course not. I'll be pleased to see both of you,' replied Renata, trying not to appear too enthusiastic about the suggestion, although secretly she was delighted at this chance to meet Jason again.

Cindy nodded, her smile widening into a rather knowing and playful grin before she backed away as someone else pushed forward to claim Renata's attention.

The rest of the day was most demanding and exhausting, as Renata not only dealt with customers but also supervised the packing up and returning of the model gowns and other clothes to the design studio in the Camino Real complex. She and Carlos then went to a celebration dinner attended by his sales assistants and the women who cut and sewed in his garment factory, as well as the models and various fashion buyers representing stores and other fashion boutiques. It was well after midnight when eventually she got back to her apartment and fell into bed.

She didn't wake until she heard the insistent ringing of the doorbell. Shocked into wakefulness, noting that the time on the digital bedside clock was ten-fifteen and remembering that she

had invited Cindy Lehrer for coffee, she bounded from the bed. Dragging on narrow white pants and a green silk shirt, she flung her hair behind her shoulders and ran barefooted to the front door.

Unlocking the door, she swung it wide open, her words of welcome dying away when she saw Jason standing there, alone. The slight smile, that hinted at secret and possibly mischievous thoughts, tilted the corners of his firm mouth upwards and his dark eyes glinted between narrowed lashes. Gone were the jeans and bombardier jacket. He was dressed like a Peruvian businessman in a light grey suit, stark white shirt and a dark tie. His hair was well brushed and shone like a raven's wing. She was so surprised at the change in his appearance that for a moment she was speechless.

'*Buenos dias*, Renata,' he said pleasantly.

'Hi,' she muttered, then looked past him into the passage. 'Where's Cindy?' she asked.

'At the last minute she had to change her plans for this morning. Her father wanted her to go with him on a trip to Lake Titicaca,' he replied easily. 'She asked me to ask you to excuse her. She also said you had invited me to come to have coffee with you too this morning. Is that right?'

'I . . . er . . . yes, I suppose I did. At least, Cindy asked if you could come with her and I agreed,' she replied, finding herself suddenly breathless with pleasure because he had come alone. 'Please come in.'

He walked past her into the small hallway. Renata closed the door, turned to face him, and immediately the memory of their first meeting sprang into her mind. That curious tension was there between them again as they looked at each other, neither of them smiling any more. Made nervous by the tension, Renata spoke quickly as she went past him towards the living room, indicating that he should follow her.

'I'm sorry Cindy couldn't come,' she

chattered, 'but I'm glad you have. Now you can tell me what you thought of the fashion show. When I told Carlos I'd given you an invitation he said you wouldn't be interested, that it was a waste of a ticket to invite a bush pilot to a show of women's fashions.'

'I thought it was great,' he replied. 'You're very talented. As for your partner's remark, it just shows he doesn't know much about bush pilots. They're usually quite normal guys who like women a lot and like to see them dressed up too. I enjoyed it. Did Kendal? I looked for him at the show but didn't see him. In fact, I was really surprised to see you yesterday in the mall. I thought that maybe Ken had finished his study of the tribe and you and he had gone back to Canada. I haven't seen him around for most of a year, not since that time he gave me the letter for you.'

Just inside the living room Renata stopped to turn slowly to face him again. It had never occurred to her that

he didn't know about Kendal's death.

'Kendal died a year ago,' she said quietly, and watched shock go through him, tautening the skin across his high cheekbones and widening his eyes.

'Hell,' he muttered, then added quickly, 'I'm sorry — I didn't know. How could I know?'

'I thought you might have heard somehow. And at one time I even thought you might have piloted the helicopter that brought him out of the jungle and back to Lima.'

'You can be sure if I had been the pilot or if I'd known I'd have been in touch with you to find out if he survived whatever happened to him,' he said, the sincerity of his feelings expressed in the deepening of his voice and the softening of his eyes. 'What did happen? Was he in an accident?'

'I . . . ' Renata broke off, biting her lip. Even now, twelve months almost to the day since Kendal died, she still had difficulty in talking about him. 'I'll tell you later,' she added quickly. She

gestured to the comfortable chesterfield and chairs. 'Please make yourself at home,' she said. 'I'll just make the coffee.'

She hurried through to the small kitchenette. Excitement was dancing through her because Jason had come to see her on his own, without Cindy. Not for a long time had her heart raced like this. Was it possible she had recovered from Kendal's death and was ready to fall in love again?

The clash of the lid of the coffee-pot as she dropped it on the floor brought her to her senses. Where were her dangerous impulses going to take her now? Go carefully, be cautious, she warned herself. You know nothing about him except that he was someone whom Kendal had liked and had obviously trusted.

And as for falling in love again, the whole idea was ridiculous. Falling in love was a once-in-a-lifetime experience, wasn't it? She had had that experience and it was over. She just

couldn't imagine herself ever falling in love again, least of all with a macho man like Jason Hernandez, who was even more different from herself than Kendal had been.

Anyway, how did she know he wasn't forbidden fruit for her in other ways? For all she knew, he could be married and have a family living in Cuzco. Picking up the lid, she began calmly and methodically to make the coffee.

3

When the coffee was made and poured, Renata returned to the living room with a tray bearing two full coffee mugs, a cream jug, sugar bowl and a small plate of almond cakes. Jason was standing at the big picture window looking down at a plaza where people swirled in colourful circles about the stalls of the street vendors. The sun was trying to break through the *garúa*, the sea mist that often enveloped Lima throughout the summer months and that was still lingering on this the last day of September.

'You have a great view,' he remarked, coming across to the coffee table as she placed the tray on it. He glanced appreciatively at the comfortable contemporary-style furnishings. 'And this is much better than the other place you lived in. I guess Muro pays the rent?'

Renata straightened up quickly to stare at him in astonishment at the implication. He looked back at her, his face a dark, hard mask revealing nothing of what he was feeling or thinking.

'A remark like that really deserves a slap on the face!' she hissed at him furiously.

He raised an eyebrow and his lips twitched with sardonic amusement.

'So go ahead, slap me if it will make you feel better. I'm used to taking abuse, especially from women who take exception to any surprise tactic of mine to find out the truth about them,' he said coolly. 'I had to find out somehow if there's any truth in the rumour I heard at the fashion show.'

'What rumour?' she demanded.

'The rumour that you're Muro's mistress and that's why he has gone to such lengths to launch you as a fashion designer.' His long upper lip lifted sneeringly. 'Maybe Kendal had reason to quarrel with you about your job

51

modelling for Muro. Maybe he guessed you were cheating on him so as to influence your employer in your favour.'

'I'm not a cheat! And I never cheated on Kendal, never. Never!' she retorted furiously, her eyes flashing with green sparks, her cheeks flaming with pink colour. 'And I would never become a man's mistress just to get him to help me further my career.' She broke off to draw a long seething breath, then added through her teeth, 'And if I knew who'd started the rumour I'd scratch her eyes out!'

'Why assume it was a woman?' asked Jason, his eyebrows tilting satirically, his lips curling into a mocking grin. He didn't seem at all abashed by her angry defence of herself. He bent and picked up one of the mugs of coffee and drank some of the hot liquid. Above the rim his black eyes glinted as they regarded her. 'You sure do have a temper to go with your hair,' he said provocatively.

Renata drew another deep shaking breath and attempted to calm herself by

turning away from him and pacing over to the window to look down at the plaza. The bright canopies covering the vendors' stalls seemed to be blossoming like flowers in the hazy sun.

'Wouldn't you be mad if you'd just heard that someone was trying to smirch your reputation by spreading lies about you?' she retorted, and turned back to look at him. He had picked up one of the almond cakes and was chewing some of it and apparently he didn't think her question was worthy of an answer. In a few strides she was back before him, determined to get his attention again. Keeping her voice low and smooth, she said, 'I assume it was a woman because Carlos employs and has employed other women besides me, both as models and designers, but I'm the only one he's taken into partnership with him. Naturally some of the others resent the fact that he's chosen to back me financially and to set up a company with me, so they could be taking their revenge on me by spreading this

rumour. They can't believe that the relationship between him and me is purely a business one.'

'I got the impression yesterday that he would like it to be more than just a business partnership.' Jason's glance was insolent as it raked her from head to foot. 'And I don't blame him one little bit,' he added softly, stepping closer to her. 'You're very seductive-looking and appear to be more sophisticated and experienced than you actually are, a great temptation to a guy on the prowl.'

For a moment Renata could think of nothing to say in reply, because his sudden closeness to her had the effect of triggering off a purely sensual reaction to him. She liked his bearlike build, she decided, and responded in an entirely physical way to the strength that she guessed lay dormant in his muscular body. She liked, too, the way his eyes seemed to glow when he looked at her and the sensual curve to his lower lip. Finding herself wondering

what it would be like to be held in his arms and kissed by him, she stepped back quickly and said with a touch of acidity, 'Is that what you are, a guy on the prowl? Is that why you've come here this morning? Is it because you believed the rumour that you've come here thinking you can try it on with me? You thought that if it was true and I was Carlos's mistress I'd be available to any man, didn't you?'

'Something like that.' He shrugged indifferently, and anger surged through her again at the thought that such a malicious rumour had been spread about her and that he had believed it and had drawn false conclusions about her.

'And that's why you came here even though Cindy couldn't come?' she challenged him.

'Could be.' Again the indifferent shrug. His face was masklike again and his eyes were black holes, mysterious, no window on his true soul. Disappointment mixed with her anger. He

was no friend after all.

'Oh, I could spit with rage!' she hissed.

'You are spitting — almost,' he said with a laugh. 'But you can cool your temper. You've convinced me by your reaction that you're not Muro's mistress and that you never cheated Kendal.' He put his empty coffee mug down on the tray. When he looked at her again the mask of cynical indifference had been lifted. He looked sympathetically curious. 'You said you'd tell me what happened to Kendal,' he added seriously. 'I guess it must be hard for you to talk about him, but I would really like to know what happened.'

As usual Renata's temper, which always flared up so fast, was dying down quickly. Not for the past twelve months had she been able to talk to anyone about Kendal's death and the empty space it had left in her life, and she was a little surprised now that she wanted to talk to Jason about it after the implication he had just made about

Carlos and herself. But there was something about him, a warmth that underlay the tough exterior, that appealed to her. Once you had his friendship you would have it for life, she thought, and he would always do his best to help any friend of his.

'It is hard to talk about it,' she admitted. 'But I'd like to tell you because you were his friend.' She sat down on the chesterfield. Jason sat down too, in the matching armchair opposite to her.

'He picked up a virus while he was living with the tribe,' she began. 'It was an obscure kind of pneumonia.'

'So why didn't he leave them and get himself into hospital?' he asked.

'I don't know. I think he must have believed he could shake it off,' she replied dully. 'There was another anthropologist staying with the tribe, a woman from England. When Kendal became so ill that he lost consciousness she informed the local Peruvian government authorities and he was brought to

a hospital here in Lima. He was so thin and wasted-looking . . . ' Her voice shook and she broke off.

'If it's hurting, stop. Don't tell me any more,' Jason suggested gently, leaning towards her.

'I . . . I want to tell you,' she insisted. 'You were a good friend to Kendal, delivered that letter for him and listened to him, so you have a right to know. And there isn't much more to tell. Even here in Lima, although everything possible was done, he didn't get better, so it was arranged to have him sent home to Vancouver. I went with him. But there seemed to be no cure. I watched him grow weaker and weaker, die slowly. It was awful.'

There was a brief silence. Renata couldn't look at him because she didn't want to show him her tears. She heard him mutter something under his breath, then he said gruffly,

'All I can say again is I'm sorry.'

'It's enough,' she whispered. 'I've always felt grateful to you for having

brought me his letter. In it he apologised for having been angry with me before he left and assured me that he loved me. It was the last time he ever communicated with me properly.' She sniffed, wiped spilled tears away from her cheeks with her fingers and looked at him again. 'If I hadn't had that letter I'd have always felt he'd died without forgiving me for losing my temper when he criticised me for working with Carlos. I'd have felt he had died not loving me, and that would have been unbearable. Now I'm glad I've had this chance to tell you what happened and to thank you again, for bringing the letter.'

'I did only what he asked me to do and what I hope anyone would do in similar circumstances,' he answered. 'But why did you come back to Lima? Why didn't you stay in Canada after his death?'

Renata picked up her coffee mug. When she had drunk some of the cooled liquid, she said,

'I couldn't stay in Vancouver — there were too many memories of Kendal there. We'd been students at the same university, had gone to the same school before that. We'd been friends for years.'

'And aren't there any memories of him here?' Jason asked with a touch of surprise.

'He was always going off to the jungle,' she said sadly. 'We were married barely twelve months and came here right after the wedding.'

'Didn't he tell you he would be away in the jungle often if you married him and came to Peru?'

'Yes, he did. But I didn't care. You see, I wanted so badly to come with him and to live in Lima again.' Renata looked at him as if pleading for his understanding. 'And I came back again six months ago because I knew I could make a career for myself as a fashion designer with Carlos's help. Having an interesting and productive career seemed to be a good way of getting over

Kendal's death. And it has been. Now, after a lot of hard work and the success of the fashion show, I feel whole again.'

Jason made no comment at first, just looked at her. Then slowly and thoughtfully he said,

'Couldn't you have gone in with someone else? Other than Muro, I mean.'

'I don't think so. There aren't too many garment companies in Lima interested in doing what I want to do. And anyway, no one else offered to give me the financial backing I needed to get started. Do you have something against Carlos?' she queried with a touch of defiance. Was he going to lecture her as Kendal had done about the unsuitability of her working with Carlos?

'Not personally. I don't really know all that much about him. But I would guess Kendal must have had some good reason for not liking you working with him.' Jason looked at her steadily. 'You say there's no truth in that rumour. Have you any ideas on how you're

going to put a stop to it?'

'Not yet, but I'll think of something,' she asserted. 'Would you like more coffee?' she offered, wondering how she could get him to talk about himself.

'No, thanks, I have to be on my way.'

'Must you leave so soon?' she complained, standing when he did. 'You're always in a hurry to go somewhere else.'

'It may be your day off, but it isn't mine,' he answered. 'I have to fly back to Cuzco.'

'Why?'

'That's where the company I own is based.'

'Then you don't live in Lima?'

'No.' His quick grin flashed out. 'And I don't have much spare time to dally with beautiful women.' The grin faded and his eyes glowed again with admiration as their glance lingered on her face. 'And you are beautiful, Renata,' he added, his voice deepening. 'Too beautiful to hurt.'

'I don't know what you mean.' The

look he had given her had made her heart begin to throb excitedly. 'How could you hurt me?'

'In many ways.' Jason's lips twisted wryly. 'I confess I came here hoping for more, but now I know I was wrong about you and that there's no chance of you and me having an affair. I should have known better than to even think of it. Kendal was a nice fellow and I should have guessed he would only be married to a nice lady who wouldn't go sleeping around. But having admitted that, it doesn't change the way I feel. I'd still like to sleep with you.'

His frankness took Renata's breath away, and while she was trying to regain her composure he bent his head and touched his lips to hers. She couldn't help but respond to the warm pressure of his lips, and for a moment she forgot Kendal as the sexual desire that she had begun to think she would never feel again blazed through her like a flash-fire.

For a few moments she was dizzy and

her hands went out to hold on to him, clinging to the fine alpaca of his suit jacket. She tasted his hot breath in her mouth as he laughed softly, and then she was melting against his warmth, feeling as if she had come home after having been out in the cold for a long, long time. She slid her hands up over his shoulders and round to the nape of his neck, and parted her lips to the probing of his tongue. Immediately his arms tightened about her and he pressed her against his hard body, until she felt the thrust of his desire and her own desire zigzagged sharply through the lower part of her body, making her gasp.

Then with an oath that seemed to singe her ears with its ferocity, Jason pushed her away from him, so that she went staggering back against the wall, her heart pounding in her ears, one hand pressed against her bruised lips. He said roughly, 'I apologise. Blame it on propinquity and your beauty. I am, after all, only a man and not a saint,' he added bitterly.

He strode out into the hallway. Urgently Renata pushed herself away from the wall and hurried to the doorway of the flat, but he had gone out into the passage. The door slammed shut in her face.

Going back to the living room, she picked up the tray and carried it into the kitchen. Her heart was still thumping and her hands were shaky. She put the tray down, clenched her hands and stamped her bare foot on the floor in a show of frustration and disappointment.

Jason Hernandez was no different from Carlos, she thought. He had come here hoping he could become her lover just because he had heard she was Carlos's mistress. And she had to admit she had been tempted for a few moments to go along with his suggestion that they have an affair, because she found him attractive.

But deep in her heart she knew she had never liked that sort of relationship, was not suited temperamentally to

having a casual affair. She would have to be in love with a man before she could let him have the freedom of her body, and she would have to know first that he loved her, put her first before all other women and respected her sufficiently to ask her to marry him before they went to bed together. That was how it had been with Kendal and that was how it would be for her for ever more. She could never separate the sexual act between herself and a man from deeply-felt emotion and complete commitment to that man.

And that took her back to the rumour. Somehow she must stop it. She would go and see Carlos and confront him with it, find out if he already knew about it and what he could do to put a stop to it.

Outside the sunshine was growing brighter, and she walked the short distance to the Camino Real. The shopping mall was bright with sunlight and noisy with shoppers and piped music. As always when she walked

through this mall or along any of the streets of Lima, taking her place among the lovely fair-skinned *criollas* of Spanish descent or the stunning *mestizas* with dark red hair and cinnamon-coloured skins, who paraded before glittering store windows, Renata felt her adrenalin rise and knew why she had come back to this city where she had been born. Even though parts of it, where the Indians from the mountains had set up their shanty towns, were desperately poor and slum-like, the rest of the city pulsed with life. Perhaps because it was built on the edge of an earthquake zone its people lived as if the next day would be their last, enjoying life to the full, reckless of the consequences.

Carlos was, as she had hoped, in his luxurious office next to her studio, and he was pleased to see her. He was sitting at his desk talking to someone on the phone, but as soon as she entered after knocking, he hung up and leaving his chair came round to greet her,

holding out both hands to her.

'*Querida!*' he smiled, and bent his head to kiss her on both cheeks. 'As always I am delighted to see you, but I thought you were taking the day off.'

Freeing her hands from his grasp, Renata walked away from him over to the desk and, turning, leaned against it to face him again.

'Carlos, something unpleasant happened at the show yesterday,' she began.

'Oh. What do you mean by unpleasant?'

'Someone was spreading a rumour that I'm your mistress and that's why you launched me as a fashion designer,' she stated baldly, and watched his smooth tanned face for his reaction. His thin arched eyebrows arched even more and his thin lips twitched as if he were amused.

'Is that all?' he said. 'What is unpleasant about that? I find it rather flattering to hear that someone would believe I've been successful in making

you my mistress.' He stepped towards her, his light hazel eyes two gleaming slits as their glance seemed to ravage her face. 'You know very well, *querida*, it is something I would like very much to happen,' he murmured. 'You are all I have ever desired in a woman.'

His lips brushed her cheek again, but as his arms lifted to go around her she slid sideways and avoided them. Going round the desk, she sat down in his swivel chair. Across the desk they regarded each other measuringly, rather like two cats, each of them trying to outguess the other.

'Who told you about the rumour?' Carlos asked smoothly, hitching one leg on to the desk and reaching forward to take a cigar from a carved walnut box.

'A friend,' Renata replied warily.

'A friend, hmm?' He raised his eyebrows again. 'Not by any chance the friend whom you invited to come to the show and who stood at the back with the American woman who spoke to you after the show was over?'

'You saw Jason, then?' she exclaimed without thinking, wondering if there was anything he didn't notice about her. Was he always spying on her?

'It was hard not to see him,' he replied wryly. 'He looked as out of place at a fashion show of women's clothing as you would look at a display of the latest aircraft,' he jibed. 'I had a few words with him. There was something about him that was familiar, I'm not really sure what it was, so I asked him where he was from and how he had come to be there.' He concentrated on lighting his cigar, then gave her a sharp cold glance. '*Querida*, I do sincerely hope now that you're not going to take up with him. All he knows is how to fly those noisy machines. You and he have nothing in common.'

'I think I'm the best judge of that. He knew Kendal and was a good friend to him,' she retorted. 'But that's not what we are discussing. Who started the rumour about my being your mistress? Do you know?'

'I suspect it would be one of our clients. Some of those wealthy women love a juicy bit of gossip, and if they don't know anything about a person's private life they'll make something up. You have come on the fashion scene out of the blue, rather like a shooting star, and they wonder how you got here. It would never occur to them that you could do it on talent alone or that my backing of you could possibly be totally on a businesslike footing.' Carlos's eyes almost closed as a smug smile curved his thin lips.

'You don't mind, then, what they're saying about you and me?' asked Renata in surprise.

'No. Why should I?'

'Well, I do mind. And I'm going to stop it,' she asserted.

'How?'

'By telling everyone it's not so.'

'And you really think you'll be believed?'

'You could help by denying it too,' she pointed out.

'I suppose I could,' said Carlos, looking across at her and smiling. 'But if you don't like being referred to as my mistress there is one sure-fire way of putting a stop to it.'

'What's that?'

'We could get married.'

'Oh, no, I couldn't ever marry you!' she blurted.

'Why couldn't you?' he demanded, his eyebrows slanting angrily.

'I . . . I . . . Your suggestion came as a surprise,' she parried. 'It was an instinctive reaction. I just haven't been thinking of marriage lately. I . . . I don't think I've got over Kendal's death yet.'

'Even so, I would like you to consider becoming my wife,' Carlos persisted.

Horrified by his suggestion, Renata could only shake her head from side to side while all the time she was saying to herself, No, no. You're too old for me and I'd die rather than let you touch me!

'But I'm not ready,' she began to argue.

'One day soon you will be. Time heals all wounds and you'll recover from Kendal's death. And, unlike you and Hernandez or even you and Kendal, you and I have much in common — our interest in good design and now in the business.' Carlos's eyes narrowed shrewdly, and he pointed to some papers on the desk. 'These are the orders we took yesterday and this morning. They add up to millions of dollars. Between now and Christmas you are going to be very busy, my dear. And so are my seamstresses, I'm glad to say. You've arrived, Renata, as a fashion designer.'

'But I would prefer to have arrived without my reputation smirched by this rumour,' she retorted. 'Because of it Jason Hernandez got the impression that I'd cheated on Kendal with you. I just can't let lies like that be spread about me. Oh, Carlos, don't you understand what I'm getting at? I don't want my clients thinking I'm a loose woman or that I'm immoral in any way!'

'Don't you mean that you don't want Jason Hernandez to think that?' he replied nastily. 'Now listen to me. I'm going to give you some important advice. You are, right now, the best up-and-coming dress designer to come out of this wild and often turbulent country, and the fashion house known as Renata is going to compete with the best houses of Paris, New York, Madrid and London, to say nothing of Milan. So if you think I'm going to let you toss away all we've achieved together over the past year just because someone has spread a rumour about you and me, you haven't read my character very well. That rumour about you being my mistress can go unchecked as far as I'm concerned if it is going to deter any would-be lover of yours from pursuing you.'

'I'm not worried about any would-be lovers!' she flared. 'I have family in this country and I know they'll be most offended if they hear the rumour. Carlos, if . . . if you don't help me to

stop it I'll break my contract with you and go it alone!'

'Oh, come, my dear, don't let's allow a bit of gossip to come between us. We work well together, you know we do, and . . . ' He began to try and pacify her, but she interrupted him.

'I mean what I say. Scotch the rumour or I stop being your partner and will let everyone know what a snake in the grass you can be. I . . . I'll ruin your business!' she finished furiously.

They glared at one another in a battle of wills that wasn't new in their business relationship.

'Then you'll ruin yourself at the same time,' Carlos flung back at her. 'You know you'd never have made it so far without my support. And do I have to remind you that we signed a contract to work together for at least two years? Break that and I'll sue you. Early on I found out that you only work well if you're free from any emotional entanglement with a man. Fortunately for me, Kendal died. Unfortunately

now, just at the moment when you have achieved success, this bastard Hernandez turns up to distract you. I'll only assist you in stopping the rumour that you feel smirches your reputation if you promise me not to have anything to do with him. Surely you could do that in return for all the support I have given you?'

'You needn't think you own me just because I've been willing to accept your help. And you can't stop me getting involved with Jason Hernandez if I want to. I'm free to have a love affair with any man I choose to have an affair with. No one, least of all you, is going to tell me how to run my private and personal affairs!' Renata retorted stormily.

'Then I shall certainly do nothing to stop the rumour. I might even add a few tasty titbits to it. And if you dare to break our contract I'd make damn sure no one else in this city or anywhere else would take you on as a designer or a model,' Carlos told her silkily. 'The only way you can stop that rumour now is to

marry me, Renata.'

Just in time she managed to control her temper, managed not to retort that she didn't want to continue to work with anyone as malicious as he was, and she was trying to think up something to say to him that would mollify him when there was a knock on the office door. It swung open and Teresa Villegas, his secretary, appeared.

'Excuse me, Señor Muro, but Señor Duenas is here. You promised to take him round the garment factory,' she said.

'Tell him I'll be with him in a few seconds,' said Carlos smoothly. The secretary, after a curious glance at Renata's slightly flushed face, went out, and the door closed.

Carlos straightened up and approached Renata. It took all her will-power not to retreat before his advance. Smiling at her, he stroked one of her cheeks with a forefinger.

'I forgive your little flare of temper, *querida*. It is understandable. You have

been under a great deal of pressure these past few weeks. Go now and enjoy the rest of your day off. We'll talk another time about my suggestion that we should get married to stop that rumour.'

Longing to defy him again, Renata swung on her heel and left the room with as much dignity as she could muster. She felt a sudden desire to confide in someone who was close to her and who might understand her, someone like her mother, whom she missed so much, ever since Carlota's tragic death in a skiing accident at Whistler Mountain in British Columbia some years ago.

Going into her own office, she phoned her mother's sister Maria and was promptly invited by that kind-hearted woman to spend the day at her suburban home. Within a few minutes she had left the Camino Real and was riding in a taxi to the more residential area of San Isidro.

4

Sunlight slanted across the golden stone of the wall that screened the house where Aunt Maria lived with her husband Francisco de Soto. Its warmth seeped through Renata's clothes, and she was glad to feel it after so many days of fog as she pressed the bellpush set into the wall by a thick wooden door under an archway. After a while the door was opened by Diego, her cousin and the Sotos' only son. The same age as herself, he had hair a little less red than her own, more of a chestnut brown, and bright black eyes that twinkled merrily in his olive-skinned face. He greeted her with a smile, and when she walked into the garden he embraced her, kissing her on both cheeks.

'It's good to see you,' he said. 'You don't visit us often enough — at least,

you never seem to come when I'm at home.'

'It's good to see you too,' she replied. 'Are you on holiday?' she asked as they walked along a flagged pathway that wound through a thick shrubbery of exotic tropical plants ablaze with yellow, orange and purple blossoms and spiky with the fronds of different varieties of palms.

'A few days only. I'm going back to the mountains tomorrow,' Diego replied as they approached the house, which was also built of golden stone in the Spanish colonial style, with many arches and wrought-iron balconies festooned with creepers. 'I'm still working for that irrigation project in an Indian village up in the mountains.'

'What exactly are you doing?'

'Supervising the laying of plastic water pipes in the old canal that their Inca ancestors built. It had been buried for hundreds of years, ever since the *conquistadores* destroyed the Inca civilisation. Soon the village will have

pure water again, running right up to faucets outside each house, and their children won't die any more from the diseases caused by drinking contaminated water.'

'It must give you a great feeling of satisfaction to be helping them improve their way of life,' Renata remarked.

'It does. But it couldn't have been done without the help of foreign aid. We had grants of money from both the Canadian and Dutch Embassies,' Diego replied earnestly. 'And the Dutch supplied the engineering know-how, showing us how to dig the ditches and lay the pipes.'

'But I thought you'd trained to be an archaeologist, not a plumbing engineer,' Renata teased him. She knew he had graduated as an archaeologist from a university in the States and that he was employed by the National Museum of Anthropology and Archaeology in Lima.

'It's because I'm an archaeologist that I know how the Incas used to

irrigate their land, even if their direct descendants have forgotten, and that's why I've been sent to the village to supervise the project,' he explained.

'How do you get to the village?' she asked.

'By plane or chopper from Cuzco,' he said. 'Same way Kendal used to go to the jungle.'

'Oh, then perhaps you've met Jason Hernandez. He's the pilot who used to fly Kendal sometimes.'

'No, I haven't met him, but I have heard of him.'

'What have you heard of him?'

'Only that he's a skilful pilot and a shrewd businessman. There are rumours going about that his company is going to take over one of the airlines that flies between Lima and Cuzco and other towns.'

They had just reached the patio, a pleasant tiled area at the back of the house, and Maria appeared through a long open window to greet Renata with outstretched arms, so that there was no

chance to ask Diego more about Jason. Diego excused himself and went inside to make a phone call to his girlfriend, he said, and since it was such a warm day Maria suggested she and Renata sat outside on the patio where humming birds, their tiny iridescent bodies shimmering blue and green, their wings forever fluttering, visited the blossoms of the plants to which their long fine beaks were especially suited for sipping the nectar that was necessary to their survival.

Maria had been to Renata's fashion show the previous day and was proud of her relationship to the new designer.

'But I did not care for what I heard about you and Carlos Muro,' she said in her forthright way.

'What did you hear?' demanded Renata, feeling a chilly shiver go through her as she guessed Maria had heard the rumour about herself and Carlos.

'That you are his mistress. That he keeps you in comfort in a luxurious

apartment in San Isidro,' said Maria her voice sharp with disapproval.

Almost as tall as Renata, Maria was plump but managed to control her curves severely. She was stylishly dressed in a white pleated skirt and a hand-knitted short-sleeved top of vivid green cotton. Gold chains encircled her neck and gold loops hung in her ears. Her dark brown hair was now elegantly streaked with grey and arranged in the latest style.

'I hope it is not true, Renata,' she added, flashing her stunned and silent niece a curious glance.

'No, of course it isn't true!'

'I am glad. Your mother, my dearest, most-lamented Carlota, would not have approved of such an arrangement. You know that in our family the women have always been chaste. They have had sexual relations only with the men they have married. I realise that these days morals are much more lax, that young women have pre-marital and even extra-marital affairs. But that is not our

way. We come from a very upright people, a people with honour, and when Carlota and I were young women we were not allowed to go out on dates unchaperoned and unsupervised. Nor were we allowed to marry a man out of our immediate social circle.'

'I know that.' Renata chuckled softly, remembering some of her father's stories of the difficulties he had encountered when courting her mother. 'Yet my mother was allowed to marry a man from Canada, a country where the social rules are different and much more liberal and where there is no class distinction.'

'That is true,' sighed Maria. 'But then Donald, your father, was so obviously a good man, with a great sense of responsibility. My father could see that and had no hesitation in allowing Carlota to have dates with him. But to get back to you and this Carlos Muro. He has a bad reputation as a womaniser, I hear.'

'Don't worry, I'm not his mistress

and I've no intention of being,' asserted Renata firmly.

'It is easy for you to say that, but you must know that often a man will help a woman along in her career hoping for a closer relationship with her because she owes him something. It happens, so I hear, all the time,' Maria pointed out.

'I suppose it does,' said Renata. 'But not with me. I owe Carlos nothing. His clothing company has profited from selling clothes designed by me. As soon as I'm established as a designer I'm sure I could make my living without his support. Already from the show I have commissions for designs from enough wealthy Lima socialites to keep me busy for the next few months.'

'That is good, and I am pleased for you. Most of all I am pleased to hear from you that you are not involved in any way other than a business way with Muro,' replied Maria.

'But how am I to stop the rumour?' complained Renata. 'Carlos says that the only way to stop it is for me to

marry him. And I couldn't do that, I just couldn't!'

'I should hope not!' said Maria fervently. 'What a pity it is you aren't married to someone else, though. Then your husband could protect you from such filthy talk. You know, Renata, that would be the best way to solve the problem. And you should marry again, soon. Not Muro, but someone closer to your own age. You are young yet and you don't want to be spending the rest of your life unmarried and alone.'

'But I don't feel like marrying again yet, and I don't want to give up my career.'

'If you find the right man, you wouldn't have to,' asserted Maria. 'You need someone solid and kind, someone who would stay with you and not go rushing off into the jungle all the time as Kendal did. You know, I never understood him. Why would anyone who had grown up with all the benefits of civilisation like he had want to live with a primitive tribe? Didn't he know

how hard a struggle it has been for some people in this country to pull themselves up out of the primitive way of life and get some education and a higher standard of living? Surely he didn't believe that going back to primitive ways is better than living in a house like this with all the modern conveniences? Why, I have heard some of the Indians from the jungle say they are glad that some aspects of civilisation have come to them. They would much rather have the services of a dentist regularly than have toothache all the time.'

'I can believe that,' said Renata with a laugh. 'But I don't think Kendal believed the primitive tribes live in a better way than us. He was just intensely interested in them and wanted to understand their social behaviour.'

'But you didn't have that same interest.'

'Oh, I was interested to a certain extent, just as I am interested in the work Diego is doing to help the people in that village up in the mountains. But

I didn't want to do that sort of work myself. And I didn't want to go and live in the jungle with a tribe like Kendal did.'

'Then you shouldn't have married him,' said Maria grandly.

'We were in love with each other. What better reason is there for being married?' exclaimed Renata, then added in a low voice, 'But sometimes I wish we had been going to have a child.'

'You would like to have children, *querida*?' Maria's attitude softened.

'Very much. If I can ever find the right man to be their father.'

'Don't you know of anyone? Haven't you met anyone suitable since Kendal died?' queried Maria with a natural maternal curiosity.

'No, not really,' sighed Renata, then she thought of Jason, remembering how she had responded to his kiss only that morning; remembering, too, how he had admitted to wanting her. Her heart thudded suddenly with excitement. Was it possible he was the man she should

marry next? 'I have met someone who attracts me, but I don't know him very well,' she went on. 'And then it's just possible he might be married already.'

'Ah, *Madre de Dios!*' Maria crossed herself hastily. 'What is it you are saying now? That you are in love with a married man? Isn't it enough that your name is linked to a notorious woman-iser?'

'I'm telling you this because I have no one else here in whom I can confide,' explained Renata patiently. 'No, I'm not in love with him, but he's the only man I've met since Kendal died that I feel I could be interested in sufficiently to consider marriage to him . . . if he ever asked me, that is.'

'If there is any chance he is married already you must stay away from him,' said Maria sharply.

'But how can I find out if he's married or not if I don't see him to ask him?' argued Renata.

Maria's brown eyes narrowed in thought.

'I am beginning to think,' she began slowly, 'that life used to be much simpler for young women in the old days, before all these ideas of having a career instead of getting married came to mix up their thinking and blind them to their natural destiny, which is to bear children and to rear them properly. I am also beginning to realise that when we were so severely supervised by our families it was much easier to know whether the man who courted us was married or not.' She flashed Renata a bright glance. 'In the absence of your father, do you want us to find about him for you?'

'Could you?' queried Renata. 'I've mentioned him to Diego, but he hasn't met him, only heard of him.'

'If we know his name and what he does for a living we can find out about him. Where did you meet him? In Lima?'

'Yes. It was when Kendal was missing in the jungle and I was trying to find out what had happened to him. Kendal

gave this man a letter to deliver to me,' Renata explained. 'He was the pilot of the helicopter in which Kendal used to travel often to the jungle.'

'Then there will be no problem. We will ask Francisco about him this evening when he comes back from the city,' said Maria.

'But how can Uncle Frank possibly know anything about him? Lima is a big city, and Jason is based in Cuzco.'

'Have you forgotten, child? Francisco is a civil servant and an adviser to the President himself. He can find out anything we want to know,' said Maria importantly.

'No, I hadn't forgotten that,' said Renata slowly, not at all sure how she could go about asking Maria's rather morose and strict husband about a man she might be interested in marrying.

Later, at dinner, Maria showed how it was possible to approach Francisco on the matter as she gently introduced the topic of flying and helicopters into the conversation.

'Renata has a friend who is a helicopter pilot,' she remarked when she had got Francisco going on the subject of how useful helicopters were and how they had helped open up the country, taking people into areas where it had been impossible to land a plane among the mountains and in the jungle.

'So?' Francisco raised his beetling black eyebrows and gave Renata an interested and enquiring look. 'What is his name?'

'Hernandez — Jason Hernandez,' said Renata rather diffidently, and braced herself for she knew not what.

'Ha! That daredevil,' growled Francisco. Black-haired, olive-skinned and rather short, he had a thick black moustache, and Renata found herself wondering irrelevantly whether all the government employees in Peru were in the same mould.

'There, I told you Francisco would know him,' said Maria complacently as she served her husband with more *pastel de choclo*, finely chopped corn

kernels combined with chicken, onions, raisins and eggs that had been baked until golden-brown. 'Is he a good man, Frank?'

'You mean, don't you, Mama, is it suitable for Renata to know him?' put in Diego with a wink at Renata. 'Is he honourable, upright and moral?'

'I wouldn't know about his morals. I haven't met him,' said Francisco thoughtfully. 'All I know is that he is related in some way to Ferdinand Hernandez who was one of our ablest diplomats and who was also an aviator. You remember him, Maria? He was killed most tragically, in a flying accident when he was Peru's representative at the United Nations Assembly in New York. He had several family connections in the USA and was just returning from a visit to see one of his relatives who lives in New Mexico.'

'Ah, yes, I remember him. So handsome he was, and such a great worker for our country.'

'He was something of a social

reformer, wasn't he?' said Diego. 'Didn't he believe in the decentralisation of government and the integration of the Indians into Peruvian society, even though he was from one of the oldest and most rich and powerful of the Spanish aristocratic families?'

'That's right,' Francisco replied. 'And his family ostracised him for his socialist beliefs.'

'Then Renata's friend is related to a good Peruvian family — on his father's side at least,' said Maria assertively, directing the conversation away from the dangerous area of Peruvian politics. 'Now we just have to find out about his mother.'

'Don't be a snob, Mother! It doesn't matter who his mother is or was,' groaned Diego. 'Who a man's parents are is not important. Besides, it's none of your business.'

'I cannot agree with you, Diego. It seems to me you are being greatly influenced by the lax moral attitudes prevalent these days in California,

where you have been studying,' retorted Maria with great dignity. 'Renata would like to marry again one day, and she should. And I owe it to Carlota's dear memory to see that she marries the right man, one who will protect her and respect her.'

'But maybe Renata and this Hernandez aren't thinking of getting married,' protested Diego. He looked directly across the table at Renata. 'Are you?'

'I . . . ' she started, but Maria's stronger and louder voice overrode hers.

'You know, Francisco, who is the mother of this Jason?' she demanded.

'No, I don't. And I agree with Diego, it doesn't matter who his mother is,' replied Francisco irritably.

'Jason is a very unusual name. It isn't Spanish or Peruvian,' remarked Maria, with apparent inconsequence. 'I have heard that American women call their children by many strange Christian names and not by the names of the glorious saints at all.'

'Jason is a classical Greek name, Mother,' said Diego with an exaggerated sigh and a wink at Renata.

'Then she is of Greek descent, his mother?' asked Maria, glancing at her husband curiously.

'I have no idea,' Francisco said curtly. 'And I can't see what business it is of ours to know everything about this man just because Renata considers him to be a friend of hers. All I know is that Jason Hernandez, like many of our fliers, has a lot of courage and dedication. He is also a survivor, as was shown last year when he survived a particularly bad storm in the mountains in which his helicopter was wrecked. Any man who could find his way out of those mountains on foot and recover from near-starvation and fever as well deserves our admiration, and I for one would have no hesitation in welcoming him to my home or in marrying him to my daughter, if I had one. Now can we talk about something else?'

'Is he married?' said Maria bluntly,

and Diego guffawed and shook his head as he exclaimed,

'Mother!'

'I don't know, and I'm not going to find out,' snapped Francisco.

'I just wondered whether any woman made enquiries about him when he was reported missing in the mountains, just as Renata started to make enquiries about Kendal when he didn't return from the jungle when he should have done,' said Maria serenely.

'I don't know,' reiterated Francisco, and looked directly at Renata. 'If you are a friend of his and you want to know more about him, why don't you ask him if he's married yourself?' he added. 'I've told you all I know.'

Although her cheeks were burning with embarrassment at Maria's direct and inquisitive questions, Renata managed to answer him calmly.

'Thanks, Uncle, you've been most helpful. I don't know Señor Hernandez very well. We've met only a couple of times,' she said.

'But she thinks he would make a suitable father of her children,' put in the irrepressible Maria and the meal ended in uproar as Francisco, speaking severely, and Diego, speaking laughingly, chided Maria not only for her snobbery but also for the way she was always trying organise other people's lives.

Later that evening Diego drove Renata back to her apartment, and as always he talked about archaeology.

'Have you visited any of the Inca sites yet?' he asked her.

'No, I haven't,' she admitted.

'You mean to tell me you haven't been to Machu Picchu?' he exclaimed.

'No. You think I should go and see it?'

'I think everyone who claims to be a Peruvian should go to see it. It is a wonderful spiritual experience to see what the Incas were capable of building.'

'How would I get to Machu Picchu from here?' Renata asked.

'You would have to fly to Cuzco first,' he replied, and was silent for a moment as if allowing the weight of his announcement to sink into her mind, 'and from there take the *autocarril* to the station nearest the site. Any travel agent would arrange it for you,' he added, as he brought the car to a stop outside the apartment building where she lived.

Cuzco. Jason's company was based in Cuzco. Renata turned to look at her cousin. In the dimness of the car she could only make out the white of his eyes reflecting light thrown back from the headlamps, the gleam of teeth as he smiled at her. Was it possible he was very subtly pointing out to her a way in which she could meet Jason again?

'You would like Cuzco,' he said quietly. 'It is an old city, once the capital of Peru. Now it is a centre for tourists and also a place from which to travel into the mountains or the jungle by plane or helicopter.'

She was silent, waiting for him to say

something more direct about Jason, but he didn't, and after a few more moments of silence she said to him, 'Thanks for the suggestion — and thanks also for driving me home.'

'You're welcome,' he said. 'And if you feel like taking a trip to see me at the site in the mountains where I'm working you'll find that the aviation company serving the mountain villages and the jungle shares a ticket desk with an airline that flies regularly between Callao and Cuzco, the one you'll probably fly with when you go to see Machu Picchu.'

'I don't see how I can go just yet,' she sighed. 'I've so much work to do.'

'You'll find the time to go if you can't find any other way out of the mess you've got yourself into with Muro,' Diego said gently, with a surprising understanding of her dilemma.

'How do you know about that?' she exclaimed.

'Mother was going on about it all yesterday after she came back from

your fashion show. I would think, goin
by the conversation at dinner, she'
been lecturing you about it. I'd take her
advice if I were you — she's usually
right. See you again soon.'

'See you,' she said, letting herself out
of the car. 'And thanks for telling me
how to get to Machu Picchu.'

5

During the next few weeks, as she supervised the cutting out and making of model dresses and suits and interviewed new customers, Renata was harassed not only by the repetition of the rumour that she was Carlos's mistress but also by his deliberate importuning of her when other people were present. Too often he slid his arm around her waist while talking to a client and made insinuating remarks about their supposed close and intimate relationship. Too often she had to avoid socialising with him by saying she had promised to visit her aunt Maria. By the end of October it seemed to her she had spent more time staying overnight in the Soto house than in her own apartment, so as not to be there when Carlos phoned her or called to see her unexpectedly.

The strain was beginning to affect her nerves too. Normally cheerful and outgoing, she was becoming morose and withdrawn. When she looked at herself in a mirror she saw that a frown line between her eyebrows was in danger of becoming permanent and that her lips were drooping at the corners instead of turning up. She often lost her temper, not only with the cutters and seamstresses, but also with Maria.

'This can't go on, Renata,' said her aunt one day. 'You must do something or I shall write to Donald to tell him what has happened and ask him to come and make you go back to Canada and finish for good with this Muro. Or I shall ask Francisco to speak to Muro and put him in his place.'

'But what can I do? Short of slapping Carlos's face and telling him to get lost, I mean? I can't just walk out of a business I've helped to build up. I've just as much invested in Renata fashions as he has. Not financially, I

admit, but I've invested a lot of myself, my time, my creativity,' replied Renata. 'What can I do?'

'I have told you — find someone suitable to marry. I have tried to introduce to you the young men we know here, friends of Diego, colleagues of Francisco. But you don't seem to have taken to any of them.'

'They're all so dull,' muttered Renata. 'Oh, I'm sorry, Aunt Maria. I know you're doing your best to help. I'll try again today to persuade Carlos to leave me alone. It's such a difficult position I'm in. If only I hadn't signed that contract last year to be his partner for at least two years I could leave the company and set up on my own. But if I did that he would sue me, and I can't afford a legal battle with him. Not yet.'

As it turned out, Carlos proposed marriage to her the next day for about the sixth time, and instead of saying diplomatically that she would think about it and let him know, Renata blurted outright,

'No, never! I've told you before, I can't marry you.'

'Why not?'

'Because — oh, because I'm going to marry someone else,' she said recklessly, tossing her head back and looking him in the eyes.

'And who is this someone else?' he queried softly, humouring her. 'I don't believe there is anyone else. You're pretending there is just to put me off.'

'No, I'm not. I'm going to marry Jason Hernandez,' Renata said defiantly.

For a moment Carlos looked taken aback, but he recovered his poise quickly and laughed scornfully.

'Ha! I'll believe that only when I see another wedding ring on your finger and the announcement of your marriage in the papers. Hernandez will never marry you,' he sneered.

'Want to bet?' she challenged him.

'But of course,' Carlos responded smoothly. 'Because I know I shall win.'

That was all Renata needed to send her scurrying to the travel agency in the

shopping mall, where she arranged to fly to Cuzco the next day. She didn't tell Carlos she would be away for at least two days and nights and maybe longer. He could stew about her absence for all she cared, but she did tell Maria.

As the blue and white aircraft out of Lima hurtled over the snow-crested peaks of the mountains on the following morning Renata felt the exhilarating sense of escape that flying always gave her. For a while she could pretend she was as free as air, without a care in the world. Carlos, the contract she had with him and couldn't break yet, ceased to exist. She had got away from him, and for the next two days she was going to do her best to find a solution to the problems she was having with him.

Within an hour the plane was gliding above the brown and green checkerboard of fields that covered the shoulders of the high sierra near Cuzco. Swerving, it followed a valley where a river was a thread of silver and a train

chugged slowly along a single line on its way to Puno. The plane tilted again, and looking out of the window beside her, Renata glimpsed a flash of blue in the distance, and beyond it the massive walls of more mountains, violet-grey in the distance, shimmering with sunlight. Above them white cotton-balls of clouds floated in a bright blue sky. Then the view was gone as the plane levelled to make its approach to the airport.

At last she was coming to Cuzco, the fabled royal city of the Incas, that had been sacked by the Spanish *conquistadores* under the cruel and malicious Pizarro. She was travelling with a group of tourists from the States and Canada and with them, tomorrow she would visit Machu Picchu.

The plane landed smoothly and taxied to the terminal building. While she was waiting for a taxi with the other tourists in the group Renata looked round the terminal building and noticed the ticket desk of the airline with which she had flown to Cuzco.

Only for a few moments did she hesitate, then, unable to ignore the impulse to try and find Jason Hernandez deliberately instead of just hoping she might run into him, she went over to the desk and asked if it was there she could book a flight on a helicopter to the jungle.

'That's right, *señora*,' the ticket agent told her. 'You want to book a flight to Puerto Maldonado?'

'No. But I'd like to speak with Señor Jason Hernandez, please.'

He gave her an admiring glance, twitched his eyebrows expressively and, after muttering something about some guys having all the luck, excused himself politely and disappeared through a door behind him. In a few moments he was back, shaking his head negatively.

'He is not here. He has gone into the mountains and won't be back until later today,' he said.

It was hard not to show her disappointment. As always when one of

her headlong impulses was blocked abruptly she wasn't able to think right then what to do next. Also she had begun to feel the effects of the *soroche*, the mountain sickness that affects travellers who have been transported too quickly to a very high altitude from sea-level. Black spots danced before her eyes and she felt dizzy.

'Would you like to leave a message for him?' She became aware of the agent looking at her closely and made an effort to shake off both disappointment and the mountain sickness.

'Could I?' she asked hopefully.

'Of course.' He smiled at her in a kindly way. 'Just write it here on this paper and I will give it to one of the mechanics to give to him as soon as he comes back, maybe this evening, maybe tomorrow. *Quién sabe*?' He shrugged his shoulders and spread his hands wide.

Renata wrote the message, telling Jason the name of the hotel where she would be staying the night and asking

him to call in to see her there. Then, leaving it with the ticket agent, she took a taxi to the hotel. Glad at last to reach her room, she lay down on the rather lumpy bed and rested until the dizziness and sickness of the *soroche* had passed.

When she felt she had rested long enough she went for a walk. Since the old hotel was near the centre of the city she didn't have to walk very far to reach the Plaza de Armas. In the large open area of the sunlit square there were sidewalk stalls tended by Indian women in their long handwoven skirts, shawls and mannish felt hats. The stalls offered various household goods for sale to passing townspeople. Small boys shined shoes. Indian families, colourful in ponchos and felt or woven hats, trudged by silently, their faces seemingly carved from eroded rock, their dark eyes sombre as if they carried the sadness of all the world on their backs.

There was a fountain in the centre of

the plaza and some benches. Renata sat down on one of them to catch her breath in the rarefied atmosphere. She consulted her guidebook and then looked around. The most outstanding building in the plaza was the cathedral, which had been constructed by Pizarro's *conquistadores* to celebrate the defeat of an Incan rebellion in which they had massacred many people. Another building, twin-towered and graceful, was a church built by the Jesuits, the granite from which it had been made glittering in the sunlight. Everywhere there were examples of Peru's two souls, Incan and Spanish.

Deciding against going into any of the buildings, Renata walked up a narrow alley beside the Jesuit church. Her heels turned and grated on rough cobblestones and the sun was blocked out by high walls of superb Inca stonework, each block of stone fitted into the one below it. No mortar held them together.

At the end of the alleyway she found

a small market where she haggled over the price of a striped poncho made not from llama wool, as she had hoped, but from acrylic yarn. The bland-eyed Indian woman who was offering it for sale explained that she was using acrylic now because the colours were brighter, did not fade and so pleased American tourists more. If she wanted to make a living from her traditional skill of weaving she had to adapt to the times, she said. Appreciating the woman's honesty as well as admiring her shrewd business sense in adapting to the reality of the twentieth century while retaining her native and ancient skills, Renata bought the poncho, paying the price originally asked.

She returned to the hotel, where she ate sparingly at dinner, mindful that she could still be ill with the mountain sickness if she wasn't careful, then went to sit in the friendly foyer of the old hotel, where a wood fire leapt in the fireplace, because the temperature had fallen quite dramatically with the

coming of night. For a while she talked to a Canadian couple, Mae and Art Cochrane from Vancouver, who were on vacation and had been on the same flight from Callao in the morning. They were also going to visit Machu Picchu the next day and, after saying they would look for her on the *autocarril*, they went to their room and Renata was left to wait, wondering whether Jason would come or whether he would ignore her message telling him where she was staying and asking him to come and meet her.

She was still slightly amazed at what she was intending to ask him to do to help her. He was the only man she could ask, and after all, he had said he would have liked to have had a love affair with her. Well, he could have her if he married her, she had decided on the flight to Cuzco. She wasn't in love with him, not in the sweetly romantic way she had been in love with Kendal. She would never be in love like that again because she would never be so

young again. But she was attracted to Jason, fascinated by the enigma of his character, sensing that beneath his cynical tough-guy armour, that had possibly been forged during the years he had spent in North America, there flowed a fiery South American passion that matched her own.

It was well after ten o'clock when the entrance door to the hotel swung open and he came in. For a few moments he stood blinking in the light, looking round. He was wearing jeans and black high-necked sweater under the same jacket he had worn the last time Renata had seen him. He looked so big and truculent that she felt a sudden revulsion of feeling. Perhaps she shouldn't have tried to see him. What did she really know about him? He could be a brute for all she knew.

While she hesitated he spotted her and strode straight towards her. In contrast to his dishevelled ink-black hair, his face was pale with fatigue and there were dark lines under his eyes.

'Why have you come here? Why do you want to see me?' he demanded in English, and the group of American tourists sitting nearby stopped talking and turned to look at him.

'There's something I have to ask you. I need your help,' whispered Renata.

He glanced round the foyer again, noting the interested onlookers and the warily watching reception clerk. Then he looked back at Renata, a warm glow of admiration replacing the hostile glitter in his eyes. His lips parted and for a moment she thought he was going to grab hold of her, haul her up from the chair where she was sitting and kiss her as he had done the last time they had met.

'We can't talk here,' he said tersely. 'Let's go to your room.'

'But I'm not sure if . . . ' she began, glancing at the inquisitive desk clerk.

'I am,' said Jason succinctly, and his grin was a sudden glint of devilry in his face, chasing away the weariness. 'Come on!' Seizing her hand, he pulled

her up from the chair on which she was sitting and drew her after him towards the stairs. 'Which floor?' he demanded.

'Second.'

'Good. I'm glad we don't have to walk up to the top floor. What made you choose this old place to stay in?'

'The travel agent in Lima arranged it all. He said this was nearest to the centre of the city and the *autocarril*. We didn't want to walk too far in the high altitude.'

'We?' he interrupted her sharply, jerking her round roughly to face him. 'There is someone with you?'

'No,' she said quickly. 'I meant the other tourists who travelled on the plane with me.'

They reached the door to her room. She unlocked it, went in and was searching for a light switch when she felt Jason's hands at her waist. As the light clicked on he kicked the door shut behind him and spun her round to face him again. His lips swooped to hers, and it wasn't the altitude that made her

117

suddenly dizzy and her legs lose their strength so that she swayed against him.

His lips slid from her mouth and began to rain kisses on her face over her cheeks, then down to her throat. Hands against his chest, she tried to push him away.

'No, no!' she cried. 'This isn't what I've come for. Please be sensible and let go of me!'

'Why should I?' he whispered, holding her more tightly. 'You've come here looking for me, and to my mind that means only one thing . . . '

'But you're wrong. You're wrong!' she insisted, still pushing. He seemed to be made of Andean rock and was immovable. Feeling a slight slackening of his arms, Renata freed herself from their embrace and backed away from him, staring at his dark face, thinking it was the face of a man who liked his own way and usually got it. But there were also lines of humour about his eyes and that hint of recklessness glinting in them, both of which appealed to her.

'Just because I've come to see you it doesn't mean I'm ready to leap into bed with you right now. You see, I don't know enough about you,' she said sharply.

Jason's face hardened. The hostile expression returned to his eyes.

'Yeah, I see,' he drawled. Giving her a raking, disparaging glance, he muttered an imprecation savagely under his breath, then, hooking his thumbs in the pockets of his jeans, he went over to the bed and sat down on the edge of it. His wide shoulders slumped wearily, but the underbrowed glance he gave her was brightly sardonic.

'So what do you want to know?' he asked, his voice rasping drily. 'I have a clean bill of health and don't suffer from any known contagious or uncontagious diseases . . . '

'I didn't mean that!' she exclaimed, feeling her temper rising.

'Then what did you mean?'

'I meant that I don't know much about you as a person. You could be

married for all I know.'

Whatever had made her think he would be kind and deal with her tenderly? Here they were at cross-purposes already, he interested only in satisfying his sexual appetites with her as if . . . well, as if she were a girl he had called in for the purpose, while she sought only his help, his friendship, his protection. She should really tell him to leave for making more assumptions about her. But she didn't. Going over to him, she sat down beside him and put a hand on his arm.

'Please, Jason,' she said quietly, 'I have to know. Are you or are you not married?'

Turning his head, he gave her a narrowed, speculative glance as if trying to assess what lay behind her question.

'But of course I am. To my ambition, to my love of flying,' he replied mockingly, his eyebrows tilting. 'No woman could take its place. Why do you want to know?'

His answer had the effect of throwing

her off course a little, but she got herself back on track and drawing a deep breath, made her next attempt.

'I would like you to marry me.'

Not a muscle moved in the dark sardonic face, and she envied him his self-control.

'Let me get this straight,' he said slowly, after a while, still staring at her as if she were out of her mind. 'Is this some sort of blackmail? Am I right in thinking you'll only go to bed with me if I agree to marry you first?'

This time her temper nearly burst through her restraint and she was tempted to march over to the door, open it and order him to leave. Instead she clenched her hands on her knees, raised her head proudly and looking him in the eyes said,

'Yes, you're right. I can't have an affair with you, as you asked me last time we met, but I am willing to marry you.'

Jason passed one hand over his face and rubbed his eyes with his fingers.

'I've had a hectic day and I'm pretty tired, so you'll have to forgive me if I'm a bit slow on the uptake,' he said slowly. 'Would you mind explaining why you would like me to marry you before I go to bed with you?'

'I . . . I'm having problems with Carlos, and the only way I could think of to get him off my back yesterday was to tell him I'm going to marry you,' Renata confessed. 'And I thought it would be best if I told you what I'd said in case he starts nosing around to find out if it's true.'

'He's been harassing you?' he asked in a voice that rasped with menace.

'Yes. Ever since I asked him to stop the rumour you heard at the show he's been pressuring me to marry him. He says it would be the best way to stop the rumour. And because I've been refusing to agree to marry him he's refused to deny that the rumour is true. He says he wants it known that I'm his mistress so that no other man will want me. He's been on and on about it for weeks

now, and yesterday I couldn't bear him any longer, so I told him I can't marry him because I've already promised to marry you.'

'*Wow!*' Jason's eyes glinted suddenly with laughter. 'That was a pretty reckless statement to make!'

'It was all I could think of,' she admitted.

'Why don't you just break your business partnership with him, leave Lima and go back to Canada?' he asked. He was very cool now, disappointingly so. Why had she ever thought he would jump at the chance to marry her?

'I've threatened to do that, but you see, we signed a contract to be in partnership for at least two years and if I break it he'll sue me for breach of contract. And I can't afford a lawsuit just now. But it isn't the business part that bothers me. It's the sexual harassment and the smirching of my good reputation that does. My aunt Maria, my mother's sister who lives in

Lima, has advised me that the best way out is for me to get married to someone else and then Carlos will have to leave me alone.' Renata looked at Jason appealingly. 'You were a good friend to Kendal and I thought you might be a good friend to me too, and help me. I don't know of any other man I could ask.'

He stared at her with opaque black eyes. Skin tautened across his cheekbones and bone showed white at his jawline. Then, with another whispered oath, he got to his feet and walked away from her to the dresser, only to turn sharply and march back to her, to stand in front of her and look down at her from under frowning brows.

'I can't believe this is happening,' he said, shaking his head from side to side as if bewildered. 'I can't believe a woman is asking me, of all people, to marry her. You must be out of your mind!'

'I thought you might say that,' she replied, with a sigh. 'And perhaps I am

a little crazy from the pressure Carlos has been putting on me to marry him.' A feeling of dismay was beginning to creep over her. It was beginning to look as if she had made the most terrible mistake in asking him to marry her.

'Hasn't it occurred to you that being married to me might turn out to be an even worse hell for you than working with Carlos is?' he asked.

'Oh? Why would it?' she exclaimed.

'I'm not exactly the domesticated type,' he said drily, sitting down beside her again. 'And I believe that men like me who risk their lives flying have no right to get married . . . '

'Then you're not married?' she exclaimed, perking up.

'No.' His lips curled cynically. 'Marriage would be like a prison for someone like me. Most women want a husband coming home at the same time every evening, and being there to do all those little jobs around the house that need doing. I've always liked my

freedom too much to get shackled like that.'

'But I don't want that sort of marriage,' Renata said spiritedly. 'I'm not very domesticated either, and I'm just as dedicated to being a dress designer as you are to being an aviator. We could have a modern marriage, go our own ways, meeting when possible, but neither of us being too possessive or too demanding. I suppose what I'm really thinking of is a marriage of convenience — convenient for me mostly, I guess, because I know if I were married to you Carlos would leave me alone, as he did when Kendal was alive.'

Again Jason shook his head slowly from side to side.

'You're incredible, you know that?' he jeered softly. 'And your thinking strikes me as being a little mixed up. Like so many women these days, I suspect, you maintain that women are equal with men and can do everything men can do, including propose marriage, yet the

next minute you're wanting to be protected by a man.'

Renata had no answer to that jibe, so she ignored it and made another appeal.

'You're the only man I've met since Kendal died that I feel I could be married to,' she said quietly. 'And you did say last time we met that you wanted me and would like to have an affair with me.'

'Blackmail again!' he scoffed. He gave her a long level look and little flames seemed to flicker in his eyes. 'I still want you,' he went on in a whisper. 'I even dream about you sometimes, and how it would be if we were to . . . ' He broke off and lunged abruptly to his feet, turning his back on her as if he didn't dare to look at her any longer, 'I'd like to help you, for Kendal's sake,' he added gruffly. 'But I can't give you an answer right now. I'll have to sleep on it.' He turned back to her, the glint of mockery back. 'This has been a new experience for me. No woman has ever

proposed to me before. It's come as a bit of a shock . . . '

'Now you're making fun of me!' she raged suddenly. 'Marriage is a serious business . . . '

'No one knows that better than I do. Marriage is a damned risky affair,' Jason retorted grimly, his face hardening. 'Did you propose to Kendal too?'

'No. We . . . we just came to some sort of mutual agreement to go out one day and get married,' she replied, trying to remember who had suggested marriage first, herself or Kendal. It seemed to her that they had slipped naturally into marriage without any forethought or any planning.

'You'll be staying here tomorrow night?' was his next question.

'Yes.'

'Then I'll try to see you tomorrow for dinner and we'll talk about this again.' He yawned suddenly, a hand across his mouth. 'Right now all I want is sleep.'

'You can stay and sleep here,' offered Renata diffidently. His glance flickered

to the bed and then back to her face. His right eyebrow lifted.

'More blackmail?' he queried. 'When I first knew you were here and wanted to see me I had hoped to do that, but now I've seen the bed and felt it and now I know you'll only do it if I promise to marry you first, I've changed my mind.'

'Oh, you've made me sorry I ever asked you!' she cried, stamping her foot on the ground.

'Want me to forget you did?' he asked quickly, almost hopefully.

'Yes — no. Oh, I don't know!' she cried furiously, her hands against her suddenly hot cheeks, her thoughts in a turmoil, anger, pride and disappointment mixing together.

Stepping towards her, Jason lifted her hands away from her cheeks and held them.

'I wish you hadn't come here. I wish you hadn't got in touch with me,' he said in a low, shaken voice. 'I was well on the way to trying to forget you. I

wish you'd break with Muro and leave Peru, go back to Canada so there would be no chance of my ever seeing you again. Ever since I brought that letter to you I've wanted you, but I couldn't do anything about it because you were married to Kendal. You've asked the wrong man for help. I'm no knight errant riding to help damsels in distress, and I once vowed I would never marry so long as I was able to fly, so you've really put me on the spot by asking me to help you.'

Putting hard fingers under her chin, he forced her head back. His lips ravaged hers brutally as if he were determined to make her hate him, and when the kiss was over she was shaking from head to foot.

'You see what you'd be letting yourself in for if you were married to me?' he jeered softly, letting her go and striding towards the door. 'Have a good day at Machu Picchu tomorrow.'

He left the room, and this time it was Renata who slammed the door after

him, angry with herself for having dared to ask him to marry her. She had blundered badly, had completely misread his character, she thought, as she got ready for bed.

It was all very well for her feminist teachers to have declared that women were just as free to propose marriage as men were. They hadn't dealt with any tough guys like Jason, who loved his freedom and flying too much to give up either for any woman, not even for the woman he desired.

6

Renata was wakened next morning by a lack of warmth. Shivering, she sat up, realising that the bedclothes had slid off her to the floor and that there was no central heating on in the hotel. Through the window she could see the sun rising, spreading rose-pink colour across the sky. Someone knocked on the door and shouted to her in Spanish that it was six o'clock and that if she wanted to catch the *autocarril* to Machu Picchu she should get up and go down to breakfast.

She called out an answer and scrambled off the bed. After a quick wash in cold water she dressed quickly in jeans, a long-sleeved shirt and a sweater, all of them suitable to wear for the ride on the railcar. She laced sneakers on to her feet and plaited her hair into a short braid so that it

wouldn't blow about while she was sightseeing. Then she went down to join the other tourists for breakfast.

Out of a postcard-blue sky the sun shone on the countryside around Cuzco as the diesel-powered single-car observation train began to climb out of the saucer-like, mountain-edged bowl in which the ancient city was located. First the train went forward and then backwards, stopped and then started forward again as it followed a zigzag pattern of railroad tracks up the steep mountainside.

Hands in the pockets of her quilted nylon sheepskin-lined jacket, glad she had worn it to keep out the early-morning cold, Renata looked down a steep-sided valley, imagining what would happen if the railcar left the tracks and plunged over the edge of the abyss. Everywhere in the mountains there were risks to be taken, even when you were tourist, she thought.

Once it was over the mountain the train passed through a wide, fertile

valley dotted with poplars and willows and large herds of cattle. At the various stations along the way Indians had gathered to watch the most exciting event of the day, the passing of the railcar. The tracks then followed the Huarcando River through a deep gorge to another river, the Urubamba. Seething between passes of sheer, solid rock, the river, brown and sometimes red in colour, was scary-looking. Renata wasn't surprised when Art Cochrane told her that the Spaniards had had trouble in chasing the last of the Inca rulers into this area.

'But they never got as far as Machu Picchu,' said Art. 'And neither did any other white man until 1911.'

When at last the train reached the station of Machu Picchu all the tourists crowded into a small bus for the rest of the trip to the plateau where the remains of what had once been considered to be the holy city of the Incas was situated.

'You can see the ruins from here.' Art

pointed up to the sugarloaf-shaped mountain that reared up from the valley of the Urubamba.

Renata looked up, overawed by the closeness of the mountains. She could just make out rows and rows of stone steps leading up to the flat top of a rocky ridge.

★   ★   ★

'They used to be covered by jungle growth,' explained Art. 'That's why they were hidden from explorers for so long.'

The twenty-minute ride was full of thrills along a narrow road that twisted around a series of startling hairpin bends and passed over a narrow bridge slung above a ravine. After lunch at a small but adequate hotel they set off to climb the rest of the way to the city, leaving coats and jackets behind because the day had warmed up.

'I'm glad the altitude is lower here than in Cuzco,' Mae Cochrane confided breathlessly to Renata as they

walked together. 'I'd never see the place if it wasn't.'

Through a narrow stone corridor they walked into a wide grass-covered area. There they all stopped to stare in amazement. The whole city, homes, temples, towers, fountains and stairs, especially stairs, because everything seemed to be connected to everything else by steep flights of stone stairs, appeared to be intact, the granite stone sparkling in the sunlight.

'It's like a halfway house to heaven!' exclaimed Mae, gazing up in awe, and Renata was inclined to agree with her.

For two hours they wandered about with a guide, who pointed out and named various places of interest including the Temple of Women, so named because in the nearby cemetery, found by Hiram Bingham, the Yale University professor who had discovered the site, most of the skeletons had been female.

'To think that the people who built this had no knowledge of the wheel, no written language and no beasts of

burden,' said Art. 'Guess they knew a lot more than the Spaniards who conquered them, and were a lot less brutal and cruel too.'

'I'm not so sure about that,' argued Mae. 'It seems to me the Incas could be cruel too. They didn't hesitate to sacrifice other humans to their gods. My guess is that neither the Spaniards nor the Incas knew they were being cruel. Behaviour like theirs was the rule during the times in which they lived. They didn't know any better. We do.'

At last the call came for the group to return to the bus, and they rode to the station to catch the train back to Cuzco. It was late coming and all the way Renata didn't think once of Machu Picchu and its glories or of the dark precipices that yawned dangerously dark on one side of the train track. She was too engrossed in wondering about the forthcoming meeting with Jason, her nerves tightening in anticipation of what he would say to her.

The lateness of the arrival of the train

at the Machu Picchu station made its arrival in Cuzco late too, and it was well after eight o'clock when Renata reached the hotel. Jason wasn't in the foyer nor in the dining room. She asked the clerk at the reception desk whether a Señor Hernandez had been asking for her. The night clerk shook his head. He knew Señor Hernandez by sight and he hadn't seen him all evening.

Trying not to feel let down, Renata ate dinner with the Cochranes, and had difficulty in keeping her eyes open after the day's outing in the mountain air. Eventually she excused herself and went to her room.

Her last thought before she fell asleep was that by not coming to have dinner with her Jason had surely given her his answer. He wasn't going to help her by marrying her, and although in a way she was disappointed because he wasn't the friend she had hoped he was, she also felt relieved that she wasn't going to be embarrassed by his refusing her proposal to her face.

Next morning she checked out of the hotel with the others, intending to catch a morning flight to Callao so that she could be back at her studio in time to keep an appointment with a new client. Much to her surprise, the reception clerk on duty handed her a note that he said had been left for her the previous day but which the night clerk hadn't seen and so hadn't given to her when she had returned from Machu Picchu.

She didn't read the note until she was in the taxi to the airport that she was sharing with the Cochranes. The handwriting was unknown to her, but she knew it was Jason's even before she read his signature at the end of the written message.

'Renata,' she read, 'Sorry I can't make it for dinner tonight. I have had to fly to Puerto Maldonado and I won't be back until tomorrow morning.'

Her fingers curled round the slip of paper, crushing it, and she dropped it in the car's ashtray. Something more important than keeping a date with her

had cropped up: a chance to go flying. Might as well face it, this was how it would always be with Jason, and it was becoming more and more clear to her that she had once again behaved too impulsively in seeking him out and asking him to help her.

The taxi stopped outside the airport terminal building. Renata got out and made her contribution to the payment of the driver. Picking up her overnight bag, she turned to the entrance doors — and caught her breath, her heart pounding suddenly with excitement. Jason was just coming out of the building, his jacket unzipped over a checked shirt, the sharp angle of his jaw blurred by the black stubble of his beard and his eyes tired-looking as if he hadn't slept much. He strode straight towards her, ignoring the Cochranes.

'Where are you going?' he demanded.

'Back to Lima. I'm booked on the next flight. I have to keep an appointment,' she said coolly, not looking at him.

'Didn't you get my note?'

'Not until this morning. Excuse me, they're calling the flight. I must go.' She tried to pass him, but he sidestepped in front of her.

'Stay until tomorrow, or even the day after,' he suggested autocratically.

'No. I've told you, I have to keep an appointment with a client.' Renata tilted her chin and looked him in the eyes. 'My work is just as important to me as flying is to you,' she added.

'I get it.' The corners of his lips curved downwards cynically. 'Muro cracks the whip and you go running to him, in spite of what you think of him.'

'No, I don't go running to any man,' she retorted defiantly. 'Now please let me pass.' Jason stayed right where he was, blocking her way, his face as hard and impassive as the mountains around Machu Picchu but his eyes beginning to gleam with humour. 'Oh, I'm sorry I ever tried to see you!' she hissed angrily. 'I made a mistake about you. I thought you were different, a friend I could turn

to. Please let me pass.'

'Renata, Renata! You'll miss the flight if you don't come now.' Art Cochrane had appeared and was striding towards her, an older man who was handsome in a distinguished way with a lean, suntanned face and silver hair. 'Is this guy bothering you?' He swung round to Jason. 'Get out of this lady's way,' he ordered in slow, painstaking Spanish.

Jason gave Art a quick sidelong glance, then looked back at Renata, his wicked grin flashing white in his brown face.

'Another of your admirers?' he queried mockingly, and before she could retort or Art could remonstrate with him further he turned away and strode back towards the entrance of the building.

'Come on, my dear.' Art had taken Renata's bag from her hand and was now urging her towards the doorway. 'Who was that guy?' he asked. 'I hope he wasn't molesting you?'

'Oh, no,' she said brightly as they

went into the building. 'He used to be friendly with my late husband.'

'Humph! He didn't look too friendly to me,' Art said as they made for the departure gate where the line of tourists going on the flight was waiting to board. 'I don't trust some of these Latin-Americans. They have a funny attitude to women. And Mae agrees with me, it isn't really safe for a young woman as lovely as you are to be living alone in Lima or travelling about the country without company. Couldn't you get work in Canada?'

'I suppose I could, but I like living here, and you have to remember my mother was a Peruvian. I have relatives here and they're very respectable — I'd like you and Mae to meet them. How much longer will you be staying in Lima?'

'Until Friday of this week,' replied Art.

'Then when we're on the plane you must give me the name of your hotel so I can get in touch with you and we'll go

out to see Aunt Maria and Uncle Frank for dinner one evening before you go back to Canada.'

'That sounds great,' said Art enthusiastically. 'A visit to a real home. It isn't often Mae and I get invited to a home when we visit a foreign country.'

The sunshine sparkled on the plane's silvery fuselage; the high-arching sky was a brilliant blue. It was a beautiful day as she walked with Art to the plane, yet Renata felt depression settling on her. Her third meeting with Jason had turned out to be even more unsatisfactory than the previous two, and now she knew he wasn't a friend after all and that she couldn't depend on him to help her. Somehow she would have to find another way of keeping Carlos at bay.

On the plane Art took her seat so that she could sit next to Mae. Although everyone seemed to be aboard and the time for take-off had come and gone, the door wasn't closed. When asked by one of the tourists the reason for the

delay, the steward explained that they were waiting for another passenger. At last there was a movement by the door. Jason had come aboard, and he was joking with the stewardess as she glanced at his boarding pass.

At the sight of him Renata felt her nerves leap. He turned to make his way down the aisle to a seat at the back of the plane. She watched him come towards her, wondering if he would speak to her, but he didn't even look at her as he passed by. The door of the aircraft was closed and in a few minutes they were taking off.

Several times after take-off Renata looked around cautiously to see where Jason was sitting. He was in the very back seat and there was an empty place beside him. The stewardess was leaning over talking to him, probably flirting with him, thought Renata acidly. He was the sort of man women would go out of their way to flirt with.

Suddenly she could stand the suspense no longer. She had to know why

he was flying to Lima. Excusing herself to Mae, she wandered slowly down the aisle until she came to the back seats.

'Is this seat free?' she asked, looking round the stewardess at Jason.

'Sure it is.' His eyes were devoid of expression.

Renata slid past the stewardess, who looked annoyed and moved away.

'I thought you hardly ever go to Lima,' said Renata lightly.

'I have some business to attend to there,' he replied coldly.

'Oh.'

She couldn't think of anything else to say for the moment, and now she was beginning to think she had made another mistake in coming to sit beside him. He hadn't moved when she had sat down and his left knee was nudging her right knee. His left elbow was on the arm-rest, leaving no room for her elbow, and he didn't seem disposed to move either his knee or his elbow. She was finding him too big, too strong, too overwhelmingly masculine, and she

couldn't stay near him a moment longer . . .

Shifting away from him, she began to stand up. At that moment the plane hit some turbulence and lurched violently, losing height. Losing her balance, Renata fell sideways across Jason's thighs.

He swore and she flinched, not being accustomed to bad language, neither her father nor Kendal having used it. It was something else to be chalked up against Jason, she thought irritably as she pushed herself up and away from him. Not only was he tough, he was coarse, and Aunt Maria, if she ever met him, would no doubt think he was highly unsuitable to be the husband of her niece, in spite of the fact that he might be connected in some way with one of the old aristocratic families of Lima.

Again, holding on to the back of the seat in front, she began to stand up.

'Sit down and fasten your seatbelt,' Jason growled at her, and taking hold of

her arm jerked her down into the seat. 'Don't you know better than to move about when a plane is being buffeted like this?' Then, his voice softening a little, he asked, 'Did you hurt yourself just now?'

'No,' she snapped, and sat up straight, looking in front of her. She wasn't unaware that with her tilted-up chin, her long, down-drooping eyelashes and her neat, straight nose she could look very supercilious.

He laughed, a pleasant sound of pure amusement, and she turned on him, guessing he was laughing at her. But he had turned his head to look out of the oval window beside him. Once again the plane sank down with a sickening lurch and two of the Indian women who were passengers screeched in fear. The stewardess appeared and went to comfort them.

Forced to stay beside Jason, Renata gritted her teeth and clenched her hands, trying to cope with the conflicting feelings he aroused in her. Not for

anything was she going to speak to him again. As soon as the plane landed she would hurry off it and get a taxi, go straight to the Camino Real . . .

Oh, no! Carlos would be there and would want to know where she had been. He would start needling her about her defiant announcement that she was going to marry Jason. He'd want to know when and where the marriage would take place and whether it would appear in the newspapers, and when she hedged, telling him that the date of the marriage ceremony hadn't been set yet, he would guess at the truth, that she wasn't going to marry Jason, and would start putting pressure on her again to marry him.

Slowly she turned her head to look at Jason, wondering how best to ask him what his answer to her proposal was. He seemed to be asleep now, his head tilted against the side of the plane. Covertly she studied his profile with its broad, lined forehead, hawklike nose and clean-cut though unshaven jaw.

Her glance went to his mouth. It was relaxed, the broad sculptured lips slightly parted, and she recalled the way he had kissed her the night before last. She shivered a little imagining she saw cruelty in the curve of his lips, the cruelty of *conquistador* ancestors who had raped and plundered with Pizarro across Peru.

And she had dared to ask such a man to marry her! She must have been out of her mind! It would be best to get away from him again, to show by her behaviour that she didn't want to have anything to do with him. Noticing that the plane was now flying more smoothly and that the sign suggesting that seatbelts should be fastened was off, she unbuckled her belt and sliding silently out of the seat returned to her place beside Mae Cochrane.

As soon as the plane landed she was the first in line to get off it, after explaining to Art and Mae that because the landing was behind schedule she would have to hurry ahead to grab a

taxi. She assured them that she would phone them at their hotel to arrange for them to visit Maria and Francisco. Without a backward glance to see if Jason had noticed her hasty leaving of the plane, she sped through the terminal building to the exit where the taxis waited. Since there were many other people de-planing and needing taxis, she had to wait a while for one. At last her turn came, and she stepped into the back of the car and sat down, her hand reaching out to the door to slam it shut.

To her surprise her hand never touched the door, because it was swung open wider to let someone else into the back of the car. Jason sat down beside her and slammed the car door shut. He was breathing heavily. The driver asked over his shoulder where they wanted to go.

'Camino Real,' said Renata quickly, and turned to Jason.

'You were in a hell of a hurry to get off the plane,' he said breathlessly.

'I told you I have an appointment to keep,' she replied stiffly.

'I think you were running away from me,' he taunted. 'I think you'd scared yourself to bits by proposing marriage to me, a man about whom you know very little.' He was so close to guessing accurately the state of her feelings when she had been sitting beside him on the plane that she turned away from him to hide her expression from him and looked out at the cars speeding along the highway.

'I assume your answer to my request for help is no,' she said in her most supercilious way.

'You really think I'd have hopped aboard that flight and raced after you to get in the same taxi if it was?' he queried, his voice lilting in surprise.

'Well, what else could I think when you didn't come to have dinner with me last night?' Renata retorted stiffly.

'So that's why you were so bitchy at the airport,' he mocked.

'I wasn't bitchy!' she exclaimed.

'Stand-offish, then,' he amended, his grin widening. 'Could I help it if the message I left for you wasn't given to you?'

'No, I suppose you couldn't,' she admitted. Then with a sudden surge of emotion, a mixture of irritation with him because she sensed he was playing with her and anxiety because she didn't know how she was going to deal with Carlos when she got back to the boutique, she said, 'Why can't you be more straightforward and tell me whether you're willing to help me or not? I'll be seeing Carlos in a few minutes' time and he'll want to know if I am really going to be married to you.' She looked at him appealingly. 'I'll understand if you don't want to go through with an actual marriage ceremony, but I wondered if you would go along with some sort of pretence.'

'Pretence?' All the humour left Jason's face and he frowned at her. 'What the hell do you mean? What sort of pretence?'

153

'We could pretend we're going to be married at some future date. We could be engaged to be married.' The taxi stopped at some traffic lights and Renata looked out. They were in San Isidro now and she could see the Camino Real mall glittering in the sunlight not far away. She turned back to Jason as the traffic lights changed and the taxi lurched forward. 'Please will you come to the Muro boutique offices now to meet Carlos and together we can tell him that at least we're engaged?' she pleaded desperately.

'You're really scared of him, aren't you? More scared of him than you are of me?' Jason accused her, looking at her with a certain hostility.

She didn't answer because again he had touched a nerve, and again she looked away from him at the traffic.

'And I'm scared, too,' he said abruptly, and she turned back to stare at him in surprise. 'Scared of what I might be letting myself in for if I marry you,' he went on, his lips curling

in a grimace of self-mockery. 'I went through hell the other night after I left you, and all yesterday as I tried to come to a decision, my loyalty to myself and to my work fighting with my desire for you and my jealousy of that creep Muro, who can be with you and near you every day . . . ' His voice rasped harshly and he broke off, leaning forward with his elbows on his knees and his head bowed to his hands so that she couldn't see his face.

After a moment of tense silence during which Renata could hear her heart pounding with excited anticipation, he lowered one hand and glanced sideways at her. He smiled, and it was like seeing a ray of sunshine light up his dark face, and her heart leapt.

'I guess desire won,' he said softly. 'When I met you at the airport this morning I was on my way to see you again at the hotel to give you my answer. I had no idea you had to be back here so soon. I've thought it all through, and if it will help you and give

you some protection against Muro I'm willing to marry you, on the condition that it will be the sort of marriage you talked about, that we'd both be able to carry on with our lives the way we do now and just meet when we can — neither of us being too possessive and demanding, I think you said. Kendal didn't like Muro and neither do I. In fact, I can't bear the thought of you having to . . . ' He broke off again, gritting his teeth together, and violence flared in the depths of his dark eyes. 'And that's why I'm willing to marry you,' he added tautly.

A feeling of elation surged through Renata, swamping all thoughts she had had of withdrawing her suggestion that they should marry because possibly Jason wouldn't be the right sort of husband for her.

'Oh, thank you, thank you!' she whispered, and on impulse leaned across to kiss his scarred cheek. He turned his head quickly and their lips met instead. It was a sweet, generous

kiss that might have developed into something deeper and more passionate if the taxi hadn't stopped outside the mall. Reluctantly Renata withdrew her lips from Jason's and smiled rather bemusedly at him. 'Will you come in with me now so that we can tell Carlos that we're going to be married? He's more likely to believe I'm going to marry you if you're with me to back up what I say to him,' she explained.

'I won't come in with you now. Not like this.' His fingers rasped against the black bristles on his jaw and cheeks. 'How long will your interview with your client take?'

'About an hour, maybe a little less.'

'I'll come up to see you then, after I've had a shave and have found out how soon we can be married. OK?'

'OK.'

The shopping mall was busy and noisy and filled with sunlight. As she went up the escalator Renata found she was smiling, smiling, smiling at everyone who was passing her on the down

escalator. Gone was the depressin
anxiety she had suffered for weeks as a
result of the rumour and Carlos's
amorous advances. Jason hadn't let her
down. She was going to marry him and
win her bet with Carlos. And with the
protection marriage would give her
against Carlos's sexual harassment she
could carry on in her partnership with
him until she had established her name
internationally as a fashion designer,
could stand on her own feet and the
contract with Carlos had expired.

7

The client with whom Renata had an appointment was Inez Dupont, the wife of a First Secretary at the American Embassy in Lima. A tall brunette of about thirty years of age, she told Renata that she had also been born in Lima and for a short time had been a model at Muro's boutique.

'I don't know how you can stand working for him,' she said frankly, after they had looked at, discussed and come to conclusions about the evening dress Inez wanted Renata to design and make for her. 'He's so domineering. And then he has wandering hands.' Inez slanted a curious sidelong glance at Renata from large brown, long-lashed eyes. 'But then perhaps you don't mind that sort of thing,' she said cryptically. 'Perhaps there is truth in the rumour I've heard lately that you are his current mistress

and that is why he's gone into partnership with you.'

'There's no truth in that damned rumour!' said Renata forcibly. 'I am not Carlos's mistress, nor do I want to be. Nor have I ever wanted to be, and I'd be glad if you would spread that little item of gossip about — and add to it that I'm going to be married soon to someone entirely different who has nothing to do with women's fashions.'

'This is interesting.' Inez arched her finely plucked eyebrows. 'Does Carlos know?'

'Yes, he does. I told him the other day.'

'I suppose you're marrying a Canadian?'

'No. A Peruvian.'

'A *Limeno*?' persisted Inez. Now the expression on her face was one of avid curiosity. 'What is his last name? I may know him?'

'Hernandez — Jason Hernandez,' replied Renata curtly. It was done, she thought; the announcement of her

forthcoming marriage had been made. To tell it to someone like Inez was to broadcast it to the whole of the Muro boutique's clientèle, giving them something else other than the rumour about her being Carlos's mistress to gossip about. 'I don't think you'll know him. He doesn't visit Lima often. He owns a small aviation company in Cuzco, flies helicopters to the interior.'

'*Por Dios!*' whispered Inez. The sharp inquisitive expression had completely gone from her face as if wiped away by a sponge. She looked almost horrified. 'You can't marry him!'

'Why can't I?' Renata demanded.

Inez stood up and started to pull on her thin leather gloves, an action that seemed to demand a lot of her attention so that her dark eyes were hidden by their black-fringed lids.

'Because . . . because . . . he's . . . ' she began, broke off and glanced sideways again at Renata, then, shrugging her shoulders, broke into a laugh. 'But it is of no matter. You don't really

belong here. You're a foreigner, so it doesn't really matter whom you marry.'

'I do belong here. I'm not a foreigner,' retorted Renata, beginning to bristle. 'I was born in Lima and my mother was the daughter of Antonio Mendoza, who was a lawyer and a legal consultant to the government at one time. Now tell me what you were implying about Jason. Why shouldn't I marry him?'

'He doesn't seem right for you, somehow,' Inez replied evasively. 'Oh, I know he's very different from Carlos, younger, better-looking, more macho . . . '

'Then you do know him! You've met him?' Renata pounced.

'Yes, I have,' admitted Inez. 'Some years ago, soon after he returned to Peru. I . . . we dated a few times, but he was so undependable and unpredictable, always going off to fly those beastly machines to the mountains, and then my parents didn't approve of him. Then I met Gary and . . . ' Inez broke

off and shrugged as though she didn't need to explain any further why she had stopped going about with Jason. 'Take my advice,' she added, turning to look fully at Renata. 'Don't marry Jason — he's the untameable type. You'll never know where he is or what he's going to do next. Personally, since you seem to have a choice, I think you would be better off marrying Carlos. At least you'd have him around every day, and his family background is flawless. You'd never have that to live down, whereas Jason's background is, to say the least, dubious.'

'Just what exactly do you mean by that?' demanded Renata, who was thoroughly irritated by now by the other woman's snobbery, which she recognised as a hangover from the times her mother had told her about and to which Aunt Maria still looked back with a certain nostalgia, when the social and economic lines in Lima had been strictly drawn and the young women of the then powerful wealthy families had

not been allowed to marry out of their immediate circle. 'I have been told that Jason is related to the late Ferdinand Hernandez, who was a diplomat and represented Peru at the United Nations.'

'Oh, he is, he is. That's why . . . ' Inez broke off again, frowning. 'Let me just say everyone knows Ferdinand was one of the leaders of social revolution in this country and believed in equality. Some say that's why he was sent out of the country. He was too progressive for the political party to which he belonged. He also believed in many European socialistic ideas, such as free love.' Inez once again looked at Renata and her smile was knowledgeable. 'Jason, it seems, has followed in Ferdinand's footsteps in more ways than one. Need I say more? And now I must go — I'm meeting my husband for lunch. You'll let me know when the dress is ready for the first fitting, won't you?'

'Of course.' Inwardly seething, Renata stood up too and followed her client politely to the door to see her out. They

had just reached the door when there was a brief knock on it and it swung open to admit Carlos. He was, it seemed, delighted to see Inez, taking her right hand and raising it to his lips to kiss the back of it with formal Latin courtesy.

When he had finished complimenting her on choosing Renata to design the evening dress she was going to wear at a forthcoming President's ball to which members of all the foreign embassies had been invited, Inez said, with a rather malicious glance at Renata, 'I've just been hearing about Renata's engagement. I'm sure you're pleased, Carlos, that she is going to associate herself with the Hernandez family. Think of what good publicity that will be for the business! *Adios*. I hope I shall be hearing from you soon about the gown.'

The expression on his tanned face as smooth and serene as ever, Carlos closed the door after Inez's tall elegant figure, while Renata went back to her

desk and waited tensely for his reaction to what Inez had said. As she could have guessed, he didn't explode with irritation but walked over to her drawing-board to study the sketches she had made of designs for Inez's ballgown. Without looking at her, he said, 'I'm glad you were sensible and came back to keep your appointment with Inez.'

Renata surveyed him from under down-drooping lashes. As always, he was neat and sleek, in a suit of pale brown with a lilac-coloured shirt of smooth cotton and a tie of a slightly darker shade than the shirt. In his right lapel was pinned a white carnation, and a silk handkerchief, also lilac-coloured, peeped from the breast pocket of his jacket. His hair was brushed straight back from his narrow, bony forehead.

'Inez is an invaluable connection for us,' he went on.

He was speaking to Renata as if they had parted on the best of terms. Had he forgotten that she had flung out in a

rage three days ago after telling him that she was going to be married to Jason?

'I suppose she is,' she agreed.

'She's the daughter of one of our leading politicians and she often appears at Government social occasions, including those which foreign visitors attend. Did she tell you she and her husband are going to Paris in January? He has been appointed to the American Embassy there. I have suggested to her that she gets you to design a couple of afternoon dresses and a morning suit for her, suitable for wearing at functions in Paris. Gratis, of course. It will be good publicity for Renata Fashions and might draw the attention of the Association of Paris Designers to our existence so that we might, in future, get invited to show your designs in Paris. Would you like to have your work shown in Paris?'

'Yes, I would,' said Renata enthusiastically.

'I thought you might. And while you

were away an invitation came from a New York organisation asking if we would consider putting on a show in January of fashions suitable for the North American spring season. But I suppose you won't be able to go.'

'Who could stop me?' she asked.

Carlos looked straight at her then, his hazel eyes as cold as a snake's beneath their heavy lids.

'Have you forgotten that you told me just before you left my office three days ago that you're going to marry Jason Hernandez? I admit that at the time I was alarmed by your impulsive decision to marry someone like him who is so very different from yourself, but while you've been away I've reconsidered. As you pointed out at the time, your private life is your own and I have no right to interfere, even though I care about what happens to you as a friend. Now don't you think he'll raise objections to you travelling places like New York and Paris in my company?'

'I'm sure he won't, not when he

knows the trip would be to help my career as a designer,' she asserted.

'Then perhaps I should put it this way, my dear,' Carlos said smoothly. 'You can be sure also that I won't be prepared to take the risk of travelling anywhere with you once you're married to Hernandez.'

Renata stared at him. How neatly and maliciously he was taking his revenge on her for having said she couldn't marry him because she was going to marry Jason! He was making it clear that if she went ahead and married Jason he would cease to treat her as an equal partner in the business.

'But that isn't fair!' she argued. 'The fact that I'm going to be married shouldn't make any difference to my status in our company. As an equal partner I have the right to go to New York or Paris if the opportunity comes up. And if you don't want to travel with me once I'm married, that's too bad. We'll travel separately.'

Carlos sighed heavily and came to

stand before her, folding his arms across his chest. Renata resisted an impulse to step back and away from the threat she thought she saw in the way he was looking at her. He looked as if he was only just holding back from taking hold of her and shaking her.

'I wish you would give up this ridiculous pretence that you are going to marry Hernandez,' he said, his thin lips curving into a smile. 'I know you didn't mean what you said the other day — it was said out of defiance. You were angry with me because of that rumour. And quite rightly so too. I shouldn't have let it spread.' He sighed again, his eyes veiled and his smile fading. 'The truth is, *querida*, I get very jealous when you so much as look at another man, and find myself behaving in strange, vengeful ways. It's as if I have no control over my emotions any more. Not only do I want to hurt the man but also you, for being what you are and for making me feel jealous.' His eyelids lifted and he

looked straight at her, his eyes gleaming with lust. 'Never have I felt for any woman what I feel for you, Renata. I want you and I'm going to have you. We'll be married as soon as it can be arranged and put paid to the rumour. You'll never regret it, I swear it. You'll have everything any woman could want . . . '

'Carlos, listen to me!' she interrupted him sharply, beginning to back away from him because he had reached out to put his hands on her shoulders. 'I meant what I said. It isn't a pretence. I am going to marry Jason.'

'No, you're not,' he insisted, coming after her. 'You're going to marry me.'

Around to the other side of her desk Renata flitted, sparing a moment to think how ridiculous the whole scene must look to anyone who might come into the studio, she retreating and Carlos stalking her, playing cat and mouse.

'Carlos, this is silly,' she said as she slid out from behind the desk and backed away again from his approach.

'If you're talking about your resistance to me, I agree. It is silly, but I'm sure you know instinctively that the one sure way to make a man want you is to resist and withdraw . . . '

His hand reached out and caught hold of the front of her blouse.

'No!' she yelled, still backing off, hearing the silky material hiss as it ripped. 'Oh, this is going beyond a joke!' she raged at him as, retaining his hold on the fabric, he jerked her towards him. Lust gleamed in his hooded eyes, sending a shiver of revulsion through her. She raised a fist to hit out at him, but he caught her wrist and, his hand tightening mercilessly, bent her arm up behind her back so that she gasped with the pain of it. Frantically she kicked with one foot at his shin while still trying to twist her wrist from his hold.

'Let me go!' she muttered through taut lips, and swung her head sideways to avoid his approaching lips, her hair flicking out at his face.

He laughed jeeringly, his slim fingers like a vice about her wrist now, his other hand holding some of her hair, pulling on it hard so that she wanted to cry out with the pain of it, pulling her head back so that her throat arched. Against her neck his lips were soft and moist, revolting, and he was pushing against her, making her aware of his arousal, while he forced her back towards the long sofa that was situated against one of the walls.

'I would have preferred your submission to me to have come more naturally and in different, more romantic surroundings,' he said breathlessly. 'But I have to admit your resistance is having a rousing effect on me. I want you to be mine, *querida*, and I'm going to have you, whether you like it or not. And afterwards I'm sure you'll be glad to marry me instead of Hernandez.'

Desperately Renata pushed back against him when she felt the edge of the sofa pressing at the back of her legs, wishing she knew some form of martial

arts to use to defeat him. All she could think of was to raise her knee to his groin, but it was too late for that. His legs, his whole body was pressing against hers so hard that she couldn't move.

Then a piece of information she had read somewhere slid into her mind. When in the process of being assaulted, in any way, scream as loudly as possible. So she opened her mouth and screamed as Carlos pushed her down on the sofa. Twice she screamed before his open wet mouth covered hers, smothering the next scream.

Vaguely she heard someone speaking sharply in Spanish. To her great relief Carlos stiffened and lifted his mouth from hers. He stepped back quickly, turning to face the intruder. Jason was standing just inside the open door, his hands on his hips, his head tipped forward slightly. He looked as if he had just stopped short from launching himself at Carlos, but menace was still glittering in his dark eyes.

Carlos strolled over to Renata's desk as if nothing unusual had happened. Renata sat down on the sofa, holding together with one hand the edges of the rip in her blouse. Never had she felt so glad to see anyone as she was to see Jason at that moment, but she couldn't have stood up and gone to him if she'd tried. She was too weak with relief.

His dark glance flicked over her observantly, but he made no move towards her.

'You OK?' he asked softly, speaking in English. Clean-shaven now, his black hair brushed until it shone, he had changed his checked shirt for a white one and his jeans for well-cut grey pants. He was even wearing a tie, but was still in the leather flying jacket. It really didn't matter what he was wearing, Renata thought, or how he looked. At that particular moment he was her knight in shining armour who had rescued her from the dragon in the shape of Carlos, and she looked at him with the utmost respect and affection.

'Not quite,' she replied shakily, answering in the same language. 'I'm glad you arrived when you did.'

'*De nada*, he said with a shrug, and turned to look at Carlos, who was behaving as if nothing unusual had happened, standing by the desk turning over some papers.

'Señor Muro? Remember me?' said Jason, reverting to Spanish. 'Jason Hernandez? We met at Renata's fashion show a few weeks ago. I guess she's just been telling you she and I are going to be married.'

Slowly Carlos laid down the sheet of paper he was holding. Slowly his eyes lifted to Jason's face, and even from the sofa Renata could see the expression of sheer vindictiveness in his glance. Nervously she stood and went over to stand just a few steps behind Jason and a little to his left so that she could restrain him from any violent action if Carlos decided to be rude and to insult him or herself.

'Renata has said several times that

she is going to marry you, but I have never believed her,' said Carlos as smoothly as ever. Was it only a few minutes ago that his hot mouth had dominated hers, preventing her from screaming while his fingers had fumbled at the opening of her blouse? Renata wondered. 'And I still can't believe that so lovely and talented a woman as she is is going to give up a blossoming career to marry a bastard like you,' Carlos added offensively, his lips curling scornfully.

Renata gasped at the insult and put a hand on Jason's as if to prevent him from hitting Carlos, but to her surprise Jason merely laughed.

'Oh, no, you can't get at me like that, Muro,' he drawled. 'I stopped reacting to that sort of underhand attack years ago. And you're wrong in thinking that Renata is going to give up her career just to marry me. She will continue with it. She will even go on being your partner in this business, at least for the period of time that is left of the contract

she signed with you. Of course, if you break the contract by refusing to continue with the partnership she'll just set up on her own. Now that she's established in Lima as a designer I don't think she'll have any difficulty in getting the financial backing she might require. I would even back her myself.'

Holding her breath, Renata watched Carlos closely, and admired his self-control. Only by the thinning of his lips and the curious hissing sound that came through them did he betray that for the time being he had been defeated.

'Whatever makes you think I would want to break the contract?' he said coolly, raising surprised eyebrows as he moved from behind the desk. 'Believe me, *señor*, I'm glad to hear that you are taking a thoroughly modern approach to marriage and are willing to allow your future wife to go on with her career. But what about yourself? Are you going to give up your business in

Cuzco to reside here in Lima with Renata?'

Renata sensed rather than saw Jason's dislike of the personal probing question. He didn't bother to answer it but said instead, 'I've come to take Renata to lunch. There are some arrangements we have to make for the marriage ceremony.'

'I understand,' said Carlos politely. 'I hope I shall be informed as to when it is to take place. I would like to attend, of course.'

'A week today, at three o'clock, to be precise. At the church of the San Pedro near the Torre Tagle Palace. I'm sure you know it,' replied Jason.

'So soon?' Renata could not help exclaiming and, seeing Carlos glance rather knowingly at her, wished she had been able to control herself and say nothing.

'That is the next free day I have,' said Jason, turning to her. 'You're not going to tell me now that you would prefer to postpone the ceremony until after Christmas?'

She looked up and into his dark eyes. Was he warning her that if she wanted the ceremony postponed it might never take place? Then she remembered Carlos, who was standing there watching and listening, no doubt hoping for her to make another mistake and to reveal that the marriage was a hastily thought-up arrangement to thwart him.

'No,' she answered. 'I don't want to postpone it, but I was just a little surprised that we could get married so soon. There's so much I have to do before then to get ready — people to inform.'

'Then let's go for lunch now and talk over the arrangements. I have to fly back to Cuzco this afternoon,' urged Jason.

She picked up her jacket, put it on and slung her overnight bag over one shoulder. Going over to him, she slipped a hand into one of his and smiled up at him.

'Let's go to my apartment,' she said lightly.

'When will you be returning to work, Renata?' Carlos asked sharply. 'Remember there is much to be done for the Christmas season, and for the show in New York should we decide to accept the invitation.'

'I'll be back later this afternoon,' she said.

Just as they were about to go out of the door Jason turned back as a sudden thought struck him.

'A word of warning, Muro,' he said softly. 'If I ever again catch you molesting Renata, or even if I only hear that you have, I won't be letting you off as lightly as I did just now. *Adios.*'

Once they were outside the mall Jason hailed a taxi to take them the short distance to Renata's apartment.

'I notice that your blouse is torn. Carlos do that?' he demanded roughly.

'Yes.'

'I thought I heard screams as I approached your office,' he told her.

'He . . . he was angry because he had just learned that I'd told my client I'm

going to marry you and he realised I wasn't pretending. He was . . . was horrible, and . . . ' A strong shudder of revulsion shook her and she touched the back of one of his hands, stroking the tanned skin with the tip of her finger. 'I was never more glad in all my life when you knocked on the studio door and walked in,' she whispered.

Jason made no further comment but slid an arm around her shoulders and held her close to him in a strangely impersonal yet comforting embrace.

'You know you have every reason now to break that contract you have with him. If he sued you for breaking it you would just have to say you broke it because he harassed you sexually,' he told her.

'I have no other witnesses,' she pointed out.

'I guess our word would be enough. And Muro must have tried it on with other women who've worked with him or for him.'

'I know he has. But they've all

welcomed his attentions,' Renata said drily. Then, more hesitantly, 'Have you really made arrangements for us to be married next week in a church?'

'Of course I have. You think I would have told him the place and time if I hadn't? I thought if I said that he would be truly convinced that in future when he tries it on with you he'll be trying it on with my wife.' Jason paused, then added with a touch of humour, 'I hope you're not thinking of having one of those showy weddings. I'd prefer not to have a lot of fuss.'

'I don't want a fuss either, because it isn't long since Kendal died,' she replied. 'I'm just surprised it's going to be in church, that's all.'

'It's the Peruvian way. But not to worry, there won't be any nuptial Mass in this case, just a quiet exchanging of vows before a priest.'

'I'll have to invite Aunt Maria and Uncle Frank and possibly my cousin Diego and some of the women I work with, like Isabella, the manageress of

the Muro boutique. She was the first to give me a job modelling when I came to Lima and has always been very kind to me. Are you sure we can do it next week?'

'All we need is a priest willing to perform the ceremony. I have a cousin, Tómas Hernandez, who is a priest, and he's quite willing to do it for us.'

At the apartment Renata cooked omelettes and they ate in the small kitchen sitting opposite to each other. Then she phoned Maria to tell her she was getting married and the time and place. As she had expected, her aunt was shocked.

'*Madre de Dios*! Why all this hurry? Why can't it be done properly with your father and Alison here? Diego too. I know Diego would like to be present. He is so fond of you,' Maria complained.

'It is being done properly. Surely you of all people are pleased it's being done in a church by a priest?' Renata pointed out with a touch of impatience. 'It's

because Jason doesn't have much free time. And then neither of us wants too much fuss. I don't because it isn't long since Kendal died and Jason doesn't because . . . oh, because he's like that, hates a fuss. But you'll be able to come, both you and Uncle Frank, won't you? I'd like you both to be there on my behalf. And Dad and Alison will understand, I know they will.'

'All right,' said Maria, mollified by the invitation. 'And you will allow me to have a little reception here afterwards, some of my friends in to meet you and the priest also, before you go away for the honeymoon. Ah, but *Madre di Dios*, where will you have the honeymoon? One night is not enough . . . '

'Oh, Aunty, you're so funny! Of course it will be enough. We can always go away together another time. I expect Jason has something arranged. I'll be out to see you tomorrow and we can talk about it then.

'Aunt Maria wants to have a reception for us after the ceremony,'

Renata said to Jason as she hung up. 'Do you agree?'

'She can do what she likes,' he said with a shrug. 'I have to go now to catch that plane. I'll see you at the church at three o'clock next Thursday afternoon. Don't be late.'

'Not before then?' she exclaimed, following him to the door. He always seemed to be in a hurry to leave her, she thought. She was always saying goodbye to him.

'No. It's considered unlucky, I believe, for the bride and groom to see each other before the ceremony,' he said with a grin. He gave her one of his appraising and admiring glances. 'My cousin is going to be surprised when he sees you. That is if he's got over the shock yet of me asking him if there was any quick way we could get married.'

'I'm still surprised it can be done so quickly. Are you sure it will be legal?'

'It will be legal,' he assured her. 'But if you want to change your mind and

not go through with it, say so.'

Renata's mind was buzzing with all sorts of questions she wanted to ask him, but she didn't know which one to start with. After all, he was still a stranger, most of what she knew of him having been learned from other people. Firstly from Uncle Frank who had said Jason was a daredevil but who wouldn't object to a daughter of his marrying such a brave man, and secondly from Inez Dupont, who had implied that Jason wasn't accepted in the primly moral social circles of Lima and who had stopped going about with him because he had proved to be unpredictable. In marrying him she would be taking a risk. But wasn't that the story of Renata's life as well as his, taking risks?

'No, I don't want to back out. But do you?' she asked quietly.

'No, not now that I'm into it so far. I hate going back on a decision once I've made it. And not now that I've caught Carlos in the act of molesting you. I

just wanted to make sure it's really what you want to do and that you're aware of what you're letting yourself in for. I'm not really husband material, but if it's the only way to stop that swine Carlos from harassing you any more I'm willing to go through with it. Just try not to expect too much of me.'

'Nor you of me,' she returned, and when he kissed her she couldn't help shrinking a little from the intimate contact. Even though Jason's lips were cool and gentle against hers and in this instance undemanding, the memory of Carlos's recent behaviour prevented her from responding completely.

'What's wrong?' queried Jason when he lifted his lips from hers. His frowning gaze was puzzled. 'Second thoughts again?'

'No. It's just that . . . ' Renata stopped, shaking her head.

'See you next week, then,' he said curtly.

She nodded and without looking at him, whispered, '*Adios*.'

She turned away quickly and hurried back to the living room, not wanting to see him open the door and go out in case she clung to him and pleaded with him not to leave her.

8

'The Church of San Pedro was built in the seventeenth century by the Jesuits and is known for its elaborately carved and gilded altar. It's one of the most fashionable churches for weddings in Lima,' Maria told Renata with some satisfaction, then sighed sadly. 'But I can't help wishing you were marrying for the first time so we could have a white wedding with lots of attendants and guests. No, no, don't go all defensive — I understand why you can't. And I am only too happy you are getting married.'

So were many other people glad Renata was getting married again. Especially the women with whom she worked, the models and the seamstresses as well as Isabella the manageress of the boutique and Teresa, Carlos's secretary. In fact everyone was downright enthusiastic, and

190

right up to the time when she rode with Maria and Francisco and Diego up to the ornate baroque façade of the church she felt as if she was being carried forward on that wave of enthusiasm.

Not that she had thought once of going back on her word during the past week. It was only when, wearing a suit of delicate rose-pink silk with a corsage of white roses, she entered the candlelit, incense-scented, gold-glinting church on Francisco's arm that she felt a sudden tremor of panic and a desire to wrench her arm from Francisco's and run out into the sunlight again.

Then she saw Jason standing with his back to her, his broad shoulders and dark head outlined against the red, blue and white blaze of light that streamed through the beautiful stained glass east window and she felt the panic subside. He hadn't gone back on his word, either. He had come. He hadn't let her down, and when he turned his head to look at her, his lips curving in a slight yet somehow mischievous smile, her

spirits soared suddenly. He had been Kendal's friend and he had come to her rescue last week. Now he was going to become her husband. He was still a little mysterious and somehow elusive, yet he was supportive of her and seemed to understand her. And wasn't understanding the biggest part of love?

The priest was younger than she had expected, a tall man with a tonsured head and a thin, ascetic face. As he spoke the words of the ceremony in Spanish, Renata studied his face, looking for resemblances to Jason, and saw none. Only in the unfathomable pitch-blackness of his eyes when they met hers in a glance of lively interest and sheer curiosity did she see any resemblance at all to Jason.

It was nothing like the quick civil ceremony she had gone through with Kendal, and she was unprepared for the effect the ceremony was having on her. Hearing Jason's voice, low and a little husky, saying his vows, she was suddenly struck by the deep silence of

the people who were sitting behind her as they listened, by the beauty of the words Jason was saying, and when it came to her turn to speak his name and to promise to love him she could only whisper, overwhelmed by the gravity of the occasion. It had never occurred to her that getting married in a church would seem more of a commitment made forever and that she would feel totally and irrevocably bound by the promises she had just made. Panic streaked through her again and she was hardly aware of what followed, only that her hand shook when she held it out to Jason to slip the ring on her finger and when she had to sign her name to the documents presented to her and Jason by the priest.

The priest spoke a few more prayers over their bent heads as they knelt for the last time, and then, her hand in Jason's, Renata walked back down the aisle, vaguely noticing that Aunt Maria was unashamedly weeping. Of Carlos there was no sign, but Isabella and

Teresa were there and several of the other women who worked for the Muro company.

Outside the big iron-studded wooden doors of the church, under the carved archway, they crowded around to give her and Jason their best wishes, and Inez was among them, much to Renata's surprise.

'What the hell was she doing there?' asked Jason roughly as he urged Renata down the steps to the limousine that was waiting for them.

'She's one of my clients,' said Renata. 'She told me you used to date her.'

'Seems to me it was the other way round. And she used to pursue me,' he said with a laugh. 'She was a damned nuisance, always turning up in Cuzco.'

'As I did last week?' she said lightly, but he made no comment.

'Thank goodness that's over,' he remarked, leaning back in the rear seat of the limousine. 'There was a moment in the church, while I was waiting for you to come in, when I had cold feet

and nearly told Tómas to forget the whole idea.'

'Well, you weren't the only one. I nearly panicked too and ran away,' she retorted.

'Perhaps you should have done,' he said, his voice sombre. 'Heaven knows I'm not much of a catch as a husband.'

'You'll suit me very well,' she whispered.

Jason looked down at her upturned face, sighed and then gently touched her cheek and leaned towards her. She read the intention in his eyes and the feeling of panic surged up in her again. Quickly she turned her head to look out of the window, and was surprised to see they were on the highway to Callao.

'Where are we going?' she exclaimed, turning to look at him. He had shifted away from her along the seat and was looking out of the other window.

'To the airport,' he replied curtly. 'I can't stay with you tonight. There's been a big earthquake in the interior,

and every available small plane and chopper and its pilot has been commandeered by the Government to fly in doctors and medical supplies. I have to go back to Cuzco now.'

'But I thought you wanted me,' Renata whispered shakily.

'I do want you,' he said roughly. 'More than you know. But remember it was you who suggested this should be a modern-style marriage in which we'll both be free to come and go as we want. No demands, no possessiveness. Well, that is exactly what you're getting. I have to leave you to fly into the interior. I have to go and help the people of those villages. Surely you can understand that?'

'Yes, I can,' she murmured, nodding. She had no right to feel disappointed, had she? This sort of thing was going to be par for the course in their marriage, both of them being free to do what their chosen careers demanded of them, neither of them complaining about the necessity of separation from each other.

'When will I see you again?' she asked.

'I'm not sure. I'll try to let you know when I'll be coming to Lima, but sometimes I might just turn up, taking a chance on your being in town, and we'll get together. If you have any problems with Muro you can always send a message on one of the regular daily flights to Cuzco and I'll get it and will come to you.'

'I don't think I'll be having any problems with Carlos,' she said, and told him how supportive of her marriage the women she worked with had been. 'And then I think he really took the threat you made seriously.'

'I hope he did, because I was serious too. If you do have any further trouble with him, that's what's going to happen.'

'Couldn't I come to Cuzco with you now?' she suggested. 'I've arranged to have a few days off work.'

'I think it best if you didn't. I'd rather you didn't come there,' Jason replied

coolly, and glanced at his watch. 'I should just about make that flight.'

His mind had already left hers. Having done what he had promised her he would do to help her, he could now return to his usual way of life. He might even forget sometimes that he was married. And wasn't that what she had wanted? Wasn't she secretly feeling relief that he wouldn't be staying the night with her, because if he did he would want to make love to her, and she wasn't sure she could make love with him yet.

Suddenly he took hold of her left hand and raised it to his lips. The expression in his eyes was soft, like black velvet.

'It's best this way,' he said in a low voice. 'You're not ready. You're still a little in love with Kendal's ghost and more than a little apprehensive of the male brute after your recent experience with Carlos. I'm not a particularly gentle lover, and if I stayed and made love to you, you might just react to me

the way you did to Carlos's harassment. You'd push me away the way you did the night I came to you in Cuzco, and I don't want that to happen, because I know myself too well. I'd be resentful and might try to force you. So I'll just have to want you and leave you for now, and . . . and maybe one day . . . ' He broke off with a muttered oath and, cupping her face with one hand, pressed his lips to hers.

It was a sweetly erotic kiss, his tongue flickering against her lips, seeking for response, and much to her surprise response flared up in her quite naturally, so that when he threatened to withdraw she put a hand around his neck to show him she didn't want him to move away. When his lips did move away from hers he continued to hold her tightly, his cheek pressed hard against her head, his breathing uneven.

'I'm sorry you think I'm not ready,' she whispered, stroking the back of his head, suddenly sensing his disappointment in her. 'It's true Carlos's

behaviour has put me off making love a little, and I have to thank you for being so understanding. But I wish you didn't have to go. We never have much time together — we're always saying good-bye. Please don't go.'

'Don't say that!' he said sharply, pushing her away from him and sitting up. 'Never say that.'

The limousine was drawing up at the airport buildings. Jason gave her another brief hard kiss and then he was gone and the limousine was moving away. Leaning forward, Renata gave the driver instructions on how to get to the Soto house, knowing she would have some explaining to do to Maria as to why she and Jason hadn't gone straight to the reception. Then, sitting back, she struggled to subdue the tears that were threatening to fall because she wasn't going to spend that night with Jason after all.

Surprisingly Aunt Maria wasn't angry; she was quite understanding, in fact.

'I was disappointed, of course, when he told me what had happened, but not

as disappointed as you must be. But he has to do his duty, after all, and we all admire him for that. Frank says anyone who can fly in supplies to those poor people is needed. Just pray to God, *querida*, that Jason doesn't get into an accident. What are you going to do now? Would you like to stay here for a few days?'

'No, I think I'll go into the studio tomorrow as usual. I am quite busy, you know,' said Renata. Work, after all, was always the best antidote to disappointment, regret and the absence of someone you loved. Someone she loved? Did she love Jason? 'Carlos has arranged for some of my fashions to be shown in New York in January and I haven't thought up the designs I want to show there yet.'

The following two weeks went by in a rush of activity. Model gowns that had been ordered for the Christmas festivities were finished and fitted on their purchasers. Cheques for large amounts of money were made out to Renata. For

the first time in her life she felt affluent.

She managed to contact her father on his return to Vancouver from his business trip to Japan and Korea, and after congratulating her on her marriage he invited her to fly on to Vancouver to visit him and Alison for a while and hoped that her husband would be with her. Carlos made no reference to her marriage, but neither did he make any further attempts to harass her. Occasionally news filtered through to her about the series of earthquakes that were still shaking villages in the interior of the country, but she received no news of Jason and she could only assume he was safe and still flying.

On the first day of December Inez came for the final fitting of her evening gown.

'I was talking to someone who knows your husband very well the other day,' Inez said as she admired her own image in the long mirror. 'She was surprised to hear that he had married you — very

surprised. Apparently he lives with her in Cuzco.' She slanted one of her dark malicious glances at Renata. 'Did he tell you about her?'

What should she say? wondered Renata as she slowly circled Inez, studying the evening dress, looking for flaws in the stitching and the fit that might need attention. Dark red satin moulded Inez's perfect figure. There were no flaws anywhere, but Renata couldn't help saying, also with a slight touch of malice, 'Excuse me for saying so, *señora*, but have you put on weight since we first measured you for this gown? It seems to me that there is a slight bulge causing a little tightness at the waist and over the hips.'

'Where? Show me,' demanded Inez, immediately distracted from what she had been saying, and regarded her reflection closely, her long white, red-tipped fingers smoothing down over her flat stomach and lean hips. 'Where is the bulge? It must be a mistake in the sewing — your seamstress has taken in

too much on one of the seams, perhaps. I know I haven't put on any weight.' She whirled to face Renata. 'You've got to fix it,' she said through viciously tightened lips.

'I think we might be able to,' replied Renata coolly, pleased that her ruse had worked. 'Let me help you take the gown off.'

'It must be done at once,' insisted Inez petulantly, as soon as the dress was off. 'The President's Ball is tonight.'

'I'm not sure . . . ' began Renata, frowning down at the gown and pretending to examine one of the seams closely in order to hide her amusement at Inez's panic.

'But it's got to be done!' cried Inez, who was dressing quickly in a short skirt and cotton sweater. 'Even if you have to stitch it yourself. I'll be back at three to try it on again. If it doesn't fit right by then, I won't be buying the gown. I'll go in one I've worn before rather than have one that doesn't fit.'

'It will be done,' replied Renata

confidently, although she had no intention of touching the gown. 'And it will fit perfectly.'

'It had better be right, or I'll be complaining to Carlos and making it known amongst your clientéle that you're capable of shoddy work!' Inez's mood was still vicious as she stalked to the door. She opened it and half turned, the expression on her face changing completely. She smiled with counterfeit sweetness. 'Came as a shock to you, didn't it, to learn that your husband of only a few weeks has a mistress hidden away in Cuzco? Carlos suggested it would. *Adios*. I'll be back at three.'

Renata hung the gown up after covering it with a long plastic envelope to protect it and slid the closet door shut. She should have guessed that Carlos was behind the juicy little bit of gossip about Jason and another woman that Inez had let drop. Her battle with him wasn't over. Vengeful and malicious in his dealings with women, he would

always find a way to hurt her since she had rejected him in favour of a man he disliked and who had made him feel inferior. The suggestion that Jason had a mistress in Cuzco he hadn't told her about was intended to cause trouble between her and her new husband and possibly destroy their marriage before it had really begun. She must try to ignore it, she decided, pretend that Inez hadn't said anything. After all, it was a modern marriage.

But the piece of information nagged at her all day, and she knew it could be true. It could be the reason why Jason had jibbed at marrying her when she had asked him. It could be why he had gone back to Cuzco instead of staying with her the day they had been married. Yes, it could explain much of his behaviour.

And it hurt. In spite of her efforts to ignore it and shake it off, it hurt that he hadn't been honest with her. It hurt very much, and as soon as she saw him again she would ask him about the

woman in Cuzco.

As the days went by and she heard nothing more from Jason, the seed of suspicion planted by Inez Dupont's seemingly casual reference to the fact he had a mistress in Cuzco grew, and was fed by even more seemingly casual remarks that were dropped one day by Carlos.

'So when is Hernandez going to take up residence with you in Lima?' he asked.

'While his company is based in Cuzco it makes more sense for him to stay there,' Renata replied.

'He doesn't want you there with him? How strange!' murmured Carlos. 'I would have thought a man like him would have wanted his wife with him, making a home for him, getting his meals ready.' He paused and then added a wicked innuendo, 'Sharing his bed every night.'

Refusing to be drawn on the subject, Renata went on sketching a new design, her head bent over the drawing-board,

her hair which she was wearing loose that day sliding forward along her cheeks and hiding the angry red colour that suffused them.

'You know, Carlos,' she said, 'it's really none of your business how Jason and I have arranged to conduct our marriage, but perhaps I should explain to you, since you don't seem to have moved with the times, there are nowadays marriages in which the partners agree to let each other carry on with their careers, living apart if it's necessary and meeting when they can. For example, I have a friend in Canada who has a very good job as a lawyer in Montreal. Her husband, on the other hand, is a business executive, the vice-president of a manufacturing company in the Toronto area. The distance between the two cities is about the same as between Lima and Cuzco. During the week they work and live apart, but at the weekends they meet, either at his place near Toronto or at her place in Montreal.'

'How very uncomfortable and distressing for them,' drawled Carlos. 'I don't understand such an arrangement. Now if you had married me instead of Jason it would have been quite different. We would have worked together during the week and played together at the weekends. We would have lived in a luxurious house that I am thinking of buying and we could have travelled to New York, Paris, Milan and other fashion centres together to sell your designs. As it is . . . ' he shrugged his shoulders as he walked over to the window to look at the plaza, 'knowing what I do about Hernandez I am reluctant to ask you to come with me on such trips.' He swung round to face her. 'Are you sure he isn't deceiving you?'

'What do you mean?' Surprised by his question, Renata was betrayed into showing her secret concern that perhaps Jason had not been entirely honest with her.

'I have heard from friends of mine

who know the Hernandez family well that he lives in a house in Cuzco with a woman, a very beautiful, well-born Peruvian. He doesn't even try to make a secret of it. And in that way he is very like his own father. But perhaps he has told you all this and you, with your very modern views of marriage, have agreed to go along with the arrangement. Do you stay at that house when you go to Cuzco to see him at the weekend, when it is your turn to visit him?'

Renata turned back to the drawing board, hoping to hide her consternation.

'I haven't been to Cuzco lately,' she said lightly. 'By the way, have you made the arrangements for us to fly to New York?'

'I have. I've also fixed up with some clothes manufacturers there to visit their factories and design studios,' replied Carlos, returning to his normal suave businesslike manner.

'When exactly will we be going?'

'Second week in January. I shall

understand, of course, if you decide not to come. January being a rather slack month, you might like to take some time off to go and check up on your husband's living arrangements in Cuzco,' he said with a touch of sarcasm.

'I shall be going to New York,' she retorted. 'And nothing you say will put me off going. You know very well that I want to be present at any show of fashions designed by me.'

Renata seethed all day with irritation at Carlos's attempt to cut her out of the trip to New York, but underneath the anger was another emotion, a strange corrosive jealousy that was slowly eating into the peace of mind she had known since she had married Jason.

It was jealousy not only of an unknown woman but also of his way of life, that freedom he protected so fiercely to go flying when he wanted to. In spite of her attempts to shake off the feeling, it stayed with her. She kept dredging the depths of her

memories of her brief meetings and conversations with Jason, and bringing into the light to examine them various remarks he had made about himself, his reaction to her proposal of marriage to him, and always his sudden departure for Cuzco on the day of their wedding. Was it possible he had had to consult with this other woman before he had been able to give her an answer? Had he left her without consummating their marriage because he had wanted to get back to his mistress as well as to go flying? Had his apparent understanding of her unreadiness for consummation been a pretence so that she wouldn't force the issue and to prevent possible demanding questions about why he wouldn't stay? Had he really been commandeered by the Government to fly to the interior to help in the evacuation of earthquake victims, or had that been a cover-up too?

Renata was even tempted to drop everything to catch the next flight to

Cuzco and confront Jason and challenge him about the woman. But to do that would be to behave in a way she had assured him she would never behave, like a jealous, possessive wife; in a way she had always disciplined herself never to behave.

Best to cool it, she thought. Best to be more suspicious of Carlos's motives than of Jason's. So she relegated the worry to the back of her mind and, instead of flying up to Cuzco for the weekend, she accepted instead an invitation to the Soto house, where Diego was at home and had brought his girlfriend to celebrate their engagement.

9

Renata was alone, lying on a lounger, sunning herself on the patio at the Soto house, when Francisco appeared. Wearing an old straw hat, he was carrying a pair of secateurs in his hand, ready to prune some of the shrubs. Bees were buzzing loudly among the blossoms and as always humming birds, known by the South American Indians as Birds of the Sun God, were flitting about, flashing with sapphire or emerald-coloured light.

Francisco paused by the lounger and said abruptly, 'Have you seen Jason lately?'

'No.' Renata looked at him. 'Why do you ask?'

'I heard yesterday that he is missing again. He didn't return from a flight to one of the mountain villages where they'd just suffered another bad 'quake last Thursday.'

'Missing?' Renata repeated in a whisper. The word brought memories of the terrible anxiety she had suffered when Kendal hadn't returned from the jungle on time.

'Is a search being made for him?' she asked as calmly as she could, suppressing an urge to express the confused emotions Francisco's remarks had aroused in her. She wanted to shout at him, even shake him, in order to show how her sudden concern for the welfare of Jason was an agony she could hardly bear.

'Not yet. There is still time for him to turn up somewhere. He was flying in medical supplies and relief workers and he might have been delayed there by another 'quake that shook the same region after he was due to arrive. More rescue teams have been sent in by chopper to check on the damage, and it's more probable they'll find him in the village.'

'When will you know that he's been found?' she asked urgently.

'In couple of days, maybe.'

215

'You'll let me know as soon as you hear something, please?' Renata felt as if the blood had frozen in her veins. Surely there wasn't going to be a repetition of the history of her marriage to Kendal? Surely she wasn't going to lose Jason as well? Francisco looked at her closely, concern showing in his dark eyes.

'You have gone very pale,' he said. 'Perhaps I shouldn't have told you yet. Perhaps I should have waited until we had more news.'

'No, no, you were right to come and tell me,' she assured him, managing to put on a brave front.

But during the next two days the strain of keeping up that brave front, of pretending that she wasn't being riven with anguish about Jason, imagining him lying in pain somewhere or raving in a feverish delirium or, worse still, imagining him dead, began to drag her down, and she was glad to be invited again by Maria for the Christmas festivities.

'You have news for me?' she whispered to Francisco at the dinner table on Christmas Eve.

'*Si*. Haven't you heard from him?' He seemed to be surprised. 'He is alive.'

'Thank God!' she whispered, and burst into tears.

'What is it? What is wrong?' Maria demanded. 'Frank, what have you been saying to her?'

'I have just told her that her Jason is alive and well,' replied Francisco blandly. 'He was missing for a while, in the region where the earthquakes happened recently.'

'Do you know where he is now?' demanded Renata.

'I believe he was taken to the small hospital in Cuzco for treatment of some cuts and bruises he sustained when a wall collapsed and he was hit by flying debris,' said Francisco.

'Then I'll go to see him tomorrow,' Renata announced determinedly.

'You can't go tomorrow — it's Christmas Day. Go the day after,' said

217

Maria forcefully, her black eyes flashing. 'And I will go with you, to support you. It is at times like these that you need the support of a close relative. Carlota would go with you if she were alive . . . '

'No,' said Renata quickly, thinking, with a flash of insight into the character of her second husband, how much Jason would dislike it if she turned up at his bedside in a hospital with Aunt Maria in tow. And then, she thought wryly, she couldn't be sure of who else might be visiting him. Wasn't it possible that the 'other woman' would be at his bedside too? And then there would be all kinds of lies to be told to Maria. 'I can go by myself. It's good of you to offer, but have you forgotten the party you're giving the day after tomorrow? I'll go by myself, and I'll manage perfectly. And please try to understand. I have to see if he's all right before I go to New York. If he's been hurt badly I'll have to stay with him. I won't be able to go.'

'Then of course you must go to see him,' said Diego encouragingly. 'It is always best to follow your heart, Renata. Then you never have to live with regrets about not having done something you wanted to do very much.'

So in spite of Maria's old-fashioned but well-intentioned arguments about it not being proper conduct for a young woman to go chasing off to Cuzco by herself, Renata left Lima the day after Christmas Day and was driven by Diego to the airport to catch the first plane to Cuzco. It never occurred to her to tell Carlos where she had gone. He and the trip to New York were the last things on her mind.

The desire to see Jason again and make sure that he was really safe and well seemed to burn holes in her insides during the flight to Cuzco. She didn't question any more her longing to be with him no matter how he behaved or how he greeted her. She knew only that she wanted to be near to him, to touch

him and tell him how thankful she was that he hadn't been lost forever.

From the airport she took a taxi straight to the hospital, ignoring the feeling of dizziness and sickness that attacked her as a result of having reached such a high altitude in a short time.

The hospital was small and was run by an Order of nursing sisters. The Almoner told her politely that it had been unnecessary to keep Señor Hernandez in hospital once his cuts and bruises had been attended to and he had been examined by the doctor. His injuries had been very superficial and he had gone home.

'Where is that? Do you know where his house is?' asked Renata, and watched the nun shuffle some papers.

'The address here is Calle Viroda. It is an old house not far from the centre of the city,' replied the nun. 'You could walk there easily from here.'

After resting for a few moments on a chair in the Almoner's office in order to

get her breath back and to shake off the feeling of sickness, Renata went out into the bright sunshine and, following the nun's instructions, walked slowly to an old narrow street that slanted uphill from the Plaza de Armas.

Elegant examples of Inca stonework, each block of stone carefully bevelled so as to fit neatly against the stones surrounding it, lined the street. On top of these remains of the times when the Incas had ruled Peru, Spanish-style houses had been built with double doors set under arches in thick walls. There were windows high up, with balconies overhanging the narrow street, casting black shadows on the sunlit brightness of the cobbles.

The house for which Renata was looking had a big decorative letter 'H' carved on each of the double doors. 'H' for Hernandez? she wondered, and felt her spirits begin to sink a little. Wouldn't that mean the house belonged to Jason? Yet he had never told her about it or invited her to it.

She rang the bell. After a while one half of the door opened and a tall slim woman, whose age she guessed was in the late thirties and whose ink-black hair was braided around her head, looked out at her. She was dressed all in black, with a black woollen skirt and a black sweater. A medallion of pure gold hung on a gold chain around her neck. Her face was oval, its skin cream-coloured, and her finely chiselled nose had a haughty downward curve to it. There was something vaguely familiar in the way the woman's deep-set black eyes were looking at her, thought Renata, expressing a certain haughty wariness as if the woman resented being interrupted at whatever she had been doing by a complete stranger and would have willingly slammed the door in the caller's face.

'Is . . . does . . . I've come to see Señor Hernandez, Señor Jason Hernandez,' Renata stammered quickly, before the door could be shut.

She felt very shaken. She had

expected a woman, but not one as serenely beautiful as this one. Swiftly she glanced at the woman's left hand, noting the band of gold and above it another ring gleaming with emeralds and diamonds. Her spirits began to sink even more.

'I was told at the hospital that he lives here,' she added, almost defensively, when the woman didn't speak but continued to stare at her.

'That is so,' said the woman slowly, and didn't move an inch.

'So please can I come in to see him?'

The woman frowned, seemed to dither as if not sure what to do, and then began to close the door.

'Please, oh, please!' cried Renata, flinging herself at the door so that it couldn't be closed. 'I've come all the way from Lima to see him. I know he's been hurt — I promise not to stay too long. Please let me in to see him!'

The door slowly opened again. The woman looked at her closely and came to a decision.

'Wait here,' she said stiffly. 'I will come back.'

The door closed with a thud in Renata's face. She stood biting her lip. If she had any sense she would leave now rather than be embarrassed by having to meet Jason in front of his mistress. She was just turning away to go back down the sunlit cobbled street to the plaza at the end of it when the door opened again behind her.

The woman in black looked out at her. She was frowning, her eyes glinting and her lips were tight with anger.

'He is not here,' she snapped, showing even white teeth. 'He must have gone to the airport.'

'You mean he's . . . ?' began Renata.

'He has left the house without telling me,' the woman interrupted angrily. 'He is mad, that one, crazy, reckless of danger! One day he will be killed flying those machines. Always he is like that. He thinks of no one but himself and what he wants to do. They tell him at the hospital he should rest at home for

a few days before going flying again, and what does he do? He goes back to the airport less than an hour after they let him out of hospital, leaving when my back is turned. Ah, I have no patience with him!'

With that final bitter remark the woman slammed the door shut again. For a moment Renata stood still, staring open-mouthed at the door, amazed by the woman's passionate denunciation of Jason's behaviour. Then she turned and began to hurry down the street, wondering what she should do now. Go back to the airport, she guessed, and ask if Jason was there. And if he wasn't, if he had already taken off in a helicopter to fly somewhere, she would just have to wait until he came back.

Half an hour later she paid off the taxi that had brought her back to the airport and entered the terminal building. It was quiet, since apparently no planes were expected to land, nor were any expected to take off, and there was

no helpful ticket agent behind the airline desk where Hernandez Aviation was advertised.

For a while Renata waited at the desk, hoping that the door behind it would open and someone would come through, but nothing happened, so she stepped over the luggage scales and approached the door behind the desk. After knocking she opened it and went through into an area behind which was obviously a storage place for freight and left luggage. Sunlight slanted in from an open doorway at the end of one of the aisles between the storage racks.

Since there was no one at the only cluttered desk in the room, she walked straight to the open doorway. Surprisingly, the dizziness and sickness had worn off and she was feeling quite clear-headed. She stepped through the wide opening and out on to a runway. Nearby were two big helicopters. Standing near one of them, talking, were two men. One of them was Jason. As Renata stared he began to turn to

the helicopter, obviously intending to climb up into it.

'Jason!' she shouted, and began to run towards him, her hair flying behind her like a red banner. To her relief he turned to look at her. The other man also looked at her. She had the impression that he was slim and dark. After looking at her he looked back at Jason. As she stopped running to catch her breath she heard him say something to Jason before he turned on his heel and walked away to the other helicopter. He climbed up into it.

Standing as still as a statue, Jason waited for Renata to reach him. There was a patch of white gauze pasted to the right side of his forehead with a crisscross of sticking plaster. His face looked leaner than ever, the high cheekbones very prominent, one of them sporting a purple bruise. He looked at her without any expression of welcome or pleasure in his eyes.

'What the hell are you doing here? Why have you come?' he snarled, and

she was in no doubt that he was furious at her unexpected appearance out there on the launching pad. 'You have no right to be out here. Go back into the building! I'm just going to take off — I'm already behind schedule.'

'I heard that you'd been hurt, in an earthquake,' she panted, gazing up at him, all her concern for his welfare showing in her eyes and face. She put out a hand to him, let it rest on his shirt-covered chest, felt the strong throb of his heart come through to her palm and was reassured that he was really alive. 'Do you think it's wise for you to go flying so soon after coming out of the hospital? The . . . the woman at your house in the town is very upset because you left while her back was turned.'

At that point the other helicopter took off, the noise of its rotor making it impossible for anyone to hear anything that might be said. Renata's hair streamed sideways in the draught created by its take-off. She was still

standing close to Jason with her hand on his chest, and he slid his fingers around her wrist to hold it tight and prevent her being blown over. He waited until the helicopter had gone some distance away and was leaping over the fields like some huge grasshopper before he spoke. Then he exclaimed, 'You've been to the Hernandez house?' The angry glitter was fading from his eyes. Slowly his fingers began to caress the inside of her wrist and she felt desire begin to tingle deep down inside her. The dangerous attraction between them was back, a live wire that twanged and sparked. It seemed that nothing he said or did could stop that attraction happening whenever they met. 'Why did you go there?' he asked.

'I went to the hospital first and was told you'd been discharged and sent home to rest. Oh, please, Jason, don't go, don't risk your life again!'

'This is exactly why I've never wanted to be married,' he muttered with an irritated groan. 'And I thought

I'd got the message through to you and that you wouldn't interfere in my life. It's bad enough having Andrea fussing over me and warning me about what might happen. I'm OK, a little tired but otherwise in perfect health. And I have to go. There's been another 'quake in one of the villages and I have to fly in another cargo of supplies because the villagers refuse to leave.' He dropped Renata's hand, his face hardening. 'Now will you get the hell out of here, go back to Lima? I'll come and see you there as soon as I can.' Turning, he began to stride towards the helicopter.

'But you mustn't go back,' she protested, following him. 'There might be another tremor while you're there. Oh, it's too risky!'

Jason swung back to her so suddenly that she collided with him. Grasping her arms to steady her, he looked down at her, his face grim, his eyes strained with torment.

'But not as risky as staying with you,'

230

he muttered between tight lips. 'Sometimes I wish I'd never met you!' He pushed her away from him. 'Go away — go on, back to Lima, to the fashion shows you love, to your work as a designer. There's no room in your life for someone like me and no room in mine for someone like you. I warned you that I'm not the kind of man a woman should marry. I guessed this would happen if we got married.'

Again he turned away, but this time she tossed all pride to the winds and grabbed his arm, hanging on to it.

'No, I won't go away!' she cried. 'I want to be with you, to go where you're going now.'

Jason looked down at her over his shoulder, his expression changing to one of speculation. He raised one black eyebrow, and his lips curled in a slight mocking smile.

'You in a helicopter? You wading about in thick, slimy mud in a 'quake-torn village?' he jeered softly. 'I can't imagine it.'

'Oh, stop looking at me like that! I'm not exactly helpless. I know some first aid and I can comfort people who are in pain. I sat by Kendal's bedside when he was dying. I'm not scared by death or destruction,' Renata retorted. 'And I want to be with you, see what it is you have to do, share in the experience. Please, Jason! I . . . was never able to go with Kendal to the jungle. I never even tried to share any of his experiences, and later I wished I had. I regretted that I'd never gone with him. Please let me come with you!'

He hesitated, his narrowed eyes considering her clothes — the tight-fitting jeans, the colourful poncho she had bought the last time she had been in Cuzco that she was wearing over a long-sleeved shirt of brushed cotton.

'You mean it?' he challenged.

'Yes, yes, I mean it,' she cried recklessly. 'I want to be with you for a while, go where you're going, see what you see when you go into the mountains.'

'You'll see the other soul of this country. You'll see what destruction and terror do to the poor people of the villages in the mountains. It won't be a pleasure trip,' Jason said warningly. 'And there might be another earthquake while we're there.'

'I don't care,' she retorted, tossing back her head. 'I want to go with you. It's my country as much as yours and I'm concerned about those people as much as you are, would do anything to help them. Anyway, it doesn't matter whether I like what I'll see or not. I just want to be with you for a few hours.'

There was a certain lightening of his face, a flicker of eyebrows, a glint of teeth as he grinned in appreciation of her recklessness.

'OK,' he said, capitulating suddenly. 'Up you go.'

In the cockpit of the big chopper he offered her a headset and fitted his own on. Renata strapped herself into the seat beside him, placed the headset on her head and over her ears and listened

to Jason informing the control tower of the airport that he was about to take off, while he started up the engine that activated the rotor blades on top of the vehicle and also the small side propeller at the tail.

When he had received clearance he moved the control column before him and the helicopter began to rise in the air. The noise was ear-shattering and Renata was glad of the headset. Through the microphones attached to the sets they could talk to each other without having to shout too loudly, and the earphones had the effect of cutting down the noise.

Up and up and then forward the helicopter zoomed over the patchwork of greenish-brown fields planted with corn and potatoes, the staple crops of the Indians. Towards a small blue lake they flew, and looking out, Renata saw the shadow of the helicopter going along beside them on the ground. Ahead were the Andes, ridges and ridges of sun-bleached greenish-blue

rocks, cleft by purple valleys and ravines, and high up, glinting distantly, the snow-dusted pointed peaks. Then they were over the lake and going straight for a pass between walls of rock.

'Ever been in a chopper before?' Jason's voice drawled in her ears, and she glanced at him. He wasn't looking at her but was looking out and down at something he could see on the ground. He seemed to be perfectly relaxed, while she was consumed by an exhilaration she had never experienced before, a delight in soaring just above the ground and being able to see such a wide panorama of scenery.

'No. This is a first time,' she replied.

'You feel all right?' he asked. 'No *soroche*?'

'No. I think I got over that while I was at the hospital in Cuzco,' she replied, and he looked at her sharply.

'I still don't understand why you've come,' he said. 'How did you know I was in hospital?'

'Francisco told me. Please try to understand, Jason. I didn't come really to interfere with you. I just had to know you were all right.'

He gave her another wary glance but said nothing, pointing down instead to something they were flying over. Green and gold, the wide floor of a valley between the mountains flowed away below them. It was spotted with sheep. Tall acacia trees lined a narrow road that led to a twin-towered Colonial church, its stone glowing in the sunlight. Then they were over it and following the course of a glittering river as it threaded its way through sloping green hillsides.

'I wasn't badly hurt,' Jason said casually.

'But couldn't someone else have flown supplies in today?' argued Renata.

'Just because I suffered a few cuts and bruises, it doesn't mean I should stop doing what I can do to help,' he replied with a careless shrug.

'She — the woman at your house

— says you're crazy,' she said, and watched out of the corners of her eyes for his reaction. As she had expected, he laughed, his face lighting up with brash humour, and she felt again that sudden surge of attraction towards him.

'She's always said that,' he remarked. 'She's my half-sister, Andrea. She's married to Juan Martinez who works at the Cuzco museum. And the house you called at used to belong to my father, Ferdinand Hernandez. Members of the Hernandez family have owned it for hundreds of years. He left it to her in his will.'

Feeling relief seep through her because the beautiful woman who had answered the door was not his mistress, glad that Jason was beginning to tell her something about his family, Renata asked, 'Why didn't your father leave the house to you?'

'I guess he left it to Andrea because he thought she had more right to it than I had. She is his only legitimate child,' he replied, and gave her a

wickedly mocking glance.

'Oh.' She didn't feel shocked. She was just surprised that he was admitting to the illegitimacy of his birth. 'Wasn't he married to your mother, then?' she asked, remembering that Carlos had sneeringly called Jason a bastard to his face and then quite recently had suggested to her that Jason was emulating his father by keeping a mistress as well as being married.

'No. He could have married her when his first wife died, but my mother didn't want to be married. She is an artist and was and still is a very free spirit,' he said. 'But don't be too concerned about him not leaving the house in Cuzco to me. He provided for me very well, and when he was killed accidentally I inherited his other house in Lima as well as his share in the aviation company I now own.'

Renata was grateful to him for at last filling in a little of his background. He had just answered many of the questions she had wanted to ask but had

hesitated to. Although other questions clamoured in her mind, wanting to be asked and answered, and she still wasn't sure he didn't have a mistress, she didn't say anything more. Right now it was best to savour every moment of being with him, of being, for a brief time, part of his way of life.

10

The helicopter swooped into another flat valley between high mountains, the sides of which were striped by wide curved terraces of earth that looked like the steps of some giant pyramid.

'They're *andenes*,' said Jason in answer to Renata's interested question about them. 'They were invented by the Mochica engineers long ago and were adapted by the Incas as a way of preventing soil erosion so that crops could be grown on steep land. They're a much superior way of farming a mountainous area than the one the Spaniards imposed upon the Incas and which did nothing to stop erosion, so that the soil that had been so carefully conserved was washed away in heavy rains. And now, after three centuries of farming the wrong way, the mountain people are being taught all over again to

terrace the land in the way their ancestors did. And with good results, as you can see.'

The valley between the mountains grew narrower and narrower, sheer rock taking the place of the terraces. Through what seemed to be merely a slit in the rock the helicopter zoomed and there was another valley opening before them. But it was very different from the one they had just left.

A river swollen by rains was spreading across the land and was washing away all before it — trees, bits of houses, even huge rocks. As the helicopter descended towards an area of higher ground on which the ruins of a village were strewn, Renata saw tents and makeshift straw huts in the main plaza, clustered at the foot of the steps going up to the doors of the church.

'You can see the mud left by the flood that came before and after the 'quakes,' said Jason. 'Some people were killed when the houses fell down and many were injured. The church was also

shaken. You'll be shocked by the mess, and you won't believe you're in the same country as Lima and places like the Camino Real. But then, not even Lima is free from the threat of an earthquake, and that's probably why the way of life there is like one long binge, as if the end of the world is expected to happen the next day.'

He landed the helicopter neatly beside another that was parked on an open flat piece of land near a cluster of houses built of mud bricks, the usual homes of villagers. Some of the huts teetered right on the edge of wide cracks that had opened up in the earth.

'The villagers are too scared to move back into their houses,' Jason told Renata when they had climbed down from the helicopter. 'They're afraid another 'quake or an aftershock might swallow them completely.'

While the helicopter was being unloaded by a team of relief workers who had flown into the area the day before, he took her through the

mud-drenched streets to the main square where the shock-numbed inhabitants were living in the tents and straw huts. In front of the partly demolished church they had gathered together for a service led by an archbishop who had been brought in by the helicopter that had flown out of Cuzco just before Jason and Renata had left. The damaged towers of the church, where bells still hung crookedly, reached upwards to the brilliant sun-bright blue sky, like two hands praying to heaven for help. Looking at the dark faces of the people kneeling in the mud, Renata saw pride and determination carved there and felt a sudden kinship with them. They wouldn't give up easily.

'Can't they be taken away from here, flown to Cuzco or some other city where perhaps they could stay in more comfortable places until the aftershocks have passed?' she asked, touched by the sadness expressed in the dark eyes of the women.

'They wouldn't want to go. This is

their home. And they would tell you they prefer it to any city. Already they're talking of rebuilding,' Jason replied.

He showed her the pile of rubble that had once been the wall of a house.

'It happened in the afternoon. I'd just flown in a medical team and their supplies and was walking back to the chopper when there was this tremendous shaking beneath my feet as if someone was testing an A-bomb underground,' he explained. 'For three or four seconds everything swayed and shuddered. I threw myself down on the ground in the middle of the street just before the house collapsed. If I hadn't moved so fast I guess I'd have been buried under that pile of bricks.'

'And killed,' Renata whispered. 'You might have been killed!'

'So what?' he said with a shrug.

They stood facing each other in the sunlit street of ruins, their feet in the mud. Renata could feel the slimy stuff soaking through the suede and nylon of her designer sneakers.

'Don't you care that if you were killed you'd leave someone behind who would be hurt by your death, who . . . who would miss you? If you'd been killed I would have cared very much, even more than I did when Kendal died. I don't think I could survive losing two husbands,' she blurted out. 'If you'd been killed up here I . . . I think I would have died too!'

Jason stiffened, closing his eyes momentarily, and muttered something beneath his breath. When he opened his eyes he looked at her with the same glitter of hostility as he had when she had run up to him at the airport in Cuzco.

'No, you wouldn't — not you. You'd have survived. You're a survivor, like these people, like me,' he retorted harshly. 'And remember you married me for convenience. Sentiment isn't supposed to enter into our relationship. Now you're making me wish I hadn't told you what happened to me here in the last 'quake and that you hadn't

come to see me. I told you never to come to Cuzco to see me, that I would come to you.'

'But I had to come to see you — I had to!' she insisted.

'It's time I took you out of here and back to Cuzco to catch the next plane to Lima,' Jason interrupted her roughly. 'This is no place for you to spend the night in.'

'But I don't want to go back to Lima,' she protested, as, with a hand under her elbow, he urged her back along the deserted street towards the square.

'So where were you thinking of spending the night?' he asked.

'With you,' she retorted boldly, glad of his support as her feet slid in the mud.

'Andrea only lets me live in her house on condition that I don't bring women to my room. She's very moral, upright and strict in the old Spanish tradition. I have to go elsewhere if I want a woman,' he said brutally, and Renata

246

guessed he was being rough with her because he was irritated with her for having come to see him.

'Well, you can be sure that if I can't stay with you there I've no wish to stay the night in the same house as your mistress!' she seethed.

'My what?' he exclaimed, and jerked her round to face him again. 'What mistress?' he demanded, glowering down at her.

'I was told that you live with a woman in Cuzco and have done for some time,' she replied.

'I have — with Andrea. And her husband too.' His eyes had begun to glint with mockery and his lips were curling into a grin. 'So that's the real reason for you coming to see me! You came to check up on me, find out if the story you'd heard about me having a mistress was true,' he scoffed.

'No, it isn't the real reason. I was truly concerned about you. Oh, stop laughing at me!' stormed Renata, and wrenching her arm free of his grasp

began to hurry towards the helicopter where two of the relief workers were assisting a woman into it.

'Her baby is due to be born any time and it looks like there'll be complications. We think it would be best if she's taken to the hospital at Cuzco,' explained one of the young men to Jason as he approached the helicopter. 'She insists on taking her two kids with her, but I don't know whether they'll be willing to have them at the hospital.'

'We'll find somewhere for them to stay,' Jason assured him.

In the helicopter Renata removed her mud-covered shoes and wiped her feet on a towel he gave her. The machine took off without warning, before she had time to put on the earphones, and the cockpit was filled with the clattering noise of the rotor turning. Everything around her vibrated.

They didn't speak on the return flight to Cuzco as golden sunset light blazed in through the windows of the

helicopters, making sunglasses compulsory. Jason seemed to have withdrawn from her completely. Feeling hurt and rejected, Renata couldn't think of anything to say to him that wouldn't result in him giving her another rebuff. Sometimes empathising with the young woman who was sitting behind her and who seemed very scared, she turned to speak to her and the two children in Spanish, doing her best to reassure them until Jason told her curtly that they didn't understand her because they spoke only the language of the Quechua Indians.

Back at Cuzco in the airport building she sat with the woman and children while Jason went to find out if the hospital could take them in.

'The nuns say the kids can stay with her, and a car is coming to get them,' he said when he came back. 'I'll wait here with you until the flight to Lima is ready to go.'

'I'll go in the morning,' she replied.

'So where are you going to stay the night?'

'In a hotel,' she said stiffly, then, unable to contain herself, she demanded, 'Why didn't you tell me you have a mistress?'

'But I don't have a mistress,' he retorted.

'Then why don't you want me to stay the night with you? Why wouldn't you stay with me on our wedding night?'

'You know why I didn't. I had to come back here.' Jason sighed heavily. 'I don't have a mistress, and I'd like to know where you got the idea that I have. My guess is that it's that dirty-minded creep, your business partner, who dreamed up this story.'

'It wasn't just Carlos,' she said defensively. 'Inez Dupont told me that she met a woman who's very close to you who was surprised to learn that you're married.'

'That would be Andrea. She was in Lima visiting relatives recently. She told me she'd heard about my marriage to you and she was angry because I didn't tell her myself or invite her to the

ceremony,' Jason replied. 'What else did Inez tell you?'

'That you lived in Cuzco with this woman she'd met,' Renata said rather lamely.

'Which I do — at least, in the same house as her. Inez was implying something quite different from the actual truth, and so you jumped to the wrong conclusion.'

'I tried not to, but it was very hard not to. I know so little about you,' she complained.

'And I know so little about you,' he retorted. 'Now let's get this straight once and for all. This is no callow youth you've married. I'm on the wrong side of thirty-five and I've not been celibate. I'd had a couple of love affairs before you came along. Once, way back in time, there was someone I was very serious about, but as soon as she started to try and tie me down it ended. Since then I've kept my friendships with women on the light side. I've told you I've always liked to be free of any

emotional involvement or commitment.' He paused, then added in a lower voice, 'And I'd succeeded for a while until I met you. Now it looks as if I'm into involvement and commitment up to my neck,' he groaned. 'Why the hell did you have to come here today?'

'Because I love you,' she said, wishing they were somewhere not quite so public, and watched a flame of desire leap in the dark depths of his eyes. 'Don't you want me to stay now?'

'*Te quiero* — I want you,' he said, passion breaking through his control so that his eyes glowed fierily into hers. 'But not in Cuzco, and not tonight. I have to fly again tomorrow, to do a risky job that I enjoy. If you stay . . . I swore after the affair with Lise that I'd never agree to get married again . . . ' He broke off, his breath hissing, and turned away from her.

'I think I'd guessed you were either married or had been married,' said Renata in a low voice. 'What happened?'

He turned back to her. There was a bitter twist to the generous curves of his lips. The black eyes were without any vestige of light.

'No, we never married. It stopped just short of marriage. I had the sense to see what a hell it was going to be for the two of us if we tied the knot. It was years ago, when I lived in the States. I worked for an aircraft factory as a test pilot. Lise and I lived together for a while. She wanted us to get married, but she couldn't stand the anxiety when I was flying. She wanted me to give it up to marry her. I refused. So we split,' Jason said bleakly. 'Ever since, I've felt I couldn't expect a woman to go through the anxiety or the loneliness she would have to put up with while I was away. Now I'm afraid to let you stay with me tonight because if you do I might not want to leave you to go flying tomorrow.' Humour began to flicker in his face again. 'You see what a fix I'm in?'

Renata nodded.

'I understand. But I'm different from Lise. I'm more like you. I have to do my own thing too. Tomorrow I have to be back in Lima, so I wouldn't try to hold you back from flying. I have a lot of work to do before I go to New York with Carlos. He's arranged a show of my fashion designs there. It's a great opportunity to get them known outside Lima.'

'Then you must get on that flight that's just being announced,' he urged.

'But I don't have to go to Lima tonight. If I go in the morning I can still get back in time for my first appointment tomorrow, as I did the first time I came to see you. I have a seat booked on the early morning flight,' Renata argued stubbornly. 'I'm staying here tonight, and if you don't want to take me to your room in Andrea's house you're welcome to visit me in my room at the hotel.'

'No,' he said curtly. He strode over to the airline desk. She followed him and reached his side in time to hear the

ticket agent tell him there were seats available on the flight. Jason turned to her.

'Where's your return ticket?' he demanded.

'But I don't want to go . . . ' she started to complain.

'Your ticket, damn you!' he snarled at her. He snatched her shoulder-bag from her, unzipped it and plunged his hand in, bringing out her ticket to wave it triumphantly at her. He put the ticket down in front of the agent. 'Change her reservation to this flight,' he ordered.

'Sure. You're the boss,' said the agent, grinning. He was the same man with whom Renata had once left a message for Jason.

'But I don't want to . . . ' she began.

'Shut up!' Jason leaned swiftly towards her and kissed her hard on the lips, cutting off her protest. 'Much as I would like it, we're not going to stay together tonight. At heart I'm a romantic, and it's not going to happen between you and me for the first

time in a crummy hotel bedroom,' he whispered.

'But why not?' she started again as, after taking the boarding pass and the ticket from the agent, he urged her towards the departure gate.

'You know something I can't stand?' he said in a silky-soft drawl. 'Women who are forever arguing or protesting. So shut up, darling.'

'Male chauvinist!' she snapped at him, but he only grinned at her and retorted.

'Not true. I much prefer women to men, but not all women.'

'Well, I won't shut up!' she flared. 'I only wanted to tell you that my father is going to fly from Vancouver to New York to visit me while I'm there. I wish you could come up to New York while he's there to meet him. Couldn't you?'

'No way.' Jason's face was grim. 'When are you leaving Lima?'

'The day after tomorrow.'

'How long will you be away?'

'About two weeks. Please try to come.'

'No,' he said curtly. 'Nothing against your father, but I just can't go on a pleasure trip while I'm needed here. I'll see you when you come back. I'll fly down to Lima.'

'I might not come back,' she flung at him in an effort to break through his stubborn refusal to meet her in New York. Close to tears and with her head held high, she turned to walk away from him, but he grabbed her arm and swung her back to face him. She had time to see the blaze in his eyes and then her lips were being blistered by a searing kiss. When he lifted his head the blaze of anger had gone, its place taken by a mocking glint.

'Just something to remember me by while you're gone and to make you think of what you've lost if you don't come back,' he scoffed. '*Adios*.'

He had the last word after all and was the one to walk away. Aware that she was being stared at by other passengers waiting to board the flight to Lima, Renata joined the line at the

departure gate, trying to pretend she wasn't regretting already that she and Jason had parted on bad terms.

During the next day she didn't seem to have a free moment and had to stay late at the studio to supervise the finishing of some of the clothes she had designed, that had been made for the show, and also to supervise the packing of them for the flight to New York. But as always she was glad to be busy. It meant that she had no time to think too much about Jason and regret that he hadn't let her stay with him for just one night before she went away.

Next morning, late getting up and full of a strange reluctance to leave Peru, she almost missed the flight to New York. Breathless from her dash through the terminal building at Callao airport, she arrived at the departure gate in time to hear her name being called. She was the last person to board the plane and entered the first-class compartment just as Carlos was getting up from his seat.

'Ah, so you've condescended to come with us, have you? I was rather hoping you had decided to stay with your dear husband,' he drawled sarcastically, and sat down again.

He was in an aisle seat, and the stewardess indicated that Renata's seat was on the other side of the aisle next to the window. Surprised that she wasn't sitting next to Carlos, Renata sat down and the stewardess put her carry-on luggage in the overhead storage bin. As she fastened her seat-belt quickly because the plane was already moving away from the terminal building, she looked across at Carlos.

He wasn't looking at her. He was half-turned in his seat and was talking to the young woman who was sitting in the window seat next to him. Renata recognised the woman immediately. She was one of the three models who were going to model Renata Fashion designs in New York, and her name was Paulina Perez. Striking in appearance, with an olive skin and fair, almost

blonde frizzy hair, Paulina had taken Renata's place as a model at the Muro Boutique quite recently. She was a very good model and had a lively disposition.

The plane reached the end of the runway and its engines were revved in preparation for take-off. Renata heard Paulina's rather loud laugh trill out in response to something amusing Carlos had said, and wondered vaguely why he had arranged for Paulina to travel first class when the other two models were in the economy-class compartment of the plane. Then the plane was lifting and she was closing her eyes, pretending she was with Jason and flying through the Andes, and wishing she could be with him that morning instead of flying away from Peru and from him, wondering when and if she would ever see him again.

She could not help being disturbed and surprised by the change in herself. A few weeks ago when Carlos had suggested they might go to New York

she had been full of enthusiasm for the project, knowing how it would boost her reputation as a fashion designer. She had thought of her career and nothing else, had put it and herself first. Now she could only think of Jason, of her strange relationship with him, of how she had this urge to improve that relationship, make it closer and more intimate, become both his wife and his mistress, possess him and be totally possessed by him.

She opened her eyes and glanced across the aisle again. Carlos was holding Paulina's left hand. His thumb was stroking over the back of it as he leaned his head close to the model's and whispered something into her ear, no doubt something salacious, judging by Paulina's giggles. Was he doing it deliberately to make her jealous? Renata wondered with a little smile, looking away and out of the window at the pristine blue of the sky now that the plane had reached its cruising altitude. If that was his intention he was wasting

his time. She was safe from him now, protected from him by her marriage to Jason, and not only by that but also by her love for Jason.

They flew first to Miami and changed there on to a flight to New York, arriving late in the afternoon. To Renata's delight her father and stepmother Alison were at Kennedy Airport to meet her. After introducing them to Carlos and the three models, she went with them in a taxi to the Manhattan hotel where they would all be staying, leaving Carlos to travel with the three models and also the boxes in which the designer clothes were packed.

'Weather isn't too good, as you can see,' her father, Donald Mackay, said as the taxi sped away from the airport and joined the traffic going towards the high grey towers of the famous city, all glittering with light in the fast-falling purplish dusk. He was the same as ever, thought Renata with a rush of warm affection: down-to-earth, practical. 'But the forecast is for milder sunnier

weather tomorrow,' he added.

'Is Jason going to fly up here to join you?' Alison asked. Tall and well-made, with greyish-blonde hair cut short at the back and swept up in a froth of curls from her temples and forehead, Alison always exuded a pleasant motherliness, and yet Renata knew that being a wife and mother had not been her sole career. She held a degree in business administration and was an assistant to the president of a company of architects. Over the years she had managed to juggle her two careers successfully.

'No, he isn't,' she said. 'He can't get away right now. There've been so many earthquakes in the interior.' Suddenly, knowing they would be interested and sympathetic, she was talking about Jason — what he looked like, how he loved flying, how she had gone with him to the village in the mountains, and she didn't stop until they had passed over a bridge spanning the East River and were turning into Fifth Avenue.

The hotel had a warm, relaxed atmosphere and Renata's room was big and elegantly furnished. Although tired after the journey she soon perked up after a shower and a change of clothes, and went down to the dining room with Donald and Alison for dinner. She noticed that Carlos was already there, sitting at another table with Paulina, and although he acknowledged her presence and that of her father and Alison he did not come over to speak to them. He was much too taken up with Paulina, Renata thought, and knew a deeply felt sense of relief. He had turned off herself at last. Her marriage to Jason had done what she had hoped it would do.

Most of the next two days were taken up with making the last-minute arrangements for the fashion show, meeting other designers who were exhibiting designs for spring at the same show, and visiting some garment factories outside the city. There was also time to attend a Broadway musical, the

latest offering from London, England, as it turned out. Renata enjoyed everything, but not as much as she would have done at one time, and every night when she went to bed she lay awake wishing with all her heart she was back in Peru with Jason.

'How did you do it — I mean, when you were younger and were first married to your first husband, how did you cope?' she asked Alison the day before the fashion show was to take place, when they were having a quiet time together in Renata's hotel room. Donald had gone off to visit an engineering acquaintance who was now with a firm of consultants based in New York. 'I know that you kept on with your own career and that he had to go away often because of his job. Wasn't it difficult? Didn't you find yourself torn in two, wanting to be with him and yet wanting to get on with your own career too?'

'Oh, it wasn't easy,' said Alison with a laugh. 'Never think that. It takes a lot of

loving on the part of both partners, a lot of understanding.' She studied Renata's face with kind grey eyes. 'Jack and I had our problems, and there were times when I felt like giving up my work. Then there were other times when I felt that the answer was to split, leave him and get and divorce so I could go my own way. But once our first child was born all that went by the board. We both changed, because suddenly we were responsible for this other person's quality of life and there were new problems to be solved, like who was going to look after the child when I felt I was able to leave her and go back to work. That was when Jack and I found we were a real team, able to give and take. He made some concessions to our new situation and found a position which didn't take him away from home so much.' Alison sighed sadly. 'He was a wonderful husband and a great father to our two kids. What more can any woman want from a man?'

'You must have missed him terribly when he was killed,' said Renata.

'I did. And it was then I was really glad I'd held on to my career.' Alison smiled a little. 'But what's all this leading to? Are you having problems already with Jason?'

'In a way. He didn't really want to get married, you see — ' Renata paused, frowned and then admitted slowly, 'As a matter of fact, I asked him to marry me to protect me from Carlos.'

'Good lord!' Alison looked astounded and then burst out laughing. 'You're kidding!'

'No, I'm not.'

'Then you're not in love with each other?'

'Well, I am in love with him now, and . . . and . . . he says he wants me, which in Spanish means the same as loving.'

'So what are you worried about?'

'Myself. A few weeks ago I wanted so badly to come to New York for this fashion show. But when the time came for me to leave Lima I'd have given

anything to have stayed there, to be nearer to Jason. Part of the trouble is he won't let me live in Cuzco where he lives. Oh, Alison, I'm so mixed up! I thought I wanted a career in fashion design more than anything else in the world. Now I don't care if I have it or not. I want to be Jason's wife and his lover, more than anything else in the world.'

'Then when this is over go back to Lima and tell him that and see what happens. Let life unfold as it should instead of trying to push it around,' advised Alison. 'You know, it could be you're more like your mother than you've realised. She was brought up in a different society from ours, remember, and she could have passed on to you some of the traditions of that society without you knowing it. The career she was educated for was that of wife and mother, and she did it to perfection. She didn't have any other ambition outside her home and her family. Yet I don't think she was ever

discontented, or resented what she had chosen to do with her life.'

'That was because she had Dad for a husband,' replied Renata shrewdly.

'Probably,' agreed Alison. 'And who knows, maybe you'll find that Jason will turn out to be the best husband for you, if you give him a chance.' She glanced at her watch. 'Now isn't it time you met Carlos to make the last arrangements for the show?'

The showing of Renata's designs was wedged in between two other shows, one of designs from a Mexican fashion house and the other, surprisingly, of designs from a new Russian fashion house. Everything went according to plan. The models did their work well and the clothes looked interesting and different.

Yet for Renata there was none of the excitement she had felt at the show in Lima. Was it because that had been her first show? she wondered. Or was it because she knew Jason wouldn't be there at the back of the audience

watching? Was it because she was missing him so badly?

She was standing in one of the wings of the stage, screened from view by curtains that draped the archway, watching the models come and go, making last-minute adjustments to the clothes they were wearing, and she felt a sense of relief when Kate Harris, the New York model Carlos had hired specially to show the evening dresses, made her last bow to the audience and swept back along the catwalk to the noisy applause of the audience.

It was over at last. Two more days spent in the company of Donald and Alison and then she could go home to Lima, to Peru, to Jason. As she turned away she almost collided with Paulina. The model was wearing an obviously new afternoon suit with a very short mini-skirt. Renata didn't recognise it as being one of hers.

'Excuse me,' said Paulina with her simpering smile just as Kate came off the stage. 'My turn now.'

'What do you mean?' exclaimed Renata. 'The show — our show, I mean — is over.'

'*Your* show, you mean,' retorted Paulina. '*Mine* is just beginning. Carlos is now going to introduce me and my line of fashions.'

'Your line of fashions?' Renata gasped.

'That's right. Carlos encouraged me to create some new designs and had them made up at the factory. He promised he would show them here in New York,' Paulina giggled a little self-consciously. 'He and I are going into business together. He says he can't depend on you now that you're married and he's asked me to take your place as his partner. Oh, get out of my way, will you? It's time I was out there.'

Renata stepped aside and Paulina teetered on to the stage in her high heels. Staring after the model, Renata could hear Carlos speaking into the microphone.

'And now, ladies and gentlemen,' he

said, 'I would like to introduce to you my latest discovery, Paulina Perez. The clothes you are going to see modelled here for the next half-hour have been created solely for this show by Paulina who is, I hope, going to replace Renata in my company. Please, ladies and gentlemen, I hope you will welcome this young and promising designer kindly.'

The audience clapped politely and, completely stunned and dismayed by Carlos's announcement, Renata left the side of the stage and went to find her father and Alison.

11

It wasn't until the rest of the morning fashion shows were over that Renata was able to confront Carlos about the way he had encouraged Paulina to create some designs of her own and then had introduced the model as his new discovery and had announced that she would replace herself. She found him behind the stage in one of the changing rooms where Paulina was in a state of undress, in the process of changing from one of her rather fantastic creations into her usual day clothes.

'Carlos, I would like a word with you in private,' said Renata coolly.

He stood up at once and came towards her but did not, as had always been his way, take her hands in his and raise her right one to his lips. He did, however, smile at her, his usual bland

smile that didn't reach his eyes. They remained cold and watchful under their heavy lids.

'Congratulations,' he said pleasantly. 'You must feel very gratified with the reception given to your designs.'

'Yes, I suppose I am,' she replied.

'So aren't you going to congratulate Paulina too?' he suggested smoothly. 'Her style is very different from yours, I admit, much more directed at younger and possibly less affluent women than yours is, but much more suited to being adapted to mass production. You see, I'm thinking of opening another line of boutiques which will offer ready-made clothes, less exclusive than the Muro boutique has been to date. That is where the big profits are these days, in mass production.'

'You mean market the clothes as if they're soap or packets of cereal?' she replied. Cautioned by her father, she had decided to keep her temper on a tight rein. There was nothing to be gained by losing it with Carlos. 'Yes, I

understand that. It goes on all the time in America and other Western countries.' She was aware that Paulina had gone behind a screen to continue with her changing, out of sight but still able to hear what was being said, so she changed to English, knowing that the model's understanding of the language was very limited. 'Did you mean it when you said Paulina would be replacing me in your company?' she asked.

'You heard me say that?' parried Carlos, raising his eyebrows, also speaking in English.

'I couldn't help hearing. I was still in the wings,' Renata said drily. 'You wanted me to hear, didn't you?'

'If you think I wanted you to hear it I'm not prepared to disagree with you.'

'What I don't understand is why you couldn't have told me that you wanted to present Paulina's designs here in New York before. Why did you have to be so secretive about it?'

'Because I guessed, rightly or wrongly,

that you would have objected to me using an invitation that was directed to Renata Fashions only to display the designs of someone else,' he replied. 'You would have, wouldn't you?'

'Yes, I guess I would. And I would have had the right to do it. Carlos, don't you see you've broken the contract we signed? It states quite clearly that you would promote only me as a designer for the Muro boutiques.'

'I see that,' he said imperturbably. 'But you'll be a fool if you sue me for breaking it. As I've already pointed out, Paulina's designs are for a new line of boutiques I'm going to open in every city in Peru. I have formed a separate company which has nothing to do with you. Gradually I shall phase out the type of boutique I've owned up to now. Or if you want it I'll sell the Camino Real business to you. I'm going all out for mass appeal instead of just catering for a certain élitish clientele. Anything produced by the new company will go out under one label, and the name will

be Muro Fashions. Of course, if you wish you can join the new company, but I have this feeling you'd rather not.'

'I see.' Renata frowned, thinking about what he had said. If she did join the new company she would say goodbye to a career as a haute couture designer. She would become just one of many designers, a faceless and nameless person, without any individuality, creating just for the sake of selling and making money. It wasn't her style. She would rather be on her own, designing the way she wanted to and promoting herself if necessary, like the Indian woman who had sold her the poncho in Cuzco. 'No,' she said slowly, 'I don't want to join your new company. But I would like to know what I'm supposed to do about our contract.'

Carlos's smile was a little wry twist of his thin lips.

'I suggest we tear it up, together, when we get back to Lima — that is if you still want to go back? I know your father and stepmother would like very

much for you to return to Canada with them. If you do decide to do that we could come to a mutual agreement here, before I fly back to Lima tomorrow to end the contract. You don't need me any more, Renata, I understand that. You're successful in your own right and can set up as a designer in any city in the world that you want to live in.'

She stared at him incredulously.

'You mean what you say? You really won't hold me to that contract?'

'Not as long as you won't hold *me* to it,' he said with a dry laugh. 'I have no wish to be involved with you any more. I find Paulina much more submissive and willing to do what I want than you are.' He turned as Paulina appeared from behind the screen and smiled at the model, speaking to her in Spanish. 'You are ready, *querida*? Good. So let's go and celebrate the success of your designs, shall we?' He glanced back at Renata. 'I know you are going to be tied up

278

with your family today and tomorrow and have arranged to fly back to Lima the day after tomorrow, but I'd like you to know that you're no longer under any obligation to me and don't have to return. I can take care of any outstanding business for you if you decide to go to Canada or even stay in this city.'

'Thank you.' Renata's sense of relief at being released from her contract with him was almost overwhelming, and it was changing her attitude to him. She was beginning to feel she could even like him a little bit. 'But I will be returning to Lima as planned. I like to tie up all my loose ends myself, and I'm committed to designing some clothes for new clients when I get back there. Also I would like to take what belongs to me from the studio, including all my drawings,' she added sweetly, and guessed from Carlos's sudden frown that he had hoped she wouldn't return to Lima so that he would have access to those drawings. 'Have a good day,

Paulina,' she said, smiling at the model. 'And good luck with your new job. See you in Lima, Carlos, and we can tear that contract up together.'

She left the changing room, thinking that she had handled the whole business rather well. She hadn't lost her temper, and now she had her freedom from that contract with Carlos. She had escaped from his dominance at last and could go it alone as a designer. She had no doubt in her mind that he had encouraged Paulina and had brought her to New York deliberately to exhibit her designs, not only because he had shrewdly seen a way of launching his new company but also to spite herself because she had thwarted his desire to dominate her completely by marrying Jason.

Now, given the new situation between Carlos and herself, now they had agreed to part company, her marriage to Jason wasn't necessary either, and perhaps when she told him what had happened he would want to end it. She hoped he

wouldn't, but she couldn't be sure what his reaction would be. She would just have to go back to Lima and wait and see what he would do.

As Carlos had suspected, when she told Alison and her father that the contract between Carlos and herself was ended and that she alone was now Renata Fashions they did their best to persuade her to go back to Vancouver and start a fashion business there.

'I can't — not right now. I have to go back to Lima, to finish some commitments I made to clients,' she replied. 'And also to see Jason, find out what he wants to do. I'll let you know how things go. If they don't work out the way I'd like them to I'll think then about returning to Vancouver.'

And so two days later she flew back to Callao alone, arriving as dusk shrouded the airport building. Once through Customs and Immigration, she made her way to the exit and asked for a taxi. One approached the kerb. The driver got out and lifted her cases into

the trunk. Renata turned away to open the rear door, and a figure loomed beside her. An arm reached out to open the door for her, and she looked up. Jason grinned down at her. He was breathing hard as if he had been running.

'That was a near thing!' he gasped, pulling the door open. 'We passed in the Arrivals lounge. You didn't see me, I guess, because you weren't expecting to see me. Get in.'

'But how did you know I was coming back today?' she exclaimed, feeling a surge of delight because he had come to meet her.

'I had to come to Lima yesterday. I phoned Muro to see if you were back yet and he told me the time and date of your arrival. Come, get in the car,' he ordered brusquely. 'We have the rest of the evening and night to talk.'

Renata needed to be swept off her feet imperiously by the person she loved most, she thought, as she slid along the back seat of the taxi. It gave

her a heady feeling of being much wanted and much loved. Jason sat down beside her, slammed the door shut, leaned forward to give instructions to the driver and then turned to her. Suddenly she was being kissed with a passion she had never experienced before in the whole of her life.

The fiery pressure of his lips on hers was no offence to her but a pleasure, and she responded wholeheartedly, winding her arms around his neck. She didn't care any more where she was and knew nothing of the journey along the highway to Lima. She longed only to be closer to him and to become a part of him, to be his mate at last, willingly and regardless of consequences. With inarticulate moans of pleasure she pressed herself against him until, laughing a little, he slid his lips away from hers.

'I hoped you'd be glad to see me,' he teased her, 'but I didn't reckon on a response like this!'

'Where are we going? To my apartment?' she asked.

'No. We're going to a place I hope you'll like and where I want to make sure you'll never want to live up to that threat you flung at me before we parted at Cuzco two weeks ago. To give you a good reason for always wanting to come back to where I am,' Jason said softly.

He claimed her lips again with a tenderness that coaxed the tiny flame of desire within her to blaze up into a fire that consumed any reservations she had ever had about letting him make love to her. By the time the taxi stopped in a tree-lined boulevard outside the walls of a house in one of the older parts of Lima, she was breathless and dizzy.

There were double wrought-iron gates in a creeper-covered wall. Jason opened one of them and guided her into a courtyard where water tinkled from a shadowy fountain. Light gleamed under arches along the front of a house. They went up three shallow steps to a double front door. He rang the bell, but didn't wait for anyone to answer his ring. Opening the right-hand

door, he ushered her into a square hallway with a low ceiling. A stairway with a wrought-iron banister curved to an upper floor.

A woman with greying hair, who was dressed all in black, came into the hallway from a passageway. Jason went over to her to speak quietly to her. Renata stayed where she was gazing round at the casual elegance of the hallway with its red-tiled floor and pots of tropical plants.

After nodding in agreement with what Jason had said, the grey-haired woman went back along the passageway and Jason came back to Renata, to pick up both her suitcases.

'What is this place?' she asked.

'The house my father left me,' he replied softly. 'Wouldn't you like to bathe and change? We could do it together, upstairs while Señora Valdez prepares dinner for us. She has kept house here ever since my father bought this house nearly forty years ago. She wants to retire but I've asked her to stay

on until I can find a suitable substitute. I'm hoping to resolve that problem while you're here.'

She followed him up the staircase and into a bedroom that was at the front of the house. She had an impression of good design in the hand-made furniture, of cool greens and blues in the curtains and bedcovering, of a thick, cream-coloured carpet and subdued lighting. There were several original paintings on the walls, canvases daubed with thick paint in abstract designs.

'This is lovely!' she exclaimed. 'But you'll have to tell me why you don't live here all the time. It's a beautiful house, not too big and not too small, with a definite homey feel about it.'

'I don't live here all the time because the company I've been running is based in Cuzco,' he replied. He helped her take off the jacket of the suit she had worn to travel in and placed it over the back of a chair. 'My father bought this house for my mother so that she could

live here whenever she came to Lima to visit him.'

'Please tell me more about them,' she urged. 'Where did they meet?'

'Here in Lima. He was already married to Andrea's mother. His was an old aristocratic Spanish family and in the tradition of the Lima society in which he grew up he married a woman from his own social circle, not for love so much as for convenience.'

'You and I have married for convenience,' she pointed out.

'Have we?' The underbrowed glance he gave her made her pulses begin to throb. 'You may have done, but I didn't.'

'Did your father fall in love with your mother?'

'He did. And she with him. They became lovers, flying in the face of the upper-class morality that pervaded Lima at the time, and set up house together here. I was born in this house and lived in it until my mother decided she wanted to go back to Santa Fe, New Mexico, where she preferred to do

her painting. Sometimes I would come back to Lima to stay with my father and sometimes he would visit us in New Mexico. Then he was posted to the United Nations Organisation in New York and was able to stay with us more often in Santa Fe. By then Andrea's mother had been long dead.' Coming close to her, he framed her face with his hands. 'My parents were not married to each other, but they cared for me and looked after me as well as if not better than many married couples look after their legitimate children. But that's enough about them for now. I'd much rather make love to you than answer questions about my family background.'

'That's enough for now,' she agreed, remembering and acknowledging as the truth what her cousin Diego had said. It didn't matter who a man's parents were as long as you loved him and he loved you.

'And you understand now why I had to bring you here instead of hiding with

you in some hotel room or even your apartment to make love to you?' said Jason, taking a moment to lift his lips from hers. 'This is my home now, even though I'm not able to live here all the time as yet. And you're the only woman I've brought here. You're my wife now, and that means I owe you all the respect and all the tenderness I have in me to offer you. What more can I say?'

'Nothing, nothing,' she cried touched to the heart by his confession of love and respect and flinging her arms around him and kissing him.

'Then we won't waste any more time,' he said huskily. 'I have to see you, all of you. If you knew how often I've dreamed of this moment, of undressing you . . .'

Her cheeks flamed. No man had ever been so frank about his desire to make love to her before. Silently and reverently he helped her to undress, kissing her often and caressing her with seductive movements of his fingers. And while he was smoothing her

clothes away from her she was unbuttoning his shirt, sliding it off him, her hands lingering on the velvet smoothness of his skin, her fingers tangling in the rough, coarse hairs. With eager fingers she found the buckle of his belt and began to undo it.

By then they were in a luxurious bathroom that opened off the bedroom. Mirrors reflected them as they helped each other finish undressing while water gushed from gilded taps into a huge turquoise blue bath that was sunk into the floor. In the bath they splashed and played, soaped each other and even shampooed each other's hair. When they were through washing they dried each other with hot, scented towels. Slowly their playfulness passed and their caresses became more lingering and arousing.

Their bodies silky and scented, they lay on the bed, cushioned by soft pillows. No questions were asked or answered, nothing was said about other people or past events. No plans for the

future were made. All that mattered to each other was the immediate present. When they talked it was only to say how much they loved each other or to make a remark of admiration or endearment. Hidden and cut off from the outside world in the quiet bedroom in the secluded house, they discovered each other's souls at the same time as enjoying each other's bodies, until at last, as the urgency of Jason's desire expressed itself in the pressure of his thighs against hers, Renata felt her whole body leap up to meet his in a wild hunger.

His laughing breath hot against her cheek, he whispered,

'Oh, how welcome you make me, *amada*, so sweetly welcome, and I adore you for it.'

Then he was thrusting deeper and deeper inside her, inciting her to an even wilder response until he lost all control too and passion erupted between them. For a while afterwards they lay sprawling in sated, breathless

silence. Then Jason moved away from her. At once she was on the alert, still unsure of him, afraid that he was going to elude her again or even leave her to go back to Cuzco.

'Where are you going?' She sat up in bed. He turned towards her, away from the built-in wardrobe which covered the whole of one wall. Taking a dressing-gown of red velvet from the cupboard, he draped it around him and tied the belt. The red velvet set off his darkness and Renata was aware again, as she would always be, of his dangerous physical attractions.

'I'm going to fetch our dinner. We'll eat up here,' he said, and left the room.

For a few moments she lay at her ease, admiring the luxury of the room and pondering over all she had learned about Jason during the past few hours. After a while she left the bed and opened one of her suitcases to take out the thin silk kimono-style dressing-gown she always took away with her when she travelled. When Jason

returned pushing a trolley laden with silver-covered dishes, glasses and white linen, she was sitting at the dressing-table brushing her hair, which was now dry.

'How did you get that up here?' she asked in surprise, swinging round to look at the trolley.

'My mother had her studio up here, in the room next to this one, so my father had an elevator built so that her meals could be sent up to her easily when she was busy painting. The elevator came in useful too when she wanted large canvases taken downstairs from the studio,' he said, and tipped the bottle of wine he had been opening over a glass to fill it. 'I'm hoping that you might consider using that room as your studio,' he added, giving her an underbrowed glance. 'Muro told me when I phoned him that you and he had decided to part company. I guess you're pleased.'

'Yes, I am. It's a great relief,' she said, going over to take the glass of wine he

was offering to her. 'Would you mind if I did work out of this house for a while?' She looked down at the bubbles of champagne winking at the brim of the glass she was holding and said what had been uppermost in her mind ever since she had realised she didn't need to be protected from Carlos's attentions any more. 'I realise now that perhaps you'll feel I don't need the protection of a husband any more,' she began slowly. 'I know you weren't too happy about giving up your freedom to marry me and . . . and I'll understand if . . . if . . . ' Breaking off, she looked up sharply, because Jason had started to laugh. 'Oh, what are you laughing at?' she exclaimed, stamping her foot. 'You're always laughing at me! Why? What have I said now to make you laugh?'

'You're so serious and so naïve,' he said. 'What on earth makes you think I would want to opt out of our marriage when as far as I'm concerned it's only just begun, right here and now in this

room? Oh, no, you're stuck with me as your husband for a while yet. Come on, let's eat and forget about your career and my career, at least for tonight. All that matters is that we're together at last in the way I've wanted us to be ever since I met you the night I brought Kendal's letter to you.' He paused thoughtfully, frowning a little. 'I guess I wasn't going to mention him, but I have. Is he going to be between us, a ghost at our table, at our bedside?'

'No, no,' Renata denied quickly, going up to him, urgent to assure him that she had at last laid Kendal's ghost and that her first marriage was now just a happy memory of another life. 'I . . . I . . . loved him, I really did. But I love you now. And it's different. I'm different . . . ' She stammered to a stop, unable to explain the difference, yet anxious to let him know that, though she would never forget Kendal, his place in her life had been taken over. 'You are the only man I want now,' she added in a whisper.

'So let's hope it's always going to be that way,' Jason replied softly, his eyes beginning to glow. He raised his glass to her. 'Here's to our future together, Renata.'

'Our future together,' she responded, feeling suddenly light-hearted. 'Mmm, this food smells good!'

They ate *picante de gallina*, a spicy, creamy preparation of chicken, and drank several glasses of a locally-produced white wine. They ignored the over-sweet dessert and coffee, going back to bed to sip more wine from tall glasses. For the rest of the night their lovemaking was steamily erotic, plunging them into short sleeps of satiation from which they woke eager for more kisses and caresses, until at last they sank into a deeper slumber.

Jason woke her at sun-up. Dressed in his usual flying clothes, he sat on the bed beside her and looked down at her sultry, heavily lidded eyes.

'I'm off back to Cuzco now,' he said.

'Oh, no, not yet. Can't you stay

longer, another day or two?' she pleaded.

'You're asking too much again,' he warned her, his face hardening.

Sitting up, she took one of his hands in hers and pressed the palm of it against her cheek.

'I'm going to miss you while you're away,' she whispered. 'I missed you very much while I was in New York. Please stay a while. Surely there's someone else who can fly in your place?'

'Sure there is,' he replied. 'But I have to be there making sure that everything is going smoothly. It won't be for long. While you were away the take-over business was straightened out. Hernandez Aviation has now taken over Sunquest Airlines, and you're now talking to the managing director of the whole shebang. When everything has been reorganised I expect to be moving my base of operations to Callao, and then I won't have to live in Cuzco.'

'Oh, wonderful, wonderful!' she

cried, putting her arms around him and hugging him.

'But I would like you to live in this house starting from today,' he continued once the kissing and hugging were over. 'Will you? And use the studio?'

'On one condition,' she said, teasing him.

'What is it?' Jason's face had hardened again and his sidelong glance at her was wary.

'I would only live in this house if I could be sure we're going to have a family,' said Renata, and waited, holding her breath, for his reply.

'I always guessed you could drive a hard bargain,' he drawled with a grin. Then, with a more sober expression, he added, 'I don't want to lose you or hurt you, because I have to do things my way as I lost and hurt Lise all those years ago, so try to remember that when you're feeling insecure and uncertain about me.' He shifted closer to her and slid his fingers through her hair, then kissed her gently. 'We'll have

a family if you want,' he whispered.

He stood up quickly and strode to the door.

'But when will I see you again?' she cried.

'*Quién sabe?*' he replied with a shrug. He had retreated from her again, was about to elude her to protect his precious freedom of action. 'That's for you to decide. If you really want me to be the father of your children you'll be here in this house when I return from Cuzco, maybe at the weekend. *Adiós, amada.*'

The door opened and closed. He had gone from her as abruptly as he had at other times, as if he were afraid she would delay him longer than he was able to stay.

But there was a difference from those other times, thought Renata, smiling to herself as she snuggled down in the comfortable bed which still held something of his warmth and the scents of his body. He would be returning to this house, and if she wanted him, really

loved him, she would be here when he came.

And she would be here, always, in the years to come, she vowed, going about her business as a fashion designer and bringing up their children, doing it all in her own way, knowing that she was loved and understood by the man whom she loved and to whom she was married.

THE END

VISIONS OF THE HEART

Christine Briscomb

When property developer Connor Grant contracted Natalie Jensen to landscape the grounds of his large country house near Ashley in South Australia, she was ecstatic. But then she discovered he was acquiring — and ripping apart — great swathes of the town. Her own mother's house and the hall where the drama group met were two of his targets. Natalie was desperate to stop Connor's plans — but she also had to fight the powerful attraction flowing between them.

Annie's real parents? Watch out!

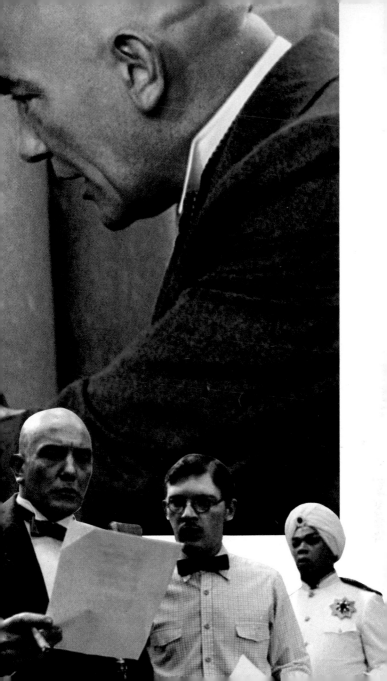

Annie tells Warbucks she can't be his little girl...

...and he searches for her parents

It may not be Buckingham Palace, but it's home to Oliver Warbucks

'You're our guest, Annie''

Caught! It's back to the Home for Annie

Answering to his name

Miss Farrell wants to "borrow" an orphan

Watch those bullies run!

And a left to the jaw!

An historic meeting—
Annie rescues Sandy

**Mr. Bundles helps
Annie escape**